WATERED down

A JACK ARMSTRONG NOVEL

James Woods

moon mountain

Watered down
A Jack Armstrong Novel

This book is dedicated to my wife, Valerie,
who makes everything possible
and to our family:
Heather, Tod, Adam, Jocelle, Nick, Dee, Mikey
and The Little Prince, Miles, our grandson,
all of whom add immeasurable joy to our lives!

"Some of us who live in arid parts of the world think about water with a reverence others might find excessive. The water I will draw tomorrow from my tap in Malibu is today crossing the Mojave Desert from the Colorado River, and I like to think about exactly where that water is. The water I will drink tonight in a restaurant in Hollywood is by now well down the Los Angeles Aqueduct from the Owens River, and I also think about exactly where that water is: I particularly like to imagine it as it cascades down the 45-degree stone steps that aerate Owen's Valley water after its airless passage through the mountain pipes and siphons."

Joan Didion, *The White Album*

CHAPTER ONE

Jack began hyperventilating as he knew that he would need all the air that he could hold in his lungs. He figured that if he could do so for at least 90 seconds, he would have a fighting chance. He also knew that he didn't have even a fighting chance against his captors, and he didn't want to let his captors know what he was doing as they would simply slug him in the gut with a rifle butt and cause him to lose his breath. He hoped that Coop, his long-time buddy, was doing likewise as he stood in front of him, which ran counter to his philosophy:

"To lead people, walk behind them," as Lao Tzu had taught.

Nevertheless, he had confidence in Coop following the same strategy given his training and background as a former Navy Seal.

He marched closer to the hole in the ground at the prodding of their five guards. The hole, if you could call it a hole, was really what appeared to be a well-head, hinged, and opened to one side creating a size-able opening presumably leading to an underground aquifer. A safe assumption as this was California Central Valley farm country.

As he stepped closer, he looked down and saw nothing but blackness below. How deep was the hole? What lay beneath? Were there rocks off which he would carom? Was the fall he was about to take, 10 feet, 30 feet or more than 50 feet deep?

And fall into what: solid ground and rocks, reflecting California's 20-year drought, or water. If water did exist below, how deep is it? Three feet or 30 feet? If he survived the fall and the landing on whatever, how was he going to get out? Or was he left to float in darkness until he and his buddy Coop couldn't tread water anymore and simply slipped beneath the surface. That was the point, wasn't it? There was no escape. He and his colleague were about to be entombed in a pitch-black underground hole from which there was no way out.

Heck, how did he and Coop get into this mess? What triggered the need for a death sentence? Clearly, they were on to something. But they didn't have proof, only suspicion and questions. Was the something that they were onto of sufficient significance to lead to this?

"OK big shot, in you go," said one of the guards. A big mussel bound guy complete with automatic pistol, most likely a Sig Sauer P226 MK25 9 mm Luger which held 10 plus rounds and recently was known to misfire, which Jack hoped would not occur now with the pistol pointed at him. The big guy gave him a shove into the bottomless, pitch-black hole. As he fell, he lost all sensory perception, so he counted to measure the distance: one thousand one, one thousand two, then he splashed feet first into some water. Thankfully, he had not hit any rocks or an out cropping during the fall as he quickly descended. He was equally thankful that his captors had not tied his hands behind his back, which gave him a fighting chance once he hit the surface. That's all he needed for the moment, he thought.

The hyper ventilation paid off as he maintained some breath while he plunged under water and began to level off many feet under the surface. Instinctually, he began to scissor kick his legs and draw his arms to his sides, in search of the surface and much needed air.

Just then an object shot by him underwater, barely missing him. What the heck was that he wondered before realizing that it must have been Coop who had been next in line behind him.

As Jack broke the surface of the water, he looked up just in time to see the cover above close shutting out all light and sealing the two of them in a watertight tomb. A moment later, he heard Coop break the surface near him, then ask, "Jack, are you ok?"

Jack answered him, "Yes, how about you?"

"I'm A-OK" he responded.

Jack thought that they must have been forced to jump into a large underground aquifer owned by the syndicate, "No doubt this was one way to dispose of syndicate problems," thought Jack.

"I doubt that we can reach the ceiling of the aquifer even if we could see it," said Jack to Coop. "I counted a full two seconds as I fell before splash down which would mean a fall of nearly 65 feet, if my calculation is correct." Jack had remembered from his high school physics class: falling objects gain distance as they accelerate so a one second fall travels 16 feet, while a two second fall covers 64 feet as acceleration increases.

"Well, if we can't go up, or down, we have to go sideways," thought Coop aloud. Although the underground aquifer offered no visible means of indicating its size, Coop knew that somewhere there had to be walls to contain the water.

If we find a wall, we may find a ledge and a place to rest and assess, he thought. On the other hand, the walls could be shear and allowing no purchase. "Each of us should swim in opposite directions until we touch terra firma then shout out any discovery."

"Agreed," said Jack. "Let's go before we run out of gas treading water."

"Kick off your shoes and take off your coat, Jack. You'll have a better chance of staying upright," suggested Coop.

Each proceeded away from the other, in an undefined and sightless direction. The only sound for the next five minutes was that of splashing water caused by their swimming in the black void. So much for stepping forward into growth, thought Jack as he recalled guidance from Abraham Maslow:

"You will either step forward into growth, or you will step backward into safety."

"I could use a little safety right about now," thought Jack as he swam aimlessly. "Now I know how blind people feel while they swim." With no visual aid, Jack used his hearing to sense the proximity of a nearby wall. A wall? Great, he thought. Then what? Whenever difficult situations were encountered what ever they were and with no apparent solution, his girlfriend, Sara, would say:

"It will all work out."

"I sure hope so," he thought.

CHAPTER TWO

A few days earlier, Jack had looked across the table at his best friend. They were at the Brazen Head, one of their favorite San Francisco restaurants. Seated opposite him was, Gary Cooper, or simply Coop. Jack and Coop went way back to their college days when Coop was a Berkeley cop and busted Jack for smoking a joint at a Cal Berkeley performance, Jack's university. Coop let Jack go and Jack reciprocated by buying him dinner over which they began to bond.

Coop thought BPD was too uneventful and decided to join the Navy Seals. Now he had his own special ops agency, aptly named, "Coop's Dark Ops," a bit of a play on words and the fact that Coop was Black. Although Black, Coop bore the name of a famous White Cowboy, bestowed on him by his mother who thought that the Cowboy was handsome, smart and a "person of integrity," she would tell him when describing her hero, Gary Cooper.

Jack exited his Big Law corporate legal practice to form "Jack's Solutions," an investigative agency. He specialized in solving complex problems for clients and had a contact list of over 4,000 names of people upon whom he could count if he needed a specialized service that he did not possess, like Coop. Together they frequently teamed up to provide clients with unusual solutions to their unique problems.

"What do you think?" asked Jack about taking a road trip to Santa Monica to visit Jack's girlfriend, Sara.

"It sounds good to me. I could use a break," Coop responded.

"Me too," said Jack.

"When do you want to go?" asked Coop.

"How about tomorrow morning?" said Jack.

"I can be ready," said Coop who was always ready, thought Jack. What a terrific partner and friend.

"We can head to Interstate 5 and travel South. We should be able to make Santa Monica in 7 or 8 hours with a couple of pit stops," announced Jack. "I'm looking forward to seeing Sara there and she promised to introduce a friend of hers to you!"

"Sounds promising," said Coop.

"Sara is staying in her old apartment on Ocean Avenue next to the Palisades Park. The park is world class, complete with a 1926 Totem pole near her apartment, towering palms, and spectacular ocean views from the bluffs high above the Pacific Coast Highway, known as the PCH, locally. And the "deer" are not bad either," said Jack.

"The deer?" asked Coop rhetorically.

"The cute girls who frequently exercise in the park!" explained Jack.

The boys had just finished a grueling and complex engagement with a client, Veronica Hill, who was divorcing from her Russian mobster husband. Veronica had inherited a note and a key from her great-great-grandfather, Graham Stackhouse, which led Jack and Coop to the Niantic, a sunken Gold Rush ship and to an 1860's poker game attended by notables of the time including Mark Twain and where Graham Stackhouse won a treasure pot and hid it for posterity in a defunct Comstock Silver Lode mine in Virginia City, Nevada.

Although the mine was defunct, through clues left by Mark Twain, Jack was able to find the hidden treasure. He and Coop fought off Russian mobsters who were searching for the same, invested the treasure in ownership of the Comstock mine which now contained rich deposits of Lithium, and earned 25% of the deposits for his services rendered in finding the treasure.

So now they were ready for some R & R and a mini road trip to Santa Monica.

"Let's take my car. I'll drive," said Coop.

"Sure, we can trade off after pit stops," suggested Jack.

"Done!" exclaimed Coop as he fist bumped Jack.

Coop had a BMW X 3 Competition SUV which not only handled well and scooted from zero to 60 in about 4 seconds, but it allowed Coop to carry his essential equipment secreted in a false floor behind the back seats. It was a nice ride.

"Born to be Wild," thought Jack, mimicking Steppenwolf. Having recently escaped death a couple of times in the last caper, "I wonder what trouble we will get into this time…," he thought to himself.

CHAPTER THREE

They headed south from San Francisco across the San Mateo Bridge toward Interstate 5. As they drove through the Altamont Pass, Jack remembered hearing about a notable Stones' concert many years ago, the location of which was now replaced with dozens of wind turbines.

"How about a little music?" asked Coop. "I have some Miles Davis which is dynamite."

"You're a fan?" asked Jack.

"Big time," answered Coop. "If I had a son, he would be named Miles."

Shortly after the Altamont Pass, they turn south onto Interstate 5, or the 5 as many called it. "In some respects, the 5 was the modern-day equivalent of El Camino Real, the King's Highway," thought Jack. El Camino Real hugged the coast of California and traveled over 600 miles from San Diego to Sonoma with 21 Missions located a day's ride apart. The modern day El Camino Real, I-5, provided a four-lane highway up and down California from the southern border with Mexico to the northern border with Oregon and then through Oregon and Washington to the Canadian border. In California, it helped whisk drivers over hundreds of miles at speeds of 70 mph and above. Coop said that he had made it from San Francisco to LA in his BMW in 6 and ½ hours. All in, it was comparable to air travel when one considered: travel to the airport, parking, TSA screening, and wait times to board, take off, land, deplane and Uber to the final destination.

"You are going to see our Nation's 'breadbasket'," said Coop.

"What?"asked Jack as he stared out the car window at the passing wind turbines.

"I grew up as a farm kid in the San Joaquin Valley," explained Coop.

"You did? "Asked Jack. "You didn't tell me."

"I don't tell you everything," said Coop.

What an interesting surprise Jack thought as he stared out the window at miles of orchards and agricultural fields.

"California has over 75,000 farms which produce 400 commodities, two-thirds of the nation's fruits and nuts and one-third of our vegetables. About one-quarter of what California produces is exported around the world," Coop commented. "Agriculture is a $50 billion annual business in the state, $20 billion more than the next state," he added. "You are looking at over 25 million acres of farm and ranch land, Jack."

"Where exactly did you grow up?"

"Hopeful," said Coop.

"Yes, you always are ..., and optimistic too," added Jack. "But where in the state did you live as a kid?"

"Hopeful," responded Coop.

"Hopeful?" repeated Jack thinking of that classic Abbott and Costello line "Who's on Second?" "Where's Hopeful?"

"About 80 miles north of Tulare, off Highway 99," answered Coop.

"How did they come up with a name like that?" asked Jack.

"Over 100 years ago, farm migrants decided to bypass Detroit, Chicago and the Midwest and headed West instead. They were attracted by the promise of thousands of acres of farmland at reasonable prices. Developers on Spring Street in Los Angeles found that they could package large tracts of farmland for 'out-of-towners' with the promise of a new beginning," Coop explained.

He continued, "For the Black community, they were 'hopeful' that there would be no more lynchings, or drinking from separate fountains, or sharecropping, or Jim Crow. Escape from what author Isabell Wilkerson calls the 'Caste' system, in her book bearing the same name. Other, non-Black migrants also were escaping discrimination and searching for an opportunity to succeed. So, when they arrived in the early 1900s, they decided to call their town, 'Hopeful'."

"Do you still have family there, Coop?" asked Jack.

"Grandpa Walker lives there. My grandmother passed away a couple of years ago," Coop explained.

"When did you last speak with him?" asked Jack.

"A couple of weeks ago."

"Want to stop by and say Hi on our way to Santa Monica?" asked Jack.

"Sure, that would be nice Jack."

As they headed along the Interstate, Jack noticed Tesla Superchargers next to an Andersen Pea Soup restaurant near Santa Nella. Well, he thought, I guess even Tesla's need to eat.

He also noticed some telling signs embedded in the orchards near the freeway; "Food Grows Where Water Flows." A few miles later he was told to "Build Dams, Avoid Man Made Droughts." Then a few miles after that, he was asked, "Why Dump 78% of California's Water in the Ocean?"

Coop turned onto Highway 152 which connected to Highway 99, which would lead them to Hopeful.

CHAPTER FOUR

The next sign they saw said,
"Welcome to Hopeful-Where Dreams Come True!"

It was not a big archway spanning the narrow two-lane country road like some city signs. Reno's "Biggest Little City in the World" and Redwood City's "Temperature Best by Government Test" were two that came to Jack's mind.

Instead, the Hopeful sign was a faded wooden sign off to the right side of the two-lane pitted road leading into the small town and standing 6 feet tall while stretching 4 feet in width, complete with chipped white paint and a slat or two missing. Instead of announcing a town of great prominence, it reminded Jack of Larry McMurtry's description of the Emporium sign in his book Lonesome Dove and the cowboys who investigated it for several hours in an effort to decipher its meaning. At least the Hopeful sign contained the proper spelling for the word it promised. It also boasted a town population of 80. Eighty "hopefuls" thought Jack. That remains to be seen.

And the road was little more than a dirt path. Not a ribbon of asphalt velvet upon which the modern-day tire would roll softly along. There were no painted markers or road icons which would guide a traveler in the center of the lane. How would Tesla's FSD ever stay centered without such assistance, thought Jack? Oh, well, first world problem, Jack said to himself.

After the sign, there were some small homes, shacks

really, together with mobile homes clearly in need of repair. All seemed to lean one way or another without the ability to maintain an upright stance. And the colorful siding used to provide shelter seemed to cover the color palate: whites, creams, yellows, magentas, blues, and browns. There was even one that bore a faded orange tint to it.

Jack saw a cluster of goats feeding out of a metal trough and a group of chickens moseying about each yard scratching the ground. Classic "free range" chickens (and goats) observed Jack as there were no fences. He wondered what morning would be like with the inevitable crowing of roosters here, there, and everywhere.

A mixture of old cars, broken washers, old tires and other "valuable possessions" were stacked in a corner of each yard, or on the front porch. Tacked to a severely leaning telephone pole was a piece of wood a foot and a half long and 4 inches wide announcing in weathered paint, "We Buy ouses" with the H missing and leaving a partially legible faded phone number that was too difficult to read for anyone interested in selling their home.

As Coop drove into "town", Jack also noticed that the houses improved in appearance resulting in several small ranch houses likely containing up to 3 bedrooms and even 2 indoor baths instead of outhouses. A few appeared to have been recently remodeled with new siding, roofs and a coat of paint.

Coop took a right onto Main Street. Several buildings offered services to farmers and ranchers: a feed store, barber shop with a "closed sign" showing in the window, a hardware store with a bench in front occupied by someone whittling a stick, a grocery store, a laundry, and a diner. The small grocery store also featured Spanish advertisements on the side of the building. All buildings were single story and in relatively rough shape: in need of paint with a few boards missing. Several small buildings were boarded up. At the end of the "town" was an elementary school bearing the name "Lincoln". The school had clearly seen better days, and Jack wondered if it was being used as he saw no children in the neighborhood and the single basketball hoop had no net. The school was located across from a church.

The church had a cross above the portico with the words "Galilee Missionary" on the long horizontal portion of the cross and "Baptist Church" in black letters down the vertical length of the cross. It was difficult to see in daylight whether the edge of the cross-bore lights which would illuminate it, if not the words, at night. It was also difficult to envision a church bearing the name Galilee set so far from the Sea of Galilee in what appeared to be a dust bowl as sand was blowing everywhere.

The sidewalks were in need of repair and there weren't many cars on the Main Street, only a few pickup trucks. Jack was sure that Coop felt out of place with his shining new BMW. Given the 100-degree temperature, Jack was surprised to notice only an occasional window air conditioner. Few people were outside as the boys proceeded through town.

"Welcome to 'Hopeful'," Coop announced. "Hopefully, you didn't blink and miss it," he added, comically.

"Where is your grandpa's home, Coop?" asked Jack.

"Down this street," said Coop as he turned left onto a small side street labeled "A street." A few doors were passed, and Coop turned into a one car unpaved, gravel driveway. The curb to the driveway bore a faint outline of numbers which were illegible. The driveway led to the right side of an old house clearly in need of paint and repair. There was no garage, only a canvas roof covering attached to the side of the house and stretched to reach a couple of rusted metal unpainted polls stuck in the ground and imitating support for a "carport".

The house itself was modest in size with a window on each side of a door center presumably in a room bearing each window. The house had a peaked roof with a broken set of louvers located where the attic would be. There was no fence surrounding the property. Instead, the lines of ownership were marked by a modest row of trees on each side of the house standing ten feet from the dwelling and presumably giving shade in the summer. The trees appeared to be a variety of fruit tree; Jack couldn't be sure as the leaves on the branches had turned brown from a lack of water.

In front of the house was what used to be a lawn when water was applied. Patches of grass appeared to be thrown on barren earth as if Jackson Pollock had splashed paint on a canvas. On the telephone pole addressing the front of the house was a basketball hoop sans net and facing the street. On the other side of the street was a similarly placed basketball hoop, together they created end lines for a court. Presumably a game could be played between the two hoops.

"Is this where you grew up, Coop?" asked Jack.

"Yes, it is where both my parents and I were raised. Unfortunately, the decline is evident everywhere," Coop indicated sweeping his arms far to the left and to the right. "Let's see if anyone is home."

CHAPTER FIVE

After mounting the two steps attached to the porch, Coop engaged the button to the right of the only door facing the street. He couldn't hear the result of his attempt to connect with a bell or buzzer located somewhere inside. As a precaution, he knocked loudly.

Some interesting woodwork framed the door and made a statement, "this home is not going anywhere." The door rested on a threshold which, in turn, rested upon the porch. The porch was anchored in cement footings and elevated 2 feet off the ground as was the entire living area of the house. Perhaps the neighborhood was in a flood plain, thought Jack. The porch also extended across the front of the house. Upon it was a single rocking chair located to the left of the door giving a view of the street, and next to the chair was an end table which was useful for resting a cup or glass, and not much more.

Jack turned, stepped to the left side of the door and inspected the "view" from the rocking chair. Several houses in a similar state of disrepair appeared across the street. None had grass or much visible vegetation. In addition to water, they each needed paint and the addition of several new clapboards. One had an American flag proudly flying atop a flagpole. The flag was tattered, and no doubt was not lowered and removed daily.

After some time, in response to Coop's repeated knocks, a deep throaty voice announced with authority, "Hold your horses, I'm coming!" A few moments later, the door flung open and a tall, lean, black man magically appeared. When he saw Coop, his smile connected his ears and his white teeth showed brightly. "Well look at what the cat dragged in! Ah ha," he uttered looking Coop over from head to toe, not once, but twice.

Coop smiled and said: "Hi Gramps," waving his hand. His grandfather stepped over the door sill and gave Coop a hug, squeezing him tightly with his outstretched arms and barrel chest.

The man stood over 6 feet tall and was dressed in black jeans, a long black sleeve shirt and a black leather vest joined in front by 5 buttons. He also wore a bolo tie around his neck and bearing a silver clasp. A turquoise ring appeared on his left hand and was large enough to make a statement. There was no watch evident.

His pants were secured by a black belt with a large silver buckle in the form of an American eagle. As for footwear, Grandpa Walker sported a pair of stylish Tecovas black boots that appeared to have been recently shined.

His grandfather stood back and continued to look him over from head to toe, "My, you have grown up nice like." Then, looking to his left he eyed Jack and asked, "Who might this be?"

"This is my best friend, Jack Armstrong, Gramps."

"Your best friend," he repeated and continued to eye Jack in an inquisitive fashion. "What makes him the 'best'?" he asked.

"He just is," replied Coop. "We go back many years and have stuck together through it all. We are a team, Gramps."

"I see," he said, both accepting and questioning Coop's statement. "Well, what brought you boys here?"

"We are on our way to LA to meet up with Jack's girlfriend, Sara, and thought we would pay you a visit along the way."

"It is very nice of you to think of me, Gary," choosing to continue using Coop's given birth name. "And nice to meet this best friend of yours. I'm Walker Cooper," he said, extending his hand for Jack to shake. "Please come in."

They entered the modest home. To the right is what looked like a living room with a sofa against the far wall under a window shaded by outside trees and venetian blinds nearly drawn, an easy chair which faced a TV with "rabbit ears". The wallpaper was faded, and the rug was worn, but the room was neat and tidy.

There was an old photo of what appeared to be Coop's grandmother on the wall. On an end table next to the sofa were photos of a man and woman holding a baby, presumably Coop. A bible lay in the center of the coffee table with a notepad and pencil next to it. A coat and hat rack were located near the front door and a black cowboy style hat hung loosely on the prongs. There was no coat visible or needed, given the heat outside.

To the left of the doorway was a dining room that could sit four around a wooden table with wooden chairs. The table was covered with a checked tablecloth. Over the table was a light hanging from the ceiling and taking the shape of four tulips. The walls were covered in a continuation of the wallpaper which began in the living room. Under the far window in the dining room, sat a long narrow serving table covering two attached shelves upon which dishes were stacked. A swinging door from the dining room led presumably to a kitchen.

Jack also observed a hallway which divided the home in two between the living room and the dining room and appeared to extend the modest length of the home. Jack imagined that the hallway likely led to a couple of bedrooms located behind the living room and the kitchen and a single bath at the end of the hall.

It was what was in the modest hallway that struck Jack as odd. Piled on top of each other were boxes. There were probably 20 boxes in all. They were neatly arranged and pushed as far to one side as possible so that a person sliding sideways could pass and proceed along the hall. Although Jack thought it odd, he didn't wish to call attention to the boxes or interpret their meaning before Coop or his grandfather decided to question or explain them.

Coop's grandfather motioned them to the dining room table and invited them to have seats. "Would you like something to drink?"

"I'll have a glass of water," said Coop.

"Me too," echoed Jack. "Before I do, can I use your bathroom? It's been several hours behind the wheel and nature is calling."

"Sure, just follow the hall. It is at the end on the left," directed Walker.

Jack proceeded sideways down the hall sliding past the boxes until he found the bathroom. He lifted the toilet seat and noticed some yellow water in it. When he finished, he attempted to flush, but the flush mechanism didn't work. He couldn't figure it out and tried again: still no results. He lifted the back of the toilet tank and looked inside. The water tank was empty. He noticed a bucket of water next to the toilet and was further mystified. He decided to return to the group without further investigation.

Coop's grandfather stepped into the kitchen behind the dining room through the swinging door interconnecting the two rooms, and Jack could hear a refrigerator door opening. Moments later he carried three glasses and three bottles of water into the dining room. The water bottles were perspiring with condensation formed by their removal from the refrigerator and the heat caused by the lack of air conditioning in the house.

Coop said, "I noticed your Bible and notepad Gramps. Are you still preaching?"

"Of course. As long as the good Lord gives me the strength to speak and people to listen to what I have to say, I will preach."

Coop explained to Jack that Grandpa Walker was the Baptist minister in town and conducted Sunday services. "Have you ever attended a Baptist service, Jack?"

"No, I haven't," said Jack.

"Well, you have missed a good part of life, my friend. It is quite an experience. We will have to arrange to be here for one of Grandpa Walker's services," Coop added.

"I would like that," said Jack.

"Gramps, what are all the boxes about?" asked Coop.

"They are my movin boxes."

"Movin boxes?" asked Coop rhetorically. "Are you movin?"

"Yep, gotta be movin on Gary."

"Movin on? You have lived here 40 years, Gramps," said Coop.

"More like 50 years," calculated Walker. "Grandma and I raised your father here, then he married your mother, a local girl, and for a short time after they were married, your mother and father lived here and had a little baby boy-you," pointing to the picture in the living room. "When they had you, the home shrunk in size: there were five of us living in this two bed, one bath house. It was time for them to move out, with you, of course. So, they headed to Berkeley where your daddy became a BPD officer."

"What is compelling you to leave, Gramps?" asked Coop.

"Follow me fellas," Walker said and motioned to the swinging door leading to the kitchen. They walked behind him into the kitchen which was painted in a yellow which had lost its luster with some wall paper featuring faded flowers. Besides the sink under a small window, a nearby stove, and small refrigerator, was a wall lined with canned goods and a kitchen counter running the length of the room on each side of the sink. Walker motioned the "boys" to the farmhouse style sink and said, "Watch this." He slowly turned on the tap and nothing came out! Instead, after a moment or two, a strange noise preceded a puff of dust which erupted from the facet.

"Where's the water?" asked Coop incredulously.

"That's a good question. I can't answer that. But I can tell you where it isn't. It isn't here!" declared Walker as he pointed to the facet.

"Whoa," said Coop. "And the lack of water is making you move?"

"You got that right!" exclaimed Walker. "We can stay and deal with trucked in water. Heck, every time I want to flush the toilet, I must pour imported water into the tank behind the toilet. When I want to take a bath or shower, what a magilla. And to do laundry, I must drive 5 miles to the laundromat in the next town. The cost of bottled or trucked in water is crazy–20 to 45 cents a gallon. The other day, one of the homes in town caught fire and there was no water to fight the fire. We had to let the home burn to the ground. Town people see no future and have stopped having children. Without water, you are nothing! Too many people don't appreciate water until this happens to them. Someone once told me:

"You know the worth of water when the well goes dry."

"Well, the well has gone dry!" declared Walker.

Coop had never heard his grandfather sound like this before, not even when his grandmother died. He sounded defeated. There was no resiliency, which was so unlike him. He always was a positive person, glass half full. But now it's empty. And, empty of what? Water?

"Besides, some guy gave me $50,000 to move," Walker said.

"$50,000 for your 50 acres? That's only $1,000 per acre, Gramps. Your property is worth much more than that," said Coop.

"Not if there is no water. The soil is as rich as ever. With water it will grow a bountiful harvest, year in and year out," Walker commented staring dejectedly at the ground.

"Gramps, what is causing this?" asked Coop.

"Well, you can start with the aliens," Walker said.

"Aliens?" questioned Coop.

"Yes, aliens are stealing our water," Walker reaffirmed. "They are taking our water right out from under us."

"Aliens?" repeated Coop unbelieving and beginning to think that his grandfather was starting to suffer dementia.

"Yes, late at night I see lights in the orchards and fields. I hear strange noises. It's as if someone from another planet has landed on my property. In the morning, when I go to check, there is no evidence that anyone has been there. But the water in my pond is gone and the water pressure to my house is non-existent. Mysterious," says Walker.

Coop raised his eyebrows and looked at Jack. Jack gave a slight nod of his head and Coop said, "Gramps, do you have a spare room where the two of us could bunk tonight and check this 'alien' thing out?"

"Yes, I do, and I would welcome your company. You can use the room your mama, daddy and you occupied."

"Let's go get a bite to eat, Gramps," offered Coop.

CHAPTER SIX

As they walked into Ruby's Diner, everyone immediately recognized Walker with a greeting, "Hi, Reverend, or simply Hi Rev!" Jack immediately thought of Reverend Al Sharpton who regularly appears on Morning Joe and is greeted the same way. Walker circulated around the tables and proudly introduced Coop as his grandson, and Jack as Coop's best friend, to those present, even introducing them to the cook, the single person wait staff, and the dish washer.

"You are a popular guy," mentioned Jack.

"Recognizable, yes, popular, yet to be determined," responded Walker.

They secured one of the six tables and Jack had a chance to survey the restaurant. It was very basic including a counter with 6 bar type backless stools each of which was anchored to the floor and borne a red vinyl covering. Behind the counter was the grill set under an oversized hood, and a set of two ovens stacked atop each other together with a large double sink and a double door refrigerator. Most of the tables were occupied and two people sat at the counter.

The server bearing a name tag that said "Ruthie" approached, handed out menus, which were encased in plastic and were printed on the front and back. Side one had the usual offerings for a small rural restaurant: hamburgers, cheeseburgers with or without fries, meatloaf, spaghetti with or without meatballs, grilled cheese sandwich, BLT and "house salad". The flip side contained a few desserts and wine and beer selections. "If you order wine, please do so by number," explained the menu and showed: 1 for Red, 2 for White, and 3 for Rose, without designated wineries or wine varietal. The beer choices were Bud and Bud light. There was also room for Coke, Diet Coke, Sprite, and coffee "with or without cream and sugar." "Simple and to the point," thought Jack.

The server asked, "Reverend, will you be having your usual drink this evening?" Walker greeted Ruthie and gave a thumbs up indicating his desire to have a Bud. Coop and Jack did likewise. Then the group uniformly ordered Cheeseburgers with house salads and fries. There was no mention of having the burgers prepared medium or medium rare as Jack and Coop preferred. Nor was a glass of water offered. Jack wondered if one would be provided upon request but decided not to ask.

Not exactly the Brazen Head restaurant in San Francisco where a bottle of Stone Edge Cabernet and medium rare rib eye steaks with grilled vegetables and Caesar salads were what Jack and Coop had become accustomed. As they were waiting for their order, Jack overheard conversations from nearby tables. Each was discussing the water situation and the drought that had plagued the state for more than 20 years.

"When will the drought end?" was a constant refrain.

"Who knows," said another customer, "The snowpack is almost non-existent again this year."

"There are simply too many straws in our water," said someone referring to the over drafting of ground water and aquifers.

"When will the politicians treat us farmers fairly?" asked a burly guy.

"Yeah" said another, "They accuse us of using 80% of the water, when we only use 50%. Now they want to ration water to farmers! Remember, 'food grows where water flows."

"When will they stop others from stealing our water?" responded his table mate.

"Seems like everyone is concerned about the water situation," said Jack to Walker.

"You bet," commented Walker, "We simply can't live without it. Can't make a living without water to grow our crops or provide for our families. In years of plenty, water is taken for granted, in years of drought, water is a privilege," opined Walker. As they were served, he said, "Bon Appetite!"

After dinner, Jack and Coop stopped by the SUV to get some of their gear as they prepared for a long night "investigating aliens".

Around midnight all through the house, not a creature was stirring, not even a mouse, thought Jack. Suddenly, he heard a clanging noise from outside. He hopped out of his single bed quietly so as not to awake Coop who was snoring soundly in an adjacent bed and pulled back the curtain covering the only window in the room. He saw several lights in the orchard and on the nearby street in an otherwise dark surrounding.

"Hey Coop," he whispered.

Instantly, Coop was alert, "What?"

"Come here and take a look."

Coop instantly rolled out of his bed and came to the

window. He looked outside and observed what Jack had seen. Lights were where they should not be and metal on metal clanging sounds interrupted the otherwise peaceful night. "Are those Grandpa Walkers 'aliens'?"asked Jack.

" I think we should head outside and do some investigating," suggested Coop.

"Good idea," Jack responded.

They dressed and packed some of their gear in a back pack that might help them in their surveillance. Quietly, they tiptoed past Walker's bedroom and exited the house not wishing to wake him.

Keeping low, they jogged toward the lights in the orchard which were a couple of hundred yards away. As they neared, they made out a couple of guys near what appeared to be an irrigation line and a pond. When they were 50 yards away, they hit the ground and began to crawl toward the men. From the back pack they took out night vision glasses and could see that one group of men were attaching a hose to an irrigation line. Another group was dipping hoses into a pond. A third group appeared to be dropping a line into an aquifer. In fact, there were a series of hoses crisscrossing the ground like spaghetti. The hoses, the size of fire hoses, were coupled together and traveled 50 yards to a nearby line of trucks with tanks. As one truck was topped off, another would roll into place.

"Those SOBs are stealing Gramp's water!" said Coop. Taking his weapon, a Glock 19, from a hostler, he said, "We are going to put a stop to that right now!"

"No, hold on," said Jack, putting his hand on Coop's gun.

"Let's see where they are taking the water. There may be more to deal with than a couple of water thieves." Coop contained his agitation and backed off.

They crawled backwards, then crouching so as not to be seen, they returned to the house where their SUV was parked. Once in the car and without turning on the lights, they proceeded to the road paralleling Gramp's ranch where the water thieves were at work. As they neared the line of tanker trucks, they saw several men opening a nearby fire hydrant and attaching a hose from the truck to the hydrant.

"Well, I'll be," said Coop, understanding the operation that was transpiring, "They're even stealing the town's water."

"And they are doing it while the town is asleep," added Jack. "Let's follow them and find out where they are 'stashing the loot'."

CHAPTER SEVEN

The line of trucks headed East, toward the mountains. They followed the water thieves for about 10 miles into the foothills, keeping a safe distance behind so they were not seen. They kept their lights off and followed the trucks by moonlight. Fortunately, the smooth country road did not offer any problems driving "blind".

In the foothills, the truck line turned onto an obscure side road and stopped at a gate maned by two individuals, one of whom held what appeared to be an AR-15 assault weapon. The guard without the assault weapon had a side arm in a holster attached to his waist, a clip board, and he spoke with the lead truck driver while the other armed guard kept an eye out for trouble. After a few moments, the gate was opened. Each succeeding tanker truck stopped and was interviewed by the guard with the clip board.

Coop said, "Looks like we should follow-on foot from here," as they turned off the road a safe distance from the gate.

"Yes, I saw a low point in the fence a hundred yards back," said Jack. "Let's back up quietly and park out of sight. We can try jumping the fence."

"I hope there are no dogs!"exclaimed Coop.

After quietly backing up, they found the side road Jack had seen which led to a ditch surrounded by brush. Coop maneuvered his SUV to a stop without using the brakes or igniting the brake lights. The ditch hid their car from the road.

After turning off the interior lights, Coop unlatched the back of the SUV and opened the floorboard where his "dark ops equipment" was located. He took two pair of night googles, a couple of Glock 19s, an M4A1 assault rifle, a couple of radio transmitters with earpieces and some other items, stuffed them in two back packs, placed the rifle over his shoulder, then closed the hatch quietly. He handed one of the back packs to Jack and led the way across the street to the low point in the fence that he had previously seen.

Once over the fence, they put on their night googles and the landscape turned into an eerie greenish light. Given the armed guards at the gate, they were on the lookout for other roving guards, trip wires and guard dogs. Carefully they began to move 50 yards from and parallel to the road that the trucks were taking up the mountain. The last of the water trucks was just beginning to navigate the road past the guarded gate. They figured that if they kept the truck lights on their distant left and quietly followed them up the hill, they would be ok.

Then Coop had another idea. Rather than climb the mountain in the dark with our night vision glasses, let's hitch a ride. "Follow me," he whispered and began to jog carefully and laterally toward the last tanker truck. With no time to question, Jack followed.

Keeping low as they approached the truck, Coop signaled to Jack toward the back of the last truck in line. Jack nodded. They both ran for the tailgate and grabbed hold of it out of sight from the driver's rear-view mirrors.

The line of trucks wound through the mountains several

miles in the dark with only their headlights guiding them. Coop and Jack could not see where the trucks were going but sensed the steep incline of the mountain they ascended. Then, without being able to view the road or land ahead of them, they sensed cresting the mountain and felt a steep decline coupled with the noise of the truck's air brakes and the use of lower gears by the driver to slow the decent down the mountain with a tank full of water. Not knowing what awaited them at the bottom, they decided to jump off and continue to follow on foot.

As the trucks gained some distance from them, they headed into the brush on the side of the road. Jack and Coop took up a vantage point at the crest of a nearby hill with a view of the valley below. What they saw amazed even them.

More accurately it was what they didn't see. The trucks had disappeared! They couldn't figure out why or where they had gone. One minute they saw truck lights and the next, there were none. "Magic," said Jack.

"Abracadabra," said Coop. "Let's unwind the mystery."

They proceeded cautiously down the mountain being mindful of the possibility that roving guards, sensors and dogs could be nearby. Jack wasn't sure how Coop would handle an adverse encounter but was confident that his training as a Navy Seal had prepared him for trailside adversities. Just then, Coop, who was leading, held up his hand in a signal to "stop". Silently, Jack halted and awaited further instructions from Coop.

They were now halfway down the mountain, and Coop pointed to the valley below. Jack could faintly see some muted lights off to the left. The lights were obscured by something they could not clearly see. They continued quietly down the mountain and could begin to decipher what had hidden their view.

Camouflage covered the left side of the valley. Nets appeared to be draped over whatever was on the valley floor, hiding what was beneath them. No doubt the tanker trucks had proceeded under some nets covering the valley road when they "disappeared".

To the right of the camouflage were a half dozen old buildings. "It looks like the old wild west," said Jack as he viewed the surroundings with his night vision googles.

"What do you make of this?" Coop asked.

"Someone is seriously interested in covering up their tracks," Jack responded. "They have hidden something next to what appears to be a couple of abandoned Gold Rush buildings."

"I thought gold was discovered at Sutter's Mill, a hundred miles North of here."

"It was, but that didn't stop miners from trying their luck elsewhere. In fact, the entire State of California was in play and nearly everyone was in search of get rich quick gold back in the mid 1800s," counseled Jack.

"We need to figure out what's going on," said Coop. "Given the armed guards we have seen; they mean to keep whatever it is, a secret. Let's start with the abandoned buildings."

Keeping low, they headed down the mountain, spotted a nearby shed and took cover in it. After a few minutes and hearing no sound, they opened the shed door and saw an old building that looked like an abandoned saloon with lights on nearby. "Let's take a look," said Jack as he began to open the door and step out.

"Wait a minute," cautioned Coop grabbing Jack by the arm. "Let's look through Tinker Bell's eyes first." Tinker Bell was a high-tech drone which was about the size of a dragon fly and controlled by an app on Coop's iPhone. He had helped develop it while in Special Navy Seal Services. Coop opened his knapsack, and prepared Tinker Bell for flight. He opened the shed door and off flew Tinker Bell quickly gaining altitude.

Jack looked over Coop's shoulder at the screen on his iPhone and watched as Tinker Bell flew over the netting which made visibility of what was beneath the netting difficult to discern from the air.

"Let's take a peek in the abandoned buildings and under the nets," suggested Coop as he guided Tinker Bell to fly into what appeared to be an abandoned saloon. Coop and Jack saw a group of five men seated at an old poker table. They appeared to be discussing something and one was clearly the leader of the group. "I think we have discovered the brain trust of this operation," said Coop.

"And they all appear to be armed," noticed Jack.

"Oh no," exclaimed Coop. "Do you see what I see?"

Jack peered closer to the monitor Coop was holding. "Whoa, what is that?"

"It is a special breed of guard dog, called a Russian Super dog," explained Coop. Years ago, scientists used genes from 17 breeds to develop a fiercely protective dog to patrol the

Russian border. It looks like these boys are serious about guarding their secrets."

"How are we going to deal with that?" asked Jack.

"Very carefully," answered Coop. "Now that we have found the hang out for their brain trust, let's check out what the tanker trucks are doing." He operated the controls for Tinker Bell, and she flew outside the saloon and under the camouflage and over dozens of canopy-covered hoop houses. As Tinker Bell flew around the grounds, Coop and Jack also noticed some roving guards with dogs on leashes.

"Nice 'safety feature'," commented Jack.

Using the images from Tinker Bell, they saw the 10 tanker trucks lined up with the lead truck opposite some pipes from which hoses were attached and connected. Each truck waited 15 minutes while its cargo was off loaded, then the next truck moved into position to be unloaded. Jack asked, "Do you know how much water each truck holds?"

"My best guess is 4500 gallons," said Coop.

"Wow, ten trucks, that's 45,000 gallons of water," whispered Jack. "This is one smooth operation. I wonder where the water is stored?"

"Either in some large tanks or underground in an aquifer," speculated Coop.

"Or both," thought Jack.

"How is it being used," questioned Coop.

"First things, first," said Jack. "Let's find out what's behind door number one, the buildings."

"How are we going to navigate the roving patrols and guard dogs?" asked Jack.

"As I said, 'carefully'," explained Coop.

Coop recalled Tinker Bell. They collected their backpacks, crouched low, and watched the guards and their dogs make the rounds. While timing the cycle of the rovers, they noticed two guards signal each other with flashlights, then disappear into one of the buildings. The two guards probably gathered to warm up, have a smoke and a chat, Coop and Jack thought. Avoiding two of the guards while on a break, Coop and Jack quietly exited the shed and tiptoed into place behind one of the buildings furthest from the saloon and away from the guards on break. Suddenly, a door to another building burst opened, and another guard exited causing a flood of light to illuminate the surrounding area. Jack and Coop quickly hit the ground and hoped that they would not be visible. They waited 60 seconds before deeming it safe to move.

"Where does their electricity come from?" whispered Coop.

"Take a look," Jack said quietly as he pointed to the nearby hillside.

Coop did as Jack suggested and said, "Son of a gun. The hillside is covered with hundreds of solar panels."

"Stolen water, captured sunlight, and there are probably even batteries storing the solar generated electricity," thought Jack aloud.

"See there," pointed Coop at a series of Tesla Power Walls which no doubt was used to store energy captured from the solar panels.

"Good for a cloudy day," concluded Jack.

"And no need for energy to be supplied by the electrical

grid," offered Coop. "Keeps things nice and quiet and untraceable through giant electric bills."

"Which makes this operation even more mysterious, "said Jack. "What are they hiding? What is so valuable?"

"We will soon find out," said Coop, as he carefully opened the door to the building against which they had been hiding. What they saw was row upon row of plants irrigated with drip lines and furnished with the equivalent of sun light from high intensity overhead lights.

"Well, I'll be," said Jack as he examined one of the plants.

"You'll be what?"

"Remember when we first met at UC Berkeley?" asked Jack.

"Yes," answered Coop.

"What was I doing?" asked Jack.

"Smoking a joint, and I busted you," said Coop remembering his days with the BPD and Jack as a student at Cal.

"And" Jack said, "what do these plants look like?"

"Marijuana," said Coop. "So, these guys are operating an illegal weed farm with stolen water and using solar energy off the grid. Pretty slick!"

"Personally," Coop continued, "I don't care if someone smokes weed. Heck, it's now legal in California after voters passes Proposition 64, and the Feds have indicated that they are loosening restrictions. Naturally, the legal has led to the illegal in growing weed like this to avoid taxes and permits. I hear that growers are taxed on the product and on the acreage. So, there is a great incentive to avoid government knowledge of where weed is being grown and sold."

"Although we can't stop organized crime from illegally growing weed, we may be able to stop them from stealing water from Gramps and the town," said Coop.

"All in," Jack said, "I count over forty large hoop houses like this one. I can only imagine the amount of water that they steal to make this work."

Unfortunately, Coop thought that this was only a drop in the bucket. He recalled what his law enforcement friends informed him that illegal pot farms draw over 5 million gallons of water a day in Los Angeles, Riverside and San Bernardino counties alone. That's enough water for over 70,000 people! I can't imagine what the number is statewide, he thought.

"There must be thousands of marijuana plants," offered Jack. "Got any ideas?" asked Jack.

"Always!" answered Coop. "Let's not make it worth their while to steal water."

"Here's what we do," explained Coop. Jack listened carefully, nodded, and then gave Coop's plan some thought.

"I like it!" Jack exclaimed.

"Ok, now let's get to work. I have what we need to 'prime the pump' in my backpack," said Coop, as he explained the plan in detail to Jack. "Let's split up and do what needs to be done. I will be stationed among the solar panels on the hillside and keep an eye on the rovers and their dogs with Tinker Bell," Coop said, then added, "Let's communicate by text and ear pod regarding the rovers whereabouts so you can avoid them."

Each then went about implementing the plan: Jack

darting quietly from building to building and Coop being ever watchful of the roving guards and their dogs.

"Watch your back, rover behind you coming around the corner," Coop informed Jack by ear piece. Jack ducked into a hoop house and quickly closed the door. He hid under an elevated marijuana table as the door opened, and the Rover stepped into the hoop house. Jack was totally silent as he heard footsteps near the door and could see feet moving toward him, a step at a time. As the guard neared to within 5 feet, Jack began to wonder what he would do if he was discovered. He could feel his heart pounding. He slowed his breathing. Thankfully, whoever was in the building, didn't have a dog as the dog would see him under the table, or smell him. Then, just as suddenly, the Rover did an about face and stepped away and proceeded toward the door through which he had entered the building. Apparently thinking all was in order after a cursory review of the building, the guard left. A few minutes passed, Jack's heart rate returned to normal and without hearing a sound, he texted Coop and asked if it was "All Clear?" Receiving the Thumbs Up emoji from Coop, Jack left the building and continued with his work.

When Jack had finished, he returned to the hoop house from which they had hatched their plan. Coop asked Jack by text if he had "encountered any problems with his installation."

Jack texted "No."

"Good," texted Coop, "I'll program my iPhone app and set it to begin in 10 minutes with a 60 second delay between.

"Now, step two, you take your walk about," said Coop as

if speaking to an Aborigine in Australia, "and I'll find my spot."

Jack ditched his backpack, exited the hoop house, and began slowly walking toward the saloon while softly whistling Snow White's Seven Dwarf's favorite tune: "Whistle While You Work."

CHAPTER EIGHT

Within a couple of minutes, Jack heard "Whoa, who goes there?" Jack turned around and saw an armed guard with a very angry dog thankfully on a leash.

"It's me," responded Jack meekly.

"Arms up," the guard insisted while holding the leash to his growling and barking dog. "Who are you?"

"I'm Jack," came his response.

"Jack who and what are you doing here? This is a restricted area," the guard asked and stated.

"Armstrong. Restricted from what?"

"Restricted from people like you. What are you doing here?" asked the guard.

"I was hiking and got lost in the hills, saw some trucks and followed them over the hill to here," responded Jack.

"Put your hands behind your head, interlock your fingers and walk toward that old saloon," said the guard pointing with his gun and holding the anxious dog who was growling and tugging at his leash.

"You going to buy me a drink?" asked Jack.

"I wouldn't kid around if I was you: you're in big trouble," admonished the guard. "All I have to do is let this dog go, and you will be torn to shreds."

Upon entering the saloon, the guard announced, "Look what I found." The men around the poker table turned and looked at Jack.

"Who, the heck are you and what are you doing here?"

asked the apparent chief of this motley tribe, a guy the others called Curley.

"Hi, I'm Jack, and I'm here to make a deal!" Jack exclaimed.

"A deal? Are you out of your fucking mind? You're in no position to make a deal with us, buddy. Cedrick you and Fred take him out and let the dogs 'play' with him," Curley commanded.

"Ok, but you will regret it," said Jack.

"We'll regret it?" asked Curley rhetorically.

Suddenly, a large explosion occurred, and everyone jumped from their chairs and rushed outside to see what happened. They saw a fire ball consume one of the canopy-covered hoop houses and begin to destroy some of the overhead camouflage.

"What the heck? Did you do that?" Curley asked Jack accusingly.

"Yep, little old me and my friend, Coop," quipped Jack.

"You're going to have hell to pay for that!" Curley exclaimed. "Give me your dog Will." Just then a second explosion occurred, and another hoop house blew up. The group was stunned and didn't know what to do.

"May I make a suggestion?" offered Jack quietly.

"What?" asked Curley incredulously.

"I said, may I make a suggestion?" repeated Jack.

"Suggest what?"

"I suggest that you return the water you stole from the town of Hopeful," said Jack.

"Do what?" yelled the boss. "Are you crazy?"

"I don't think so," responded Jack.

Just then a third explosion occurred, and another hoop house was consumed by fire. "Why don't we just shoot you, instead?"

"Well because every 60 seconds another hoop house will explode unless you agree to return the water. Does everyone see the red dot on the Curley's forehead?" shouted Jack over the excitement.

All turned and looked at the boss and stared in disbelief at the dot placed squarely in the middle of the Curley's forehead. They all began to point at Curley's head. "The dot is a courtesy of my pal, Coop, who is an ex-Navy Seal, and who is aiming his M4A1 assault rifle at you presently. No harm to me and no harm to you, Curley," declared Jack. "Now let's make a deal before your whole marijuana farm goes up in smoke. If you agree and I give Coop the signal, the explosions stop!" Just then a fourth explosion occurred.

"You think you know what you are dealing with, but believe me, you don't," declared Curley.

Seems to me I have heard that before, Jack thought to himself.

Curley thought for a few seconds, and asked: "So to stop the destruction of our green houses and remove the armed threat, we have to return the water that we took from the town of Hopeful?"

"Yep, that's it," agreed Jack. "Clean and simple. And, of course, don't go near the town ever again," Jack added.

Curley thought for a moment longer, then said, "The syndicate won't be happy with this, and you guys are going to be sorry. You will be in the cross hairs, but that is your problem." Then he nodded his agreement, and simply said, "Ok."

With that, Jack raised his hands as if signaling a touchdown, like Touchdown Jesus at Notre Dame, which alerted Coop that they had an agreement. Coop pulled up the detonator app on his iPhone, and the explosions ceased. "Now line up your ten trucks and begin filling them to the brim with water to be returned to Hopeful," commanded Jack.

While the trucks were loading, Curley slid back into the saloon and called Big Joe. "We have trouble."

"What trouble?" asked Big Joe.

Curley explained.

Big Joe said, "With armed guards and attack dogs you let a couple of hikers take control of our farm and stash? What do you guys have? Rocks for brains? There is going to be Hell to pay for this." Then borrowing a line from Butch Cassidy, he concluded, "Who are those guys? Whoever they are, tell Cedrick and Fred to get even with them!"

After the crack of dawn, a parade of 10 tanker trucks carrying 45,000 gallons of water made its way into the town of Hopeful. The town's people were beginning to move about their morning business and noticed the parade with wonderment, then as word spread excitement grew. "Look, it's truckloads of water being delivered," said one excited on looker. "Where did that come from?" asked another. "I don't know, but we'll take it!" It was like carrying water to hopeful people in the Desert. Or, as Gramps would say, "Manna from Heaven."

Coop and Jack accompanied the trucks in their parade

through town and led them to Grandpa Walker's home. Coop ignored the doorbell and knocked on front door. When Gramps answered, he looked sleepy and bewildered. Coop asked him "Where do you want your water delivered Gramps?" Walker looks up and down the street in front of his home in astonishment and scratched his head. "Where did this come from?" he asked.

Coop said, "It's from those aliens you mentioned."

Still mystified, Walker said, "Well, I guess they can return it from where they got it." Coop nodded agreement and motioned for Jack to organize the trucks to proceed as directed.

That night, there was new life in town with the return of the stolen water. The town took on a fiesta atmosphere, with music, dancing and colorful lights brightening the town. There was even a Mariachi band.

The next day, Sunday, Coop and Jack attended Grandpa Walker's Baptist sermon at the Sea of Galilee church. Walker was stunning: a tall black man dressed in his black robes and greeted warmly by the congregation who stood throughout the ceremony in true Baptist style.

"Today is our Thanksgiving," implored Walker. "Our Thanksgiving," he repeated. "For today, we have water while yesterday we had little. As Jesus taught us by ordering his disciples to divide the few fish and loaves of bread among the many, today we share with our brothers and sisters the return of our water! Hallelujah, Hallelujah, Hall-el-ujah!," he shouted to the congregation who returned the praise.

Then music began and a choir sang "Amazing Grace".

Everyone in the church was on their feet and joined in with hands clapping and bodies moving to the music.

Coop looked at Jack and said, "Reminds me of Glide Memorial in San Francisco and Reverend Cecil Williams" as he clapped his hands with the music. Jack nodded back also keeping time to the music with his hands and feet.

"We all know that Jesus walked on water because he had faith. Now we have water which gives us faith. Hallelujah!" Walker declared. "As we know, faith is the substance of things hoped for and the evidence of things not seen. Through faith we understand that the worlds were framed by the word of God, so that things which are seen were not made of things which do appear," Walker preached.

"As we slept last night, our water was stolen by unknown forces and by this morning, the water returned in a mysterious way. Keep the faith my brothers and sisters, and your faith will set you free!" Walker declared. "Remember Daniel and the Lion's Den," Walker reminded the congregation. "What set Daniel free from harm? It was his faith. Faith in God set him free."

"I'm glad we could assist with Walker's faith," whispered Jack to Coop who was smiling from ear to ear.

After the sermon, Coop and Jack caught up with Grandpa Walker. Coop said, "Well Gramps, that was a terrific sermon. The return of the water should suit you and the town well. Keep the Faith. Now you need not move," concluded Coop.

"Not so fast, Gary. What happens when it runs out?" he asked.

"Runs out?" repeated Coop.

"You don't think that what was restored will last forever, do you?" asked Walker.

"I never gave it much thought," said Coop.

"Look, I'm no hydrologist, but we have been suffering a 20-year long drought in California, and our water supply is not replenishing itself. Some say our aquifers are being depleted by Big Ag. All I know is that my well has run dry, and it may show some life now that it has been partially replenished with the water that was stolen by the aliens, but it certainly won't last forever," said Walker.

"I have an idea: how deep is your well?" asked Jack.

"I'm not sure, probably about 50 feet," answered Walker.

"What if it were several hundred feet deep?" offered Jack.

"I expect that would certainly help," answered Walker.

"Coop and I will see what we can come up with in regard to drilling a deeper well for you," said Jack. "We really don't want you to have to move because of a lack of water."

CHAPTER NINE

"What do you think, Jack?" asked Coop.

"We need to find a well driller," responded Jack. "But before we do, we need to keep an eye out for some bad guys who may not like what we made the illegal marijuana guys do in returning Hopeful's water. The marijuana boss made it clear that 'the syndicate' would not be happy with what we did," explained Jack.

"The syndicate? What syndicate?" asked Coop.

"Beats me," said Jack. "Maybe it's the water syndicate, or the marijuana syndicate, or the alien syndicate," joked Jack. "Whatever it is, we should keep an eye out, I think they may have some retribution in mind. His exact words were: 'You think you know what you are dealing with, but believe me, you don't'."

"I think you could be right, Jack. Wasn't that a line from the Jack Nicholson movie 'Chinatown'?" said Coop. "For now, let's see if we can line up a drilling company for Grandpa Walker's well."

"I'll give Google a try," as Jack manipulated his iPhone and found reference to the Lundy Well Service. He gave the service a call and received a recorded message: "Sorry we can't take your call right now as we are in the field servicing our clients. Please leave a message and we'll get back to you." Coop did as instructed and left his name and cell number.

Jack suggested trying another well service. They found Arnie's Well Service and gave Arnie a call. They received the same response and left another message. O for 2: "one more and we strike out," said Jack laughing.

The third well drilling service at least answered the phone. The response though was no better as they both listened on Coop's iPhone speaker: "We are booked for six months, and if you can find another available service, we suggest that you go with them," said the receptionist.

"Do you know where the boss is," inquired Jack.

"Oh, you mean Red?"

"Yes, Red," responded Jack tying the name to Red's Well Service.

"He is in Corcoran today on a job," the receptionist answered.

"Thanks," Jack signed off not telling the receptionist that they would track him down. "Coop let's take a side trip to Corcoran.

"OK, I'll drive. We will head south on Highway 99," answered Coop.

Soon after they left Hopeful, they began to see "those" signs again:

"Governor Stop Throwing Our Farm Jobs and Water in the Ocean."

"Is Growing Food Wasting Water?"

"Save California Water, Build More Dams."

"Governor Stop Wasting Our Dam Water."

"People certainly have strong feelings about water in California's central valley, Coop," observed Jack.

"They sure do," agreed Coop. "As Gramps said, "You can't live without it. Didn't Mark Twain say, 'Water is worth fighting over, whiskey isn't'?"

Then they saw a sign announcing, "Tom McCleod Slept Here."

"Cute," said Jack. "Everyone is jacked up about water, or the lack thereof, and some jokester announces who slept here. And where is 'here'? There is nothing around for miles. And who is Tom McCleod?"

"One of those unanswered mysteries of life," answered Coop as he noticed a car in his rear-view mirror, "I think someone is following us. "

Just outside of Fresno on Highway 99, Jack leaned forward and checked the side view mirror and lowered his visor to align the mirror it contained to show what was behind them. Spotting a black SUV with two men in it caused Jack to say, "Well, it didn't take long for the syndicate to become unhappy. What do we do now, partner?"

"They don't know where we are headed," said Coop. "So, a bit of a 'wild goose' chase may be in order for them," he said as he floored his BMW X3 Competition and the car leapt forward. In seconds, they were doing over 100 mph and the car following them was having trouble keeping up. Highway 99 was generally a straight four lane highway heading North and South through California's Central Valley, about 300 miles long. It merged north into Highway 50 in Sacramento and South into Interstate 5 near the Grapevine. What a name for a town, thought Coop remembering that it got its name from some Spanish residents who planted grapevines nearby. "Shall we invite some company to check them out?" asked Coop.

"What do you have in mind?" asked Jack.

"Hold on," Coop said as he dialed his car phone and continued driving at a lightning-fast pace. He called Murph, a Captain at the BPD, his old Berkeley police department. "Murph, it's Coop," Coop announced over the car's speaker phone.

"Whoa, Coop, it's been a while. What's up?"

With both hands solidly on the wheel Coop explained, "Jack and I are headed South on 99 near Fresno toward Corcoran. We think there are a couple of bad guys who are after us. I wonder if you can call your friends at the CHP and ask for a stop and ID?" Coop asked.

"What makes you think that they are bad guys?" asked Murph.

Rounding a curve at 95 mph and fishtailing Coop regained control of the car and continued to explain nonchalantly, "We busted an illegal marijuana farm last night and made them return 45,000 gallons of stolen water to the town of Hopeful where my grandfather lives. The gang's boss, a guy named Curley, said some guys in the syndicate would not be happy with what we made them do. We think that they may be up to some retribution," said Coop, remembering a certain Presidential candidate who also used that word.

"Got it," said Murph. "I'll make the call. Are you driving your BMW?"

"Yes, at a rather high rate of speed," Coop offered, fishtailing again out of another turn. They are in a black SUV. "I'll take them 'off road' on Highway 41 toward Lemoore then cut it back on 198 so the hunter has time to set up and intercept its prey near Visalia on 99," suggested Coop.

"Sounds like a plan," acknowledged Murph. "I'll pass it onto CHIP. Be careful!"

"Thanks, Murph," concluded Coop as he discontinued the call.

"This is the Heart of the Valley," Coop explained to Jack in a matter-of-fact style while continuing his high rate of speed on a country road with dust flying everywhere. Gesturing with his wheel free hand, he described the Central Valley is "Where hundreds of farming families live and eke out a living."

"I once met a fellow by the name of Ramon Resa. He grew up in Goshen, a small town off Highway 99 near Visalia. He had an unknown number of brothers and sisters and a mother who did not want to keep him, so he was raised by others. The family was composed of migrant farmers who would travel up and down the Central Valley harvesting fruit, cotton and anything that needed hand picking, irrespective of the weather: well over 100 or well below freezing, it didn't matter as the pickers had to do their job.! The kids would often have to travel in the trunk of the car well before dawn to the next job site with the hatch partially open so they could breathe. Little Ramon at only three years old had the responsibility of piling the picked cotton in a mound so the older kids and adults could bundle it for collection and shipment.

"Despite the difficult life Ramon and his family lived, he made the best of it. One of his teachers observed that he had a unique difficulty reading which placed him at the bottom of his class. Upon further observation, the teacher concluded that he was dyslectic. Once diagnosed, Ramon was taught appropriately and jumped ahead of his class given his raw intelligence.

"Today, Ramon Resa is an MD and practices pediatrics in the Central Valley's Potterville, not far from where we are. He wrote a book entitled: 'Out of the Fields' as we see around us." With Coop's sweeping his arm in a broad gesture in front of their speeding car, "Dr. Resa helps the people of the fields obtain the medical needs they desperately require. Sometimes, those with the greatest struggles in life rise to the top. Dr. Resa is an inspiration to us all." Coop exclaimed, and "The jerks following us are not."

About then, Coop swung left onto Highway 198 doing over 80 mph in a 30-mile zone and continued to lead the prey trailing them toward Visalia and the trap that awaited them.

As they turned onto the main highway, Coop and Jack noticed a California Highway Patrol car closing in on the black car and suddenly red lights and siren could be seen and heard. Then over a loudspeaker, a deep voice stated: "Pull over to the right side of the road, safely stop your vehicle and remain inside."

Coop began laughing. "So much for those guys." Next, he called Murph and thanked him for interceding. He also asked if Murph would "share with him the names of those stopped when that was available."

"Happy to do so," responded Murph.

About an hour and a half from Hopeful, they saw a sign welcoming them to Corcoran, population 24,000, elevation 200 feet. Coop began to laugh out loud. "Elevation 200 feet. Hum."

"What are you laughing at?" asked Jack.

"Corcoran is noted for two things: the home of Charles Manson who was housed in the California state prison located here until his death in 2017 and land subsidence, not elevation," commented Coop.

"What do you mean 'land subsidence'?" asked Jack.

"Corcoran is subsiding nearly a foot a year: over 11feet in the past 14 years," offered Coop. "It has subsided over 30 feet in the past 50 years. Heck the subsidence could swallow up a whole house in some cases."

"Thirty feet!" exclaimed Jack.

"There is a famous photo of a fellow next to a telephone pole in Fresno County's West side on Panoche Road, not far from here," Coop explained. "I read about him in Mark Arax book, 'The Dreamt Land,' which described in detail the Central Valley and water issues. At the top of the telephone pole is a sign that reads '1925', where the road once stood. Halfway down is a second sign painted with '1955' indicating where the road was in that year. At the bottom, where the road was when this fellow was standing, a third sign that says '1977.' The distance between the top of the pole and the bottom is 30 feet showing the discrepancy of where the road used to be at the top of the telephone poll and where is sat in 1977. We don't know where the relative road depth is today as the telephone poll which served as a marker in 1977 can't be found.

"The fellow in the photo is Joe Poland, a government scientist who was Harvard educated," Coop continued. "Joe was a man of average height, pictured with pork pie hat, glasses, short sleeve white shirt with pocket protector. His life's mission was to study land subsidence, much of it in California's Central Valley."

"Why the subsidence?" asked Jack.

"Depletion of the underground aquifers by farmers," answered Coop. "Farmers are poking so many holes in the ground—some say too many straws in the soup—that the earth is sinking. Farmers have been sucking water out of the ground for years. Groundwater accounts for about 40% of the state's water supply in a normal year, and as much as 60% during droughts like the one we are currently enduring. Annually, aquifers are replenished with rainwater and snowmelt from the Sierras; however, the replenishment does not overcome the overdrafts by farmers. An estimated 2 million acre-feet of water is pulled out annually from the ground and never replaced. About 80% of groundwater is used for farming. And when the earth sinks, so do roads, aqueducts, bridges, dams, and canals. These are very expensive to repair and replace and are essential to modern life."

"I imagine that folks who work the farms are not exactly flush with cash," offered Jack.

"No, they are not, generally. It is an agricultural community with low earnings—about half the national average—16% unemployment and little capacity for increased taxes to fix what essentials need repairing," stated Coop.

"And there is little transparency or accountability about the governance of water in the area," he continued. "The LA Times recently published an article about the Tulare Lake region which includes Cochran. It concluded that when it comes to water, 'this is a region that operates more like a secretive fiefdom ruled by a handful of legacy farming clans than a publicly governed jurisdiction where decisions affecting the well-being of residents are made on a foundation of transparency and accountability'."

"Sounds like a hornet's nest. So where do we go from here?" asked Jack.

"Let's go to the local water district office and try to figure out where Red is drilling."

After driving a few minutes around town, they passed a one-story stucco building labeled Tulare Lake Basin Water Storage District. "In, we go," said Coop.

CHAPTER TEN

"Hi, I'm Gary Cooper and this is my colleague, Jack Armstrong. We are searching for Red of Red's Well Service. Do you happen to know where he is?"

"Not off hand. Are you sure he is in Corcoran?" the bright eyed, pretty young Latino woman asked.

"Well, this is where his receptionist said he would be," answered Coop. "Presumably he is drilling a well here."

"Oh, a well driller. I will check our records and see if we can locate a permit describing where the well might be located," the young woman said. She left the Water District counter, turned, and opened a file cabinet next to the back wall, as Coop and Jack gave her the once over and nodded in agreement that she had a dynamite figure. After a few minutes, she returned with a small folder. "I see here that Red's has been issued a license to drill a well out of town a couple of miles from here on Whitley Avenue. Take a left out of the parking lot and then make the first right onto Whitley Avenue. Whitley Avenue proceeds through town and is named after the man who founded Corcoran in the early 1900's when he brought 30,000 acres. Hobart Johnstone Whitley," she explained.

"Thanks for your help," offered Jack as he winked at her, and she smiled. He and Coop then exited the office.

They drove as instructed along Whitley Avenue and exited the small commercial part of town and entered a rural part of Corcoran. After a couple of miles, Coop pulled over and they exited the car to get a better view of the surroundings. Standing on the door sills to gain a better look, they surveyed the area and, in the distance, saw some rigging and presumably some drilling gear. "Let's take a look over there," said Coop pointing to the rigging and motioning Jack to get in the car.

As they neared the rigging, they notice signage on the side of a truck announcing in bright red letters against the truck's black background: "Red's Well Service". Effective advertising thought Jack.

Seeing an older roughneck shouting orders to two Latinos, they approached and introduced themselves. "Hi, I'm Gary Cooper and this is my friend, Jack Armstrong."

"You sure don't look like the Gary Cooper I saw in the Westerns," declared Red laughing.

"My mother's dream was to have a son like Gary Cooper. A smart, good-looking, long-legged cowboy. Instead, I'm what she wound up with," explained Coop with a smile on his face.

Red laughed again. "And my father wanted a son like the oil well firefighter, Red Adair. He got the first half, a well driller, but not the oil well fire fighter he wished," answered Red said also with a laugh. "So we have something in common: not measuring up to parental aspirations!"

"Did he give you a last name?" asked Coop.

"Somewhere, but people just call me Red," he said.

"You look busy, and we don't want to waste your time, Red," said Coop. "My grandpa lives in Hopeful, and he needs his well to be drilled deeper. The town is running out of water. We called a couple of other drilling services and only got their recordings to leave a message. When we connected with a live person, your receptionist, we thought we might be onto something. So here we are," explained Coop.

"Well, you are, and you aren't," said Red. "You found me, but I can't help. I'm too busy to take on any new business. Seems like the whole Central Valley is watered down. Even if I could take on your job, it would have to be cleared by the Big Boss."

"The Big Boss?" asked Jack. "I thought you worked for yourself as Red's Well Service."

"I do work for myself, but any new well drilling work in the Central Valley has to be 'commissioned' by Big Joe Thornley," explained Red.

"Commissioned?" asked Jack.

"Yep, approved," responded Red.

"Is that legal? Is Thornley some sort of government official?

"No, he isn't, and it doesn't matter if it's legal," said Red. "It's the way things are done in the Central Valley."

"I thought a permit and license is all that is needed to drill a water well," commented Jack aloud expressing his frustration.

"What happens if a well is drilled without being commissioned by Big Joe Thornley?" asked Coop.

"Let's see," said Red quizzically staring at the sky, "Sometimes, fertilizer nitrates are poured down the well making the water undrinkable. Sometimes, a well driller's rigging is mangled up and made unusable. Occasionally, the driller's laborers are harassed and run off the job. And every now and then, a drill owner goes missing and is found weeks later, floating in an aquifer," said Red.

"Those are pretty stiff alternatives. How does one get a well 'commissioned'?" asked Jack.

"First, you must meet a representative of Joe's, who will size up the job and assess an appropriate 'Administrative' fee. Once the fee is paid, the job will be placed on a 'To Be Performed' list. Then, after a few months, a well driller is assigned by Big Joe and will come to the site and begin work for which you will pay a fee by the foot. Usually, about $60 a foot for shallow domestic wells to as much as ten times that for agricultural wells with stainless steel casings," Red explained.

"Where does the money go?" asked Coop.

"The administrative fee goes directly to Joe as does 20% of the drilling fees," responded Red.

"Joe must be rich," said Jack.

"Either he is, or his syndicate is," said Red.

"Syndicate?" asked Jack.

"Yes, Big Joe Thornley's syndicate. Rumor has it that his syndicate is controlled by organized crime, overseas interests and is connected to politicians," said Red.

Just then, a shot rang out and they all took cover behind Red's well drilling apparatus. "What was that?" asked Jack.

"Seems like we stimulated some interest from someone in Joe's syndicate," answered Red.

"Heck, we were just talking to you," commented Jack.

"Sometimes, that's all it takes if Joe's boys think we are up to no good," said Red. "Joe likes to keep a tight lid on his operations and eyes are on his well drillers as we control water access."

"And we crashed one of Big Joe's marijuana parties last night. He is likely pissed about that," offered Coop.

Another shot was heard as it pinged off the well drill.

"What do we do now," asked Jack.

"Usually, I simply wait it out until they leave," answered Red.

"So, this has happened before?" asked Jack.

"You bet," said Red. "Every so often I could be meeting with someone who Big Joe's guys view as 'suspicious' and bam, the guns come out scaring the heck out of everyone."

"Are those the guys who were following us?" asked Jack of Coop.

"Appears to be," answered Coop. "At least it looks like the same black SUV that was following us."

"You carrying?" asked Jack.

"Yeah. Apparently blowing up part of their marijuana grove and making them return 45,000 gallons of stolen water to Hopeful wasn't enough. I think they need another lesson," said Coop as he pulled his handgun, a Glock 19, the latest Navy Seal handgun, which is replacing the Sig Sauer P226. The Glock is small, lightweight, and reliable. Coop stood behind the big well drilling auger for cover and took aim at the two men hiding behind their SUV. He shot the passenger side window and the rear seat window of their car. This caused the gunmen to hit the ground, which is what Coop had intended. He then shot 4 rounds quickly under the SUV causing the bullets to ricochet off the ground and "motivate" Big Joe's boys to jump into their car and speed away. "I don't think that they will be back or will bother you again, Red."

"Thanks, I needed that," said Red.

"Red, if we hung around today, would you have time for a beer after work?" asked Jack.

"Why not?" answered Red "I kinda like you hanging around town for a while. Let's meet at Harry's Bar on 6th street at 6 pm."

"Done, see you at 6," said Coop as they shook hands and departed. As Coop and Jack closed the doors to Coop's BMW, they looked at each other, smiled and said in unison: "You think you know what you are dealing with, but believe me, you don't."

CHAPTER ELEVEN

"Don't you find it interesting, Coop?" asked Jack. "During our last adventure, we were on a treasure hunt for gold and this time, we are on a treasure hunt for water. Who would have thought of something as plentiful as water being treasure?"

A few hours later they met up with Red at Harry's Bar in Corcoran. Harry's was the basic saloon in a rural town except that water posters predominated the wallpaper. Clearly, farming ruled in Corcoran. "Thanks for joining us," said Coop. "The beer is on us."

"Thanks, Fellas, for the beer and for swatting away those insects this afternoon," said Red.

"We assume that you had no further trouble from them," stated Jack.

"No, never saw them again," answered Red. Then he said, "I take it that you guys are new to 'Water World'. And I don't mean Kevin Costner's movie."

"You got that right!" said Coop. "We are virgins when it comes to understanding the water system in California. All we want to do is help my grandfather have enough water to continue to live where he has for 50 years."

"Simple enough and yet it isn't," said Red. "The water system in California is complex. There are four primary sources of imported water for the Central Valley and Southern California: The State Water Project, the Owens Valley/ Los Angeles Aqueduct, the Colorado River and the Central Valley

Project. Since your Grandpa lives in the Central Valley, let's focus on that Project.

The CVP benefits farmers greatly. In effect, the Sacramento River area in Northern California acts as a giant sponge which receives nearly three quarters of the rain fall in the Valley while the larger San Joaquin Valley to the South receives about 25%. Using 20 reservoirs in the foothills of the Sierra Nevada, the CVP stores about 13 million acre-feet of water, that's the equivalent of 13 million acres covered a foot deep with water, and releases more than half of it annually through its canals and aqueducts."

Red continued, "Historically, the CVP was the world's largest water and power project when undertaken during FDR's administration. Because of the Great Depression and the lack of funds, the State of California had to turn to the Federal Government to complete the project and administer it through the Bureau of Reclamation," recounted Red.

"What about California's shrinking groundwater, like Grandpa Walker's? Isn't state government doing anything to protect it?" asked Coop.

"Yes and No," responded Red. "California until recently was one of the few states that did not regulate groundwater. A few years ago, the state enacted the Sustainable Groundwater Management Act. This requires water districts to regulate the removal of groundwater from aquifers. Although enacted in 2014, the regulation does not take effect until 2040. In the meantime, hundreds of wells are being drilled and groundwater is being removed ahead of the effective date of the regulation. That's one reason why I'm so busy!" commented Red.

"New research predicts that thousands of drinking water wells could run dry in the Central Valley by the time the law's restrictions take full effect in 2040. The simple fact is that we are pumping too much groundwater."

"Isn't there effective state regulation of water in the interim? asked Jack.

"The Water Resources Control Board's job is to ensure that existing rules are followed pending the 2040 regulations," answered Red. "The Water Board needs to routinely implement water right curtailments—analyzing how much water is available, determining which water users can and cannot divert water, issuing curtailment orders to prevent water users from taking water that is not theirs and carrying out enforcement when violations occur. Unfortunately, the Board does not effectively do this."

"Why?" asked Coop.

"Because numerous bureaucratic, political and policy obstacles stand it the way. And enforcement laws and options are too light. Recently, the San Francisco Chronicle reported that 80 ranchers were caught for diverting half of the Shasta River flow. They were fined the maximum, a whopping $4,000 which amounted to $50 per rancher! Besides, there are only 80 statewide investigators assigned to discover water violations. Need I say more?" asked Red.

"In addition to the race against the 2040 regulations, sustainability of the Central Valley is battling Wall Street investors. Some of the world's largest investment banks, pension funds and insurers have been depleting California's groundwater to grow high-value nuts, leaving less for surrounding farmers and communities. Its David versus

Goliath all over again and the little guy, like your grandfather, Coop, is losing."

Red continued to explain, "During the last few years, one of every six of the deepest wells in the Central Valley has been drilled on land owned or managed by outside investors, according to Bloomberg. Deep wells drain shallower wells. One investor drilled a well over 1200 feet deep which is capable of extracting 2400 gallons of water per minutes. Besides depleting water resources, the vast amount of water extracted from the ground has caused land subsidence. In some instances, as much as a foot a year. Just look at Corcoran, where we are today, the town has subsided more than 30 feet over the years which has caused aqueducts, road, and buildings to be damaged."

"Yes, we drove through town and noticed some of the effects of land subsidence," said Coop.

"Because of the scarcity of water, some of the world's largest financial entities have sought control over lakes, rivers, and underground aquifers," added Red. "They need the water to grow the crops in which they have invested, principally almonds and pistachios which have the highest returns on capital invested."

"And to add insult to injury, Red continued, "these same investors and farmers export their high value products overseas, oftentimes to countries with which we do not have friendly relations. For example, as much as 30 percent of California almonds are exported to China."

"So, in effect, we are exporting water to China! How do you like those apples?" asked Coop.

"Or egg rolls," said Jack.

"How do politics enter into water allocations?" asked Coop.

"Does a bear do what where?" responded Red. "Of course, politics plays a hand in water allocation. Where are the votes?" He asked rhetorically. "In the cities, not in the farmland."

"So, if LA or Phoenix are severely reduced or cut off from water, politicians would suffer?" concluded Jack.

"And the leader of the Red party, no relation to me," asserted Red, "represents a Central Valley district. So, a Blue President may not look favorably upon that Central Valley district, and they lose water while nearby cities benefit because that is where the votes are. Within the farming districts, let us not overlook the value of Big Ag over the fishes (aka the environmental movement). A Red President will favor Big Ag every time."

"Recently, however, you may have read that our politician staged a publicity stunt by ordering the federally controlled Central Valley pump station to release 2.2 Billion gallons of water. The water was wasted as it ended up in the Tulare lake bed and by-passed farmers who would need the water the following summer."

"Why would he do that?" asked Jack.

"Just to show that he could," responded Red.

"As you can imagine, water is the life blood of a farmer. A lack of water is a death knell to the farmers like Grandpa Walker," added Coop.

"What are the three things that one needs for life to exist?" Red asked rhetorically.

Jack answered, "How about food, air, and water, not

necessarily in that order. Take any one of those away for varying amounts of time and life will cease to exist."

"You got it! Water is also essential for real estate development (aka the movie Chinatown)," added Red. "Without water, there is no real estate development."

"Remember what Grandpa Walker is experiencing now," said Coop. "After fifty years, he is moving because of the lack of a consistent flow of water."

"He who controls water, controls life, agricultural food and real estate development," said Red. "That makes water a very important and valuable commodity. Big Joe's syndicate and Wall Street have figured that out and are asserting control over water allocation to increase the amount they control and its value."

Then he added, "And during drought conditions, like what we have experienced for the past 20 years, the value of water skyrockets, about 1,000 to 1,500 California households a year have dry wells and farmers are plowing under their crops and selling their farms at rock bottom prices rather than attempting to water them. Researchers estimate that about a third of the nearly 30,000 domestic wells analyzed are at risk of failure. A higher proportion, as much as 40% of these wells, affect disadvantaged communities.

"Adding further value to water are the wildfires," explained Red. "Fires burn until water extinguishes them or they run out of fuel. Annually, wildfires cost many lives, destroy thousands of structures, and create billions of dollars in actual and economic losses. With climate change and more frequent drought conditions, California has suffered major wildfires since 2017 including two exceeding one million acres each."

Coop's phone rang. "Hello," he answered. "Murph, what's the latest? Ah. Ok. What are their names? Any priors? Ok, I see. And for the record, Murph, we think those were the guys who took some shots at us a few hours ago and who we ran into at the illegal marijuana farm. No, we cannot say positively they were the guys, so no need to arrest them. Yes, we will be careful," he signed off.

Turning to Red, Coop said, "Before we leave, I think we need to visit Big Joe Thornley if we are going to make headway with Grandpa Walker's well. Do you know where we can find him?"

"He is not far from here, in Tulare," responded Red. "He has one of the largest orchards in the state. Over 50,000 acres. Head to Tulare and ask anyone in town where Big Joe's ranch is. You will have no trouble finding it. But be careful!"

"Thanks again Red for the tutorial." remarked Jack as they got up and left Harry's.

CHAPTER 12

As they walked to the car, Coop briefed Jack about his call with Murph. "The two guys in the car that were trailing and shooting at us, were ID ed as Cedrick Brown and Fred Struggles," Coop said. "Both have records: Brown was busted for assault and battery several times and spent some time in the can. Struggles also has a record of A&B with time served."

"Classic heavies," commented Jack. "Weren't those the guys called out by Curley at the pot farm?"

"Yes, I think I heard him say their names. We need to keep an eye out for these guys. No doubt they will try again," said Coop.

"At least they know that they are on our radar screen," commented Jack.

Within 30 minutes, Jack and Coop were entering the Tulare city limits. "Let's find a place where we can crash for the night and visit Big Joe tomorrow all fresh and presentable," suggested Jack as they drove along South Blackstone Street and noticed the Village Inn.

"Before we turn in, let's get a bite and a beer," said Coop.

"I'd like to shower up first," said Jack. "Ok with you?"

Coop nodded his agreement and they checked into the Village Inn requesting two rooms and a one-night stay at the registration desk. After a shower, shave and some clean up, Jack met Coop in the lobby and remembered passing a Mexican restaurant called Hacienda on the way into town. You up for some Mexican tonight?" asked Jack.

"Sure, let's give it a try," said Coop.

They headed to the restaurant and, upon entering, found it to be upscale with classic Latino décor and nearly full. Jack noted that there were a couple of empty bar seats. "Let's grab those," said Jack pointing to the two empties.

As they took their seats, Jack noticed a cute young woman seated next to him. She was wearing nicely pressed levies, probably Isaias, a flowered Armani blouse together with Yves Saint Lauren sandals. Jack noticed that she had finger and toenails painted blue which matched her eyes. He also noticed a light necklace that dazzled in the evening light and likely was from David Yurman. She had no wedding ring. Top it all off with a very appealing figure too, thought Jack.

"Hi, I'm Jack and this is my friend Coop," he introduced himself and Coop to her.

"I'm Samantha," she responded reservedly.

"Good to meet you Samantha," he said. "I must say, you certainly dress stylishly."

"Thank you," she responded demurely while checking out Jack's attire as well.

"This seems to be a very popular place," said Jack. "Yes, it is. Reservations are tough to land, so I frequently sit at the bar. The food is quite good, and ambience is very nice," she said.

"Are you local?" asked Jack.

"Yes, born and raised in Tulare," she commented.

"Are you schooling or working, Samantha? asked Jack.

"I work for the town newspaper, the Tulare Telegraph."

"What do you do there?" asked Jack.

"I'm an investigative reporter."

"That sounds cool. What led you to being an investigative reporter?"

"I graduated top of my class and wanted to stay local and work with the townspeople in Tulare."

"And what do you investigate?"

"Whatever strikes me as odd," she responded. "The Telegraph editors give me wide latitude in what I research and write," Samantha explained.

"What do you consider as 'odd'?" repeated Jack.

"I am investigating the effect Big Ag is having on the little farmer. Also, I am interested in the dirty water and dying wells that low-income people in the Central Valley are suffering," she responded.

"Coop and I are interested in some of the same. Coop's grandfather is being forced to sell his ranch and home of 50 years in Hopeful, because of a lack of water. Also, we found that a group of thieves were stealing water from him and the town's aquifer."

"It happens all too often around here," said Samantha. "The little guy is nearly defenseless. Perhaps with a little publicity some change will occur," she offered.

"Would you like to join us for a bite and a drink," Coop said invitingly.

"That would be nice given our common interest. Call me Sam, Sam Curtis" she responded and offered her hand to shake.

Jack asked a nearby waiter for a booth where the three of them could sit when one is available to continue their discussion over some food and drink. "I think one is opening up as we speak," said the waiter as Jack slipped him $20. "Right this way," said the server.

CHAPTER THIRTEEN

"Sam, our immediate concern is finding a driller who can provide Coop's grandfather a deep enough well for fresh water. We met with Red of Red's Well Service earlier today in Corcoran, and he said that the drillers are locked up by some guy by the name of Big Joe Thornley. Do you know him?" asked Jack.

"Sure," replied Sam, "Everyone knows of Big Joe."

"We understand from Red that Thornley controls who gets well drilling and who doesn't," said Jack. In effect, he decides who gets water and who doesn't in the Central Valley."

"I am working on a story now about control of the well drillers and Thornley's name keeps coming up. He does seem to have great influence on who gets to hire a driller and the cost of the well," said Sam.

"Do you know where he hangs out?" asked Coop.

Sam described a very large ranch in Tulare County which is Thornley's headquarters and is located about 5 miles North of town.

"What does he grow on his ranch?" asked Coop.

"Almonds," replied Sam.

"Almonds? Aren't they big water sucks?" asked Coop.

"Sure are," replied Sam. They lead the pack: a gallon of water per almond!"

"What other crops are large water sucks?" asked Coop.

"Wheat, alfalfa, lentils," replied Sam. "And, beyond crops, there is beef. Beef requires from 300 to 800 gallons of water to produce one pound depending upon whether precipitation is included in the calculation. Check out Beef Research.org."

"No way," said Coop exasperatedly.

"It's true," said Sam.

"No doubt many of these products are exported overseas as well," commented Jack. "Maybe the road signs rhetorically asking, 'Is Growing Food Wasting Water?' should be rewritten to say: 'Growing Food Is Exporting Water!'."

Coop nodded in agreement, "Let's order and continue our conversation." After some discussion, the three decided to share a combination of chicken and shrimp fajitas, brown beans, rice, chips with guacamole and accompanied by some "awesome" margaritas.

During dinner, the three discussed what was likely to happen at Big Joe Thornley's. "Do you guys even have an appointment with Big Joe?" asked Sam.

"Not really," replied Coop.

"So, you thought you would simply knock on the gate to his 50,000-acre ranch and expect to be let in?" she questioned.

"We kinda play it by ear," said Coop.

"That doesn't sound like a recipe for success," said Sam.

"You have a better idea?" challenged Coop.

"Why don't you guys join me during my scheduled interview of Thornley tomorrow afternoon? You can be my news assistants," suggested Sam. "Besides I wouldn't mind a bit of company confronting Big Joe."

"You have a scheduled interview tomorrow afternoon?" repeated Jack.

"That's what I said."

Jack looked at Coop. Coop nodded. Jack said, "We would be pleased to be your 'bodyguards,' I mean 'news assistants,' when you visit Big Joe."

"Good. Settled," affirmed Sam.

CHAPTER FOURTEEN

They drove Coop's BMW along rolling countryside North of the City of Tulare. After 5 miles they saw a turn off the highway for Thornley's Big Valley Ranch. The road led them to the foot of a hill where a half mile drive up the hill was highlighted on each side by alternating palm trees and agaves. The agaves were of the Americana and Chiapensis variety while the palms were of the Queen Anne type. At the top of the drive, several hundred feet above the valley floor, two large Royal Palms greeted them and led to an ornate home that looked like an out of place Mediterranean villa. They parked Coop's car in a spacious circular courtyard with an ornate fountain centered upon exotic tile and throwing water high in the air. Also, parked in the courtyard was a black Rolls Royce. "Someone is doing well," muttered Jack.

"Is Mr. Thornley available," asked Sam as she spoke into the intercom near the large, bronze door fit within a horseshoe arch frame.

"Do you have an appointment?" came the response from behind a small hatch that opened separately near the top of the door.

"Yes, I do. I am Samantha Curtis of the Tulare Telegraph."

"And who are the two gentlemen accompanying you?" which caused Sam, Jack, and Coop to notice a video camera mounted high above the door.

"They are my news assistants, Jack Armstrong and Gary Cooper," responded Sam.

"Wait one," came the response.

About 5 minutes later, the door buzzed and automatically opened. The three entered and were met by a large, muscular man dressed in a smart blue suit and standing 6'3". "Follow me," he said. They proceeded along an intricately laded stone path, down a large style reception room through the middle of which flowed a little stream. On one side of the stream was what appeared to be a sitting room while a two-story library adjoined the other side. The reception area and its stream stepped down into a two-story atrium and emptied into a large reflecting pool at least 50 feet long and 10 feet wide. The reflecting pool caused Jack to remember Jack London's magnificent unfinished residence in Sonoma called Wolf House, which was destroyed by fire.

Big Joe's reflecting pool was home to lazily floating lilies and a gentle fountain which sprayed water casually about. It was surrounded by what appeared to be living quarters under horseshoe arches and panoramic view windows. The walls reached to the sky as there was no roof over the atrium. The home was finished in the latest Ralph Lauren style polo lounge motif.

As they approached the end of the reflecting pool, they noticed a large piano upon which was placed a dozen or so framed photos, presumable of family members. One picture in front showed a large, distinguished man together with a truly beautiful Asian woman in a wedding pose.

The room at the far end of the atrium had no door blocking entry. Instead, the room opened spaciously into the atrium like the reception area located at the opposite end of the reflecting pool. They entered and viewed a large room lined on two sides with two-story bookshelves complete with a ladder. The back wall of the room was a wall of glass fitted within arches and magnifying a magnificent view of an enormous orchard lying hundreds of feet below the home and extending north for as far as the eye could see.

Seated at a massive table facing the atrium, was the distinguished looking man in the piano top wedding photo, this time dressed in Isaiah jeans, Hermes slip-on's, and Sid Mashburn shirt with sleeves rolled one quarter up each arm. He was enormous in size as his name implied: Jack estimated that Big Joe was 6 feet 5 inches tall and probably weighing 255 pounds. Although he was size-able, Jack viewed him as being quite fit for his 55 plus years in age.

"Ms. Curtis, please introduce me to your 'assistants', the man said.

"This is Jack Armstrong gesturing toward him with her right hand and Gary Cooper motioning with her left hand," Sam announced as they stood beside her. Jack and Coop are my news assistants," she said.

"I will take your word for it, Ms. Curtis," said the man behind the table in a not too subtle questioning attitude. "How can I help you?"

"Thank you for meeting with us," responded Sam. "Your home is spectacular and makes a statement with its Mediterranean motif." Big Joe nodded in acknowledgment. After a brief pause, Sam continued: "I am writing a story for my paper, The Tulare Telegraph, regarding the influence that Big Ag has upon the small farmer. You have one of the largest ranches in the Central Valley, and I thought it would be important to gain your perspective from a 'Big Ag' point of view."

"I may qualify as 'Big Ag', as you say, with over 50,000 acres of almonds," he responded.

"Perhaps you can tell us a little about your business," Sam asked.

"We have rich soil and Mediterranean climate in California which makes growing conditions idea when water is added."

"I have heard that almonds require an enormous amount of water, and the almond industry consumes 10% of the state's water. Is that correct?" Sam asked.

"We are proud that California produces close to 100% of commercial almonds in the United States and 80% of almonds worldwide. The real culprit when it comes to water is dairy and beef. Almond milk is less water intensive than cow's milk and a single pound of beef requires hundreds of gallons of water. About one-third of the state's entire water budget is used to produce meat and dairy. California's livestock industry uses more water than all the homes, businesses, and government in the state combined," counseled Thornley. "And let's not overlook cattle feed, alfalfa, which consumes 15% of the state's irrigation water," he added.

"Is it true that one-third of California produced almonds are exported overseas. Aren't we, in effect, exporting water to those countries?" asked Sam.

"I believe that America is the land of the free and home of the brave," responded Thornley. If it is legal and a good profitable business, then why stop it! Besides, water is a commodity controlled by individual property owners, not a resource to be managed collectively by the state. Water is not a public resource. It is owned and controlled privately."

"I am sure that you appreciate that the drought and current water usage is having a significant effect upon many in the state, Mr. Thornley. Mr. Cooper's grandfather, for example, is moving from his home of over 50 years because he has no water for his home or ranch," recounted Sam.

"Well, I'm sorry to hear that Ms. Curtis. I hope that Mr. Cooper's grandfather finds a peaceful place to reside."

"We do too, Mr. Thornley. You wouldn't happen to know any well drillers who could assist Mr. Cooper's grandfather in extending his well, would you?" asked Sam.

"We understand that to drill a water well, it has to be cleared by you, Mr. Thornley," added Coop.

"We are interested in maintaining quality control of the drilling process in the Valley, as I am sure you can appreciate," explained Thornley.

"Quality control, or simply 'control'?" asked Coop rhetorically.

"If we wished to 'control' drilling Mr. Cooper, we would not permit landowners to drill on their property. That, of course, is not the case. Property owners may drill to their hearts content on their property," added Thornley.

"And where do they obtain the equipment and expertise to do that?" persisted Coop.

"I expect that they can rent the equipment and ask advise from the rental company,"

"Doesn't that undermine 'quality control'?" asked Jack.

"That's why it's best to work with Thornley Drilling to accomplish what is needed," responded Thornley.

"There are fees associated with Thornley Drilling?" asked Coop.

"Yes, of course, there is an administrative fee associated with assessing the site, the equipment and the manpower needed to accomplish the desired well. Then, there is the cost of the drilling usually assessed by the foot drilled as well," explained Thornley.

"What if someone can't afford your fees?" asked Sam.

"Then they do not receive a well," Thornley flatly stated.

"Then they must move," concluded Coop.

Jack thought aloud, "I wonder how much property is affected by this well drilling regime?" No one responded. "Incidentally, have you become aware of organized attempts to steal water for illegal purposes, such as growing marijuana?" offered Jack.

"No, I haven't. I'm not surprised though as water is essential for crops and even life itself, so it is a valuable commodity," Thornley opined. "If you really want to pin the tail on the donkey, look at urban use of water and its waste thereof such as swimming pools and golf courses for the privileged. Or the 'environmental, no dam, save a salmon, brigade' which allows water to run unimpeded to the sea. How about Northern California's possessiveness of 'it's' water which has inhibited the creation of an efficient system of transporting water south through a peripheral canal, or Delta tunnel. Agriculture is big business for the Central Valley, for California, for the United States, and for the world, Ms. Curtis."

"You have helped us understand more completely the 'Big Ag' point of view," commented Sam. "We hope that you would be receptive to a follow up interview with some additional questions," she added.

"Sure, Ms. Curtis. Call me anytime," Thornley offered.

With that, the trio left the house on the hill and headed back to town. What they didn't know was the series of calls that Joe Thornley made after their departure.

CHAPTER FIFTEEN

"We have trouble brewing," Thornley spoke softly into his phone to his overseas syndicate member and the biggest contributor to the enterprise. In answer to a question, he explained, "A story that is being prepared for the local newspaper about 'Big Ag' and our exploitation of CV water. Once they realize that we are exporting a significant portion of the state's water overseas through the sale of almonds, beef, alpha, and other products while residents of the state suffer a multi decade drought, we will have hell to pay. And they will likely touch on our control of CV well drilling which affords us nice fees and assurance that we will always have sufficient water for our business needs by controlling who has access thereto."

"Have they connected us to the theft of water?" the syndicated member asked.

"Not yet, but I expect them to hit upon us stealing water for our collateral needs such as growing illegal marijuana. I think the two 'assistants' joining the reporter were the guys who raided our greenhouses outside of Hopeful. They fit Curley's description. They need to be watched."

After listening to further comment, Thornley volunteered "I think I was able to redirect their inquiry into the effect that environmentalist, urban dwellers, beef producers and Nor Cal possessiveness may have on the exploration of water."

The syndicate member then asked whether Big Joe had special arrangements in place with the local newspaper.

"Yes, I can catch and kill the story given the agreement we have with the Tulare Telegraph editor. Nevertheless, it may not be too soon for me to alert others in the syndicate that trouble is brewing."

"Other steps?" Big Joe repeated the question asked of him then answered, "I think a call to our political partners, Senator Nunley and Congressman McNitt could be helpful as well. It is time they begin to earn what we pay them for their 'service'. Perhaps they can sponsor some Federal legislation vesting water title to the property owner where it rightfully belongs."

"Also, I think calls to our lobbyist and the person we had placed on the state's water control board should be made. We have a good thing going and I don't want anything to interfere with the interests of our members or the income we have earned," he said. "A heads up to the Sheriff's Department is probably in order as well," he added.

"No, I don't think they are onto Operation Watered down" Thornley replied to a sensitive question over the phone. "But we should snuff out the risk before it becomes a reality. Indeed, it is time we put a tail on them. We need to know what they know, what they are learning and where they are headed. I have just the medicine to take care of that."

Next, he made another call and said: "Cedrick, it's Joe Thornley. I have a job for you and Fred. Be in my office at my hilltop home tomorrow at 2pm."

He texted someone else, "Call me asap, use a pay phone," he instructed.

CHAPTER SIXTEEN

Sam invited the boys back to her office to discuss the meeting with Thornley and asked what steps next should be taken. Jack immediately commented: "The guy is part of an organization which has connections everywhere. Much of his business is most likely criminal in nature—his syndicate. They participate in stealing water and either using it for illegal purposes or reselling it. They also control well drilling and export water-based products overseas which is likely legal if not socially unacceptable during drought conditions. Together these operations are making enormous profits for their syndicate."

Coop nodded his agreement and added, "Thornley's syndicate takes advantage of the 'little guy' through their theft of water and depriving small farmers from drilling for more water. It's a classic 'squeeze play' and if one is not big enough to protect oneself, they move or are history like Grandpa Walker."

"It doesn't seem fair, does it?" questioned Sam. "Perhaps we can even the score a little by writing a feature story about the same."

"What will that accomplish?" asked Jack.

"As for the illegal activities and the theft of water, we can hope that law enforcement will step in and put an end to it," said Sam. "Shinning a bright public light on questionable activities frequently result in legal action," she added.

Jack said that as a lawyer, he had noted numerous times

that the US Attorney in various jurisdictions religiously read the press and considered investigating highlighted questionable activities and taking legal action as appropriate. "I agree with Sam, this is often times where law enforcement gets its inspiration."

"And if it doesn't, perhaps we can intercede," added Coop smiling and no doubt thinking about his Black Ops business.

"I intend to write a story, and we will see where that takes us," offered Sam. "I'll shoot for a draft to provide my editor by next week. I think I will title it:

'The Great H2O Heist'.

I am noodling a lead reading: 'Did you know that during this 20 plus year drought, your irreplaceable water is being stolen from beneath your very feet? That's what is happening in Tulare County and perhaps elsewhere!'"

"Clever and intriguing," said Jack. "We look forward to reading an early draft. Coop and I will continue our journey south to Santa Monica, for a bit of R & R. Let us know when you have made some progress."

CHAPTER 17

"It really is built on a desert, isn't it?" commented Coop as they drove south on Interstate 5 past four huge pipes supplying water from the California aqueduct to Los Angeles near the Grapevine.

"Yes, it is," agreed Jack as he searched both sides of the highway over the Tehachapi mountains for signs of vegetation. The desert-like conditions continued into Los Angeles and even over the Sepulveda pass and past the Getty Center.

"Were you able to reach Sara? Is she expecting us given our delays in Hopeful and Tulare?" asked Coop.

"Yes, she is and with bells on," responded Jack happily as they turned onto Sunset Drive and headed for San Vicente. As they proceeded down San Vicente toward the ocean, Jack asked Coop if he knew how many Coral trees were planted in the center divider.

"Not really," answered Coop. "But they sure are beautiful flowering trees."

"There are 126 of them," said Jack. "They were planted by LA Mayor Sam Yorty when the Pacific Streetcar Line was replaced by the dividers on San Vicente which dead end at Ocean Avenue. Another favorite of mine is the Jacaranda tree with its purple leaves. And let's not forget the Palm trees that are in abundance here.

Coop eyed the cute young women running and biking along the road.

Jack noticed the same and said, "You will have to check

out the Palisades Park along Ocean Avenue. The Palisades Park is world-class with swaying Palm trees leaning toward a magnificent view of the Pacific Ocean. It is a prime spot for girl watching. And Montana Avenue is a terrific street lined with nice restaurants, shops, and young lovelies," added Jack.

"What is it about LA that the young ones like?" asked Coop.

"The sun, scenic beauty, movies, music, restaurants and just a great atmosphere for fun and entertainment," answered Jack.

"I'm sure that being on the edge of the Pacific with great beaches attracts the beauties too," said Coop.

"And beautiful people beget beautiful children," said Jack as they turned right off San Vicente onto Ocean Avenue Extension as the road began to decent into the Santa Monica Canyon. On the left they spotted the address for Sara's apartment and pulled into the carport. A brief flight of stairs down the side of the apartment house led them to a breezeway across which the apartment entrance was located. A rap on the door resulted in a jubilant Sara greeting the two of them.

"I missed you guys," she gushed. "Particularly, you, Mr. Armstrong," as she hugged and kissed him.

"I missed you too," said Jack as he squeezed her tightly and met her embrace with a long, slow kiss on her lips. As they broke apart, Sara faced Coop and said, "And I have a surprise for you Mr. Cooper." With that, she invited them in and from one of two bedrooms out walked Veronica Hill whom Coop had met while the boys helped her recover a treasure inherited from her great-great-grandfather, Graham

Stackhouse. Coop had become infatuated with her during what they fondly called, The Niantic Caper.

"Wow, this is a surprise!" exclaimed Coop as he stepped forward, swallowed her up in his arms and kissed her tenderly. "I sure didn't expect to see you here."

Veronica looked down blushing.

Sara motioned for them to step onto the deck. When they did, a breathtaking view of Santa Monica Bay and Santa Monica Canyon unfolded below them. All took in the breathtaking scenery: the coastline, surfers, boats and an endless view of the Pacific Ocean. Sara also mentioned that a famous actor who once played Batman rented a writing studio above them, while another famous actor who also played Batman owned a home below them.

Coop laughed, "How does it feel to be squeezed between two Batmen?"

Sara volunteered that in the late 1930s and early 1940s F. Scott Fitzgerald lived in an apartment next door to hers.

Jack was impressed by the nearby neighbors who surrounded the Sara's apartment and asked her who owned the building.

"It is owned by a family who raised their daughter here. They are terrific people. I sublet my apartment to a girl friend who is traveling in Europe currently. There are two commercial units at street level and six residential units below. As you can see my apartment is a two bedroom with a deck and the view of a lifetime, a breeze way over another deck, and it is rent controlled. Even though I am living in San Francisco, I hope to never give it up. Let's sit outside, have a drink, and catch up."

They spent the next hour or so bringing the ladies up to speed on their water adventures. "So, you think that you are onto something?" asked Sara.

"You bet," said Jack. "We believe that Big Joe Thornley, his men, and his syndicate are a form of organized crime manipulating water. We simply do not know the extent of it. I doubt that they will stop at growing illegal marijuana, controlled drilling and water diversion. We must do some more digging."

"And who is paying for this 'digging'?" asked Sara.

"Nobody," said Jack. "It is pro bono, as we say in the legal trade. At least for now. And let's not forget that this all started with Grandpa Walker, his need for livable water and an insufficient well which is causing him to move after 50 years."

"That's generous," added Veronica. "I assume that you are 'scraping by' from The Niantic Caper payoff."

"Exactly," said Jack remembering the millions that he and his team earned from their discoveries in Virginia City while working for Veronica. "I don't mind spending a few bucks in the interests of Coop's grandfather and our great state while investigating some corruption."

"Just make sure that your 'digging' doesn't lead to internment or incarceration," said Sara prophetically.

"That's why I'm along for the ride," said Coop. "I'll make sure my partner doesn't suffer a bad fate."

"You guys must be hungry. Why don't we head to Michael's on Third near Wilshire and get a bite? Thereafter, you can bunk here if you wish," offered Sara.

"Do you have room? asked Coop.

"Veronica can continue to occupy the guest bedroom, one of you can sack out on the living room sofa and the other can make yourself comfortable on the deck couch, the sea air and sound of the ocean will put you to sleep in the mild temperature," said Sara. "Unless each of you wish to keep us girls warm."

"Just like my old college days," thought Jack.

At Michael's they were seated in the restaurant's great three story atrium dining room. With the roof retracted, the sky above met the taste-full garden surrounding the dining room. Sara said that Michael, the owner, also has a first class restaurant in mid town New York. It took a couple of drinks for the group to soak in the ambiance before ordering their meals.

Veronica, eying Coop, asked Jack "how long do you expect to be in town."

"We're not sure," responded Jack. When we started south, we were simply looking for some R & R and to catch up with Sara "and a friend," explained Jack. "One thing led to the next and here we are several days later. We expect to receive a draft of an article that a reporter named Samantha is preparing for the Tulare Telegraph. She is trying to shine a public light on what's going on. After that, who knows? While we are in town, it would be great if you guys could show us some of the sites. I understand that there is a fabulous Academy Motion Picture Museum that recently opened.

"Yes, there is. The Motion Picture Museum features how movies are made, the background regarding some of the all-time greats like Citizen Kane and featuring some amazing actors. Near the Motion Picture Museum is the Peterson Automotive Museum," offered Sara, "Where some truly priceless cars are exhibited."

"How about the La Brea Tar Pit?" asked Coop. I understand that it was recently labeled one of the first 100 Geological Heritage Sites documenting archaeological findings over 15,000 years ago.

"Well, that's easy," offered Sara. "Those are all located a few miles from here and are near each other, including the LA County Museum of Art, if you are interested in expanding your imagination. Even closer to the apartment is the Santa Monica Pier with its lighted Ferris Wheel: quite a site at night."

"I've always been drawn to the Hollywood sign, Sara. Do you have any background information about it?" asked Veronica.

"It was originally labeled 'Hollywoodland' to recognize a housing development in the early 1920s," replied Sara. "Originally, the sign was to be taken down after 18 months. Only the word 'Land 'in the name was dropped about 30 years later. Today, we are celebrating the sign's 100th birthday. In celebration, each of the 45-foot-tall letters have been painted. A total of 250 gallons of primer and paint was applied. The Hollywood Sign draws an estimated 50 million visitors a year, accordingly to the Hollywood Chamber of Commerce."

"And I hear that the Getty Museums are world class," suggested Veronica.

"Yes, both the Villa at the beach with its priceless sculptures and the Getty Center on the hill are worth visits," agreed Sara. "And don't forget the Broad and MOCA in downtown LA as well as the Huntington and Norton Simon in Pasadena, if you are in the mood for museums and art."

"Too much to see and so little time to see the sights," said Jack. "Sara let's go for a walk." Sara nodded her agreement as Jack reached to help her from her seat. "Meet you guys back at the apartment." And walk they did: to Ocean Avenue, then to the Santa Monica Pier where the Ferris Wheel was brightly lit and in full glory. Thereafter, holding Sara's hand, they proceeded down the steps from the Pier onto the beach and walked north along the paved bike and walking path toward Malibu. Enjoying the surf and moonlight, Jack said how much he missed Sara's Dream-Girl smile and beauty. She squeezed his hand and put her head on his shoulder as they walked. About 2 miles along the path, Jack felt refreshed. The walk and talk did him some good, he thought. From Sara's loving ways, he was sure that it did her some good too.

As they entered the tunnel under the PCH which led up some stairs to Mabery Road and the back of Sara's apartment, Jack noticed some guys at the top of the stairs who did not look friendly. "Sara, is there another way to your apartment without using the stairs to Mabery? Jack asked. "

"Yes, follow me," she said and led Jack along a narrow sideway next to the PCH which took them past Patrick's Roadhouse to Ocean Avenue Extension. They carefully proceeded and were on the lookout for trouble. When they reached the apartment, Jack gave Coop a call and alerted him to the unfriendlies and advised him to "keep his eyes open."

When Coop and Veronica returned, Jack took Coop aside

on the deck and asked him whether he thought Big Joe's men had found them, or whether the unfriendlies were just locals looking for trouble.

Coop said that one can never be too careful and added, "We should assume that Big Joe is 'onto us.' He certainly has reason to be after our demolition of his marijuana facilities, the gun battle with his hoods while talking to Red and our association with Sam and her investigative nature."

"I agree," said Jack. "I just don't want to expose Sara and Veronica to any danger we may invite."

"I will be extra vigilant, partner," responded Coop.

CHAPTER EIGHTEEN

The next morning, Sara noticed Coop standing by the deck rail taking in the magnificent view of the Malibu coast up to Point Dume. While handing him a large cup of black coffee, she asked, "Did you know that Point Dume was named after a Padre in the 1700s? It is a great place to see the Gray Whales migrate." Coop simply nodded in acknowledgment.

Sara pointing said, "not far from here is where the Santa Monica Long Wharf existed. Southern Pacific built the Wharf in the 1890's and it stretched almost a mile into the ocean to make a deep-water port for Los Angeles. It was the longest wooden pier in the world at that time and lasted to the early 1900s as San Pedro became the Los Angeles port of choice."

Changing the subject, Coop looked to Jack who joined them with a cup of coffee in hand and asked, "It's been a couple of days, should we give Sam a call about progress on her article?"

Jack said, "Probably wouldn't hurt. I'll give her a call," as he pulled his phone from his back pocket while appreciating the convenience men had over women in using and storing their cell phones in their pants pockets. Sara said that she would check on Veronica.

"Hi Sam, it's Jack and Coop," Jack said holding the phone with its speaker activated so Coop could hear, "How is your story progressing?"

"I'm on the right track, but it needs more work, fellas," she said.

"As in what kind of work?" asked Coop.

"We don't know how big Big Joe's water empire extends, and what the syndicate plans to do in the long run," offered Sam.

"I've got some ideas to assess the size of Big Joe's Water World," said Jack. "We'll make a few calls and do some looking around, then get back to you as your 'research assistants,' Sam. Can you meet us at the Tulare airport tomorrow afternoon?"

"Sure, what's up? she responded.

"I think we will go for a plane ride over the Central Valley and Big Joe's empire," answered Jack.

"Great idea. I know that I am onto something big and could use all the help I can get," said Sam.

CHAPTER NINETEEN

"HI E," said Jack to his phone, "can you meet me at the Santa Monica airport tomorrow morning, say 10 am with one of your trusty planes? We need to do a bit of air recon of California's Central Valley."

"Sure, Jack, see you there and then." E responded happily.

"How do you know him?" Coop asked.

"He is my financial advisor, and he has done a great job introducing me to MLPs which pay quarterly distributions," Jack said. "They are a nice, safe investment, in my opinion."

"Ok, but what about flying?" asked Coop.

"He is also an airplane nut!" responded Jack. "He has done some free-lance stuff for me in the past and used to fly in Viet Nam. He loves flying and has acquired several planes which he houses at the Santa Monica airport. I wonder which one he will unveil for us," added Jack.

"I didn't even know that Santa Monica had an airport," said Coop.

"Santa Monica has a great little airport only a couple of miles from the apartment," explained Jack. It is a general aviation airport and one of the oldest in the United States. At one time, it was the busiest single runway airport in the world. On average it handles about 300 operations a day.

"It is located two miles from the ocean and six miles North of LAX. In 2015, Harrison Ford was riding in a plane that crash landed on a nearby golf course. Fortunately, he was not seriously hurt. Unfortunately, the Santa Monica airport is scheduled to close at the end of 2028. We will have a chance to check it out with E."

After a good night's sleep, Jack and Coop headed to the airport. They told Sara and Veronica that they would return that evening and were doing some air recon of the Central Valley to learn more about water.

At the airport they spotted a plane that had to be associated with their ride: it was a single wing, single prop plane wearing camouflage paint. As they parked, a wiry, medium height fellow approached them and stuck out his hand to Coop, "Hi, I'm E." Jack gave him a bear hug and a big smile, then explained to Coop that E was short for Eric.

"Glad you could break away so quickly," said Jack. "We appreciate you meeting us here on short notice."

"No problem, Jack," said E, "anything for you! Besides I had an early morning meeting at the Dimensional Fund nearby in Santa Monica on Ocean Avenue. Shall we load up and get going? Incidentally, where are we going? And what recon are we doing?"

"We are working with a Central Valley newspaper, the Tulare Telegraph, in researching a story about water. Specifically, water theft and the squeeze of Big Ag on the little guy causing him to fold his cards and move for lack of water," said Jack.

"And, even more specifically," added Coop, "My Grandpa is being forced to move after 50 years because of theft of his water and the depletion of the aquifer by Big Ag from which he draws water."

"Got it," said E. "And what do you want to discover from the air?"

Jack explained, "We are hoping to see hidden wells in the agricultural fields as well as water lines that appear to be out of place as well as water diversions. We also want to assess the extent of Big Ag water over drafting that could be tied to a syndicate led by a guy called Big Joe Thornley who lives on a 50,000-acre almond ranch North of Tulare," summarized Jack. "All of this should provide ammunition for the investigative news article being written by a friend of ours. So, the Tulare airport, Southeast of Tulare will be a good place to head," instructed Jack. "First, tell us about this air beauty with which you have entrusted our lives, E."

"It is a U-10 Helio Courier which was an unsung hero in Vietnam," responded E. "It is an airplane that could fly into airfields built crudely by farmworkers. It is also a short take off style plane. Its maximum speed is 180 mph; cruising speed of 160 mph, rate of climb is 1,150 feet per minute, ceiling of 20,500 feet, range of 1,100 miles and takeoff distance of less than 350 feet."

"Sounds perfect for our mission, E," commented Jack.

"When we land in Tulare, we can introduce you to Samantha Curtis with whom we are working. She is an investigative reporter at the Tulare Telegraph. As a general route of flight, let's follow the 405 north to I-5 and then to Highway 99 as it splits from the 5. That should lead us directly to Tulare. I figure about a little over an hour of flying time and covering about 170 miles in the process," said Jack.

"Roger that," said E.

As they touched down in Tulare, Sam appeared and approached the plane. Jack and Coop each greeted her warmly and introduced her to E, as their pilot. "Thank you for arranging this, Jack and Coop," said Sam.

"Let's spend an hour or so crisscrossing the Central Valley looking for anything unusual, water wise," suggested Jack. "We will be looking for hidden wells, any siphoning from the California Aqueduct, or other water diversions and neighboring properties lacking water as well as illegal dams.

As they lifted off, Sam explained that Tulare is the heart of the San Joaquin Valley which produces about 15% of the state's agricultural products. They could see the outline of Tulare Lake, which was once the largest freshwater lake, west of the Great Lakes. "It covered 600 to 800 square miles at one time. It has been reduced dramatically by water usage, diversions; and drought," Sam explained. "The lake is winter dependent on whether it will be size-able or not. During drought years it is nearly bone dry and will only recover in a wet winter. Nevertheless, even in a wet winter, the damage has already been done with the depleted aquifer under the lake which will never fully recover."

They flew south above Highway 99 and over a small town, named "MacFarland, whose high school cross country team was featured in a movie starring Kevin Costner," Sam related. She explained, "Given the flat terrain, the team had to train running up and down covered piles of agricultural and cow waste. The underdog McFarland team won multiple state cross country championships with runners often working in the fields early in the morning before and after school."

The power of perseverance thought Coop.

As they flew over the surrounding farmland, they did notice multiple well heads in some farms and even some pipes and hoses dipping into the California aqueduct. Occasionally, they spotted what appeared to be a small dam capturing water from a nearby river.

Then they turned north to Big Joe Thornley's 50,000-acre farm. As they flew over his ranch, Jack asked E to fly lower over the orchard so they can check out the wells. They noticed what appeared to be wells partially hidden by the almond trees. They also saw a runway no doubt used for crop dusters and private planes together with a large pipe emanating from a branch of the nearby California Aqueduct presumably leading to Big Joe's ranch and one of his well heads.

"Convenient source of water when needed," said Jack noting the illegal diversion of water.

"Wait until I confront him with that," said Sam, as she took pictures from her iPhone camera.

Not too far away, they also saw evidence of a small farmer who did not appear to have access to water as his orchard and the surrounding grounds were brown and fruitless. "I guess we found one who didn't pay to play," said Jack.

"Or could not afford Big Joe's 'administrative fee'," commented Coop. "Can you do another fly-by of the brown orchard?" asked Sam. "I'll take a few shots."

"How do we know whether the small farmer's water plight is caused by water theft or inability to access an aquifer like Gramps?" asked Coop.

"We don't know, Coop," said Sam, "but we can take an

educated guess. First, each well is supposed to be permitted by the county. And the counties have been shall we say generous in issuing permits ahead of the effective date of the Ground Water Sustainability Act which will limit the number of wells that can be drilled starting in 2040. I happened to have a list of the permits issued to Big Joe and his Big Ag neighbors with me. So, we can do a rough count during our fly over of his property.

"Second, I learned during my master's year that scientists are putting the finishing touches on identifying farms that overdraft water," commented Sam. "It is a new frontier being investigated after two decades of drought. Historically, California's farmers could pump without limit from their wells. As a result, aquifers have been depleted and the associated ground has sunk significantly."

"You mean like the town of Corcoran?" asked Jack.

"Exactly," said Sam. "In essence, regulators need to quantify how much water each farmer is using and do so with some accuracy and without water meters or even knowing how many wells there are in each area. As we have seen, many of these wells are hidden in orchards or corn fields. And farmers are loath to invite regulators onto their property to investigate how many wells exist to figure out how much pumping of groundwater exists. Farming and ranching interests as well as some conservative legislators believe that water is controlled by individual property owners and is not a public resource. They oppose water meters saying, 'Once it's metered, it's going to be taken'."

"So how do regulators estimate water usage?" asked Coop.

"Researchers have developed a way to estimate the amount of water used by agricultural crops from images recorded by NASA-operated satellites," said Sam. "The technique involves several steps: first, figure out which crops are growing on each field via satellite images which are frequently updated. Theoretically, each crop, at a particular point in its life cycle, consumes a predictable amount of water and releases it though its leaves, depending on local weather conditions. From this data predictions can be made as to how much ground water is being used to farm. And that data can be compared to estimates of available water in the underlying aquifer."

"You sure know your water stuff," commented Jack.

"Thanks," said Sam. "I have been studying water hydraulics for years and have developed a little expertise."

"So, if Big Joe has 50,000 acres of almonds, one of the thirstiest crops, there is a good chance he is over drafting water from the aquifer under his property to the determent of surrounding farmers," suggested Jack.

"You got it, Jack. Big Ag can squeeze the little guy like Coop's grandpa," confirmed Sam.

"Eventually, even farmers like Big Joe will run out of water if he continues to overdraft," said Coop. "So, what is his long game?"

"Especially with over 20 years of our most recent drought, climate change and the unpredictable future of water availability for farmers," said Sam. "With the recent break in the drought, many view state water restrictions to be too severe, no doubt you have seen the many signs along the highways expressing some of that criticism. Many have decided to plow under their crops and convert their property into huge warehouses covering hundreds of thousands of square feet to beat the water restrictions."

"Big Joe's long game remains to be seen," thought Jack aloud. "Once we get our ducks in order, I think we should visit him again," said Jack. "He did invite us back if we have more questions."

"Although we are not able to estimate how much ground water Big Joe is using, our fly over can provide a rough estimate of how many wells he has. We can then compare that estimate with the number of permits the county has issued to him," suggested Sam.

Over the hour of Central Valley fly time, they crisscrossed Big Joe's property many times and counted over 80 well heads. Glancing at the permit sheet, Sam found permits for only 40 wells.

"Surprise, surprise," said Jack.

Just then, a shot rang out and a pinging sound came from the right wing. Someone yelled: "They're shooting at us!"

"WTF," said another.

E immediately pulled the yoke back hard and placed the U-10 in a steep climb. As the plane climbed, E yelled "Hold on!" then he made a hard right turn away from Big Joe's almond orchard.

All had been pushed back into their seats, and another bullet creased the cockpit. E asked, "How many of you have been in a plane crash?" as another bullet hit the fuselage. He then glanced over his shoulder and saw Coop and Jack raise their hands confirming their near-death experiences with airplanes. E laughed and was grateful for his Viet Nam war experience as a pilot while he soared through the Central Valley California sky and out of rifle range. He turned toward the Tulare airport.

After landing, they huddled outside the plane and reconnoitered. Jack said, "I think it is time we take Big Joe up on his invitation to meet again."

"He has some questions to answer," said Coop.

"Jack asked Sam to give him the list of permitted wells, and told E to stay with the plane, patch it up and be prepared to take them back to Santa Monica after their meeting." said Jack.

Given the gun shots, Sam said she felt that she would be safer with E and decided to stay behind, admonishing them to "be careful" as they parted.

CHAPTER TWENTY

Jack and Coop pulled up in front of Joe Thornley's home in an Uber and approached the front door. Before they could knock, the door opened, and Big Joe greeted them: "What's up?" he asked curtly.

"We have a few unanswered questions and accepted your invitation to visit again," said Jack.

"What questions?" asked Big Joe, not inviting them into his home.

"Well, for starters," said Jack, "Where do you get all your water for these thirsty almonds?"

"From wells," answered Big Joe.

"How may wells do you have?" asked Jack.

"I don't know and why is it any business of your business?" responded Big Joe.

"Do you have permits for those wells?" asked Coop.

"Sure," responded Big Joe.

"We counted over 80 well heads from the air, and I only see permits for half that number," Jack said, waving a sheet of paper in front of him.

"Let me see that," demanded Big Joe grabbing the sheet from Jack. As he glanced at it, ripped it to shreds, threw it on the ground and said, "I think you have asked enough questions about my operation. Please excuse me. Cedrick, Fred," he shouted. When they quickly appeared, Big Joe said, "Please show Mr. Armstrong and his friend our special water feature."

The two burly guys that Jack and Coop had seen at the marijuana farm, chased them and took shots at them while they were with Red of Red's well service, said "Right this way, yous guys." Big Joe whispered in the ear of one of the muscle men.

As Jack and Coop were unarmed, they proceeded without resistance around the corner of Big Joe's home and down a path which led to a large area devoid of trees and covered with cement. In the middle of the cement was what appeared to be a well-head secured by a wheel. Three more armed men approached them from behind and sprinted ahead to the well-head. Five armed against two unarmed. Tough odds to overcome, thought Jack.

The one in the lead opened the well covering by twisting the wheel atop the hatch several times. No doubt the cover would be resealed once they were finished with Jack and his friend.

Then the one who had received whispered instructions from Big Joe took Jack aside and said, "Before you step into eternity, Mr. Armstrong, Big Joe wanted me to tell you that unfortunately, you will not be around to see the full effect of Operation Watered down. I am sure it will give you something to think about while you settle into liquid blackness."

Pushing him toward the well-head, the other thug said, "Ok, big shot, in you go!" while pointing his Sig Sauer P226 MK 259 mm Luger 10 round pistol at Jack. As Jack hyperventilated and prepared to jump, the man said, "Be sure to tell us what you think of our special water feature," and gave Jack a shove into the black, bottomless hole.

Jack and Coop each disappeared following one another into the hole below. Fear of falling on unseen rocks resulting in broken bones quickly subsided as their fall was abruptly interrupted by their plunge into water the depth of which was unknown. Fortunately, their held breath allowed them to struggle upward toward air. As they breached the surface of the water, they found each other by sound while in complete darkness. After a brief discussion, they agreed to swim in opposite directions in search of something to hold or stand upon.

Coop yelled out: "Don't swallow the water! It might contain nitrates and other poisonous elements." He was aware that many of the Central Valley aquifers had been contaminated with fertilizers that were harmful if swallowed making the water undrinkable.

"Now you tell me!" shouted Jack as he spit what he had partially swallowed.

After 5 minutes of swimming, Coop yelled that he had found a foothold. Of course, Coop would be first to "land" thought Jack, he is an ex-Navy Seal. So now Jack had to decide whether: to keep swimming in the direction in which Jack was headed, or to turn around and try to find Coop in this black watery hole.

Coop answered the conundrum, "Head over here, I think I have found something and have an idea," he said to Jack. So, about face he turned and after several more minutes of sightless swimming, he zeroed in on Coop who was singing "Zippy Do Dah" loud enough for Jack to be guided to him.

"What are you so happy about?" asked Jack.

"Do you remember when we were flying over Big Joe's orchard, we spotted what appeared to be a rather large pipe embedded in the side of the California aqueduct?" asked Coop.

"Yes. So, what?" challenged Jack. "No doubt he likely uses it to replenish his aquifer at the expense of others. Heck water theft seems to be the norm in the Central Valley!"

"What if I told you that I found where the end of the pipe connects to the aquifer," said Coop, as he sat upright atop something.

"That's nice, you win a cigar, Coop," offer Jack who was treading water. "I'm more interested in getting outta here."

"A cigar and more," claimed Coop as he slides off his pedestal to uncover the end of the California aqueduct pipe located under the aquifer waterline. "Here, let me show you." Taking Jack by his hand, he told him to "hold his breath and duck under water with me." Underwater he guided Jack to feel the circumference of the pipe.

When they surfaced, Jack excitedly said: "Holly crap, Batman! You mean that there might be a way out of this Hell hole?"

"Yes, because this pipe's diameter is large enough for us to enter individually and swim underwater to the outside aqueduct," explained Coop.

"And you think we can hold our breath long enough for each of us to survive the swim?" asked Jack.

"Just before we 'jumped' into the hole, I took a final look around and noticed on my right that the aqueduct was about 40 yards away from the well head hole into which we were forced to jump." responded Coop. "After our 'jump' and swimming to my right in this black pit for a few minutes I literally bumped into the pipe. As I like to say: 'even a blind squirrel finds a nut occasionally'."

"I figure I covered about 20 yards swimming before bumping into the pipe, making the end of the pipe about equal distant from the adjoining aqueduct. It will take roughly 20 strokes and about 90 seconds to swim underwater through the pipe to reach the aqueduct and, hopefully, fresh air," said Coop.

"That's assuming the valve is open at the other end and there is no restraining grate which imprisons us," quipped Jack.

"The valve should be open," observed Coop, "because I feel a gentle flow of water from the pipe into the aquifer. Swimming against the gentle flow shouldn't lengthen the swim by much," estimated Coop.

"Maybe no closed valve, but let's hope that there is no restraining gate with wire mesh at the other end," prayed Jack.

"If there is, I should have sufficient lung capacity to manage a return swim," said Coop. "Then we can figure something else out. Assuming no obstruction, Jack, you seem to be a strong swimmer, so I don't think the length of the pipe should be a problem for you. I will go first," proposed Coop. "Give me a chance to reach the end of the pipe. If everything is according to our plan and there is no restraining grate, I will find a rock or something and will knock three times on the end of the pipe. Sound travels well in water. So, that will be the signal for you to enter the pipe. I will wait at the other end and if I don't see you within 2 minutes after I knock on the pipe, I will reenter the pipe from the other end and look for you and will guide you out."

Jack verbally gave assurance that he understood the plan. "Let's start hyperventilating," said Coop. After several deep breaths, Coop entered the pipe and began his swim to its end and the hoped-for escape from the aquifer. He figured that he would exert 30 underwater breast strokes and frog kicks within 90 seconds to reach the end of the pipe. Even if he had to perform 45 strokes, he figured that he had plenty of capacity given his Navy Seal training. Probably enough for a return trip, if necessary.

As he neared the end of the pipe, Coop encountered a wire mesh grate covering the pipe opening. While his breath began to dissipate, he felt around the edge of the grate. He could see the end of the pipe a few feet away and the light colored water told him that the aqueduct was near. If he could only hold on another 30 seconds or so, he thought he could find a grate release and freedom, otherwise he would have to return to the aquifer before he ran out of air. Then he felt it: a small release holding the grate in place. Hopefully, it was not rusted and frozen. He pressed the release firmly and the grate sprung open allowing him to escape the pipe. After a couple more strokes he broke the surface of the aqueduct gulped in some fresh air and quickly looked around while holding the end of the pipe. Seeing no danger, he found a rock on the edge of the aqueduct and knocked three times as a signal to Jack, that it was safe for him to proceed.

Hearing Coop's three knocks, Jack took a giant deep breath after hyperventilating for 30 seconds and started his underwater swim. He began losing some steam as he neared the end of the pipe but gained needed strength when he saw the open grate and lighter water toward the end of the tunnel. "Come on Jack, he told himself. You can do it!" Out he popped into the aqueduct and quickly was grabbed by the collar by an unseen hand before he drifted down the swiftly moving aqueduct. After catching his breath and seeing Coop for the first time, Jack spit out some water and asked, "Now what?"

"Just a second," said Jack as he took in a big breath and went back under water. Thirty seconds later he resurfaced and said, "I had some unfinished business. Now we float down the aqueduct for a few miles and exit as it passes by the Tulare airport. Let's just say we found a 'water taxi' to the airport."

"Brilliant," said Jack.

"Let's get going. Simply float on your back feet first and the aqueduct will do the work for you. I'll lead the way. And let's keep quiet as we don't want to alert Big Joe's water tour guides of our Great Escape."

Down the man-made river they began to float at a relatively rapid speed. As they approached an overpass, they saw one of Big Joe's henchmen on guard with a rifle. He noticed the boys, he raised his rifle and began to shoot. Bullets zipped by each of the floating targets fortunately without a hit. No doubt the shooter was radioing others about their escape.

The over passes were spaced a couple of miles apart and the line of travel for cars and trucks did not follow beside the Aqueduct. So, by the time the two passed under the next overpass, the pursuers were only arriving and had little time to take aim. The Tulare airport was still a couple of miles away and Coop hoped that they would make it there before Big Joe's gang arrived.

Soon, they began to see planes overhead landing nearby, Coop took the lead in finding a spot from which to exit the aqueduct knowing that they were near the airport. Although they were soaked from head to toe as they exited the aqueduct, they were exuberant in surviving the "special water feature" and "target practice" for Big Joe's boys.

From a distance, they saw E working on his plane. A shot rang out and they hit the tarmac. "Darn," said Coop. "I thought we had put more distance on the shooters. After a few seconds, another shot was heard. Quickly, they sprinted to the hanger where E was working on his plane. He heard them approach in fast moving crouches and began to laugh. You guys look like a couple of drown rats."

"Did you hear the shots E?" questioned Jack.

"Shots? What are you talking about?" After a moment, he began to laugh again so hard he almost fell from the ladder upon which he was working. "Those weren't shots. I was using a pop rivet to repair the holes in my plane from the rifle shots we took. Here look at this."

He then squeezed the rivet holder behind a piece of the plane fuselage and a loud bang occurred as the rivet popped into place binding the pieces of metal being repaired. The two soaking wet refugees from Big Joe's water feature began to laugh. They quickly briefed E on Big Joe's riflemen and the need to evacuate asap.

"So much for Big Joe's 'friendly' invitation," said E.

"Are you ready to fly?" asked Jack, "We need to get out of Dodge and figure out what's going on, here. Where's Sam?"

"Sam mentioned something about getting back to the newspaper office to work on the story," E responded.

"I thought she would stick around to learn what happened at Big Joe's," said Coop.

"Let's just get the Hell outta here," screamed Jack, before the bad guys arrive.

E threw the pop rivet aside, took down the ladder, grabbed the tail of the plane and with Coop and Jack's help, swung the plane into position to enter the runway from the hanger. All three then wasted no time and climbed into the plane. E quickly grabbed his headset while flipping the necessary switches to start the prop and a moment later, the plane began taxing toward the runway. He summoned Jack to grab the 'second seat' up front to assist visually.

As they turned onto runway 31, for a Northern take off into the wind, they heard a ping as a bullet creased their wing. E looked down the 3,900- foot runway they were about to travel and saw three armed men with rifles in the back of a pick-up truck heading toward them at a high rate of speed. "Hold on," he shouted to his passengers and gave the plane full power.

"Any of you ever play 'chicken'?" E asked the group.

"Not recently," shouted Jack as he saw the gap between the oncoming truck and the plane narrow.

"Well, here we go," yelled E. "This will be close," he screamed. "Giddy-up!" he said as if encouraging the plane to speed up.

"Time for a prayer," added Jack.

The truck was also picking up speed and quickly closing on the plane, having traveled half of the 3,900-foot runway toward them. As the plane gathered the necessary speed for take-off, E rotated and the plane immediately began to climb after only 350 feet.

Another bullet whizzed through the right wing. "That's it," declared E. "That's my gaul darn plane you are messing with!" he yelled to the oncoming truck. Just as he was about to clear the truck, he eased forward slightly on the yoke, took aim at the truck and the U-10 dipped just enough to cause the plane's landing gear to crease the top of the pick-up's cab and knock the riflemen out of the bed of the speeding truck. In attempting to avoid the collision, the 80-mph truck swerved, the driver lost control and the truck began to roll. Having cleared the truck, E shouted, "Take that you bastards!" as he pulled back on the yoke and again the U-10 gathered speed and altitude.

"Whoa, that was close, E. Great piloting!" said Jack.

"What a maneuver," bellowed Coop. "You touched your plane on the top of a speeding pick-up about to collide with us while we were taking off. Amazing! Where did you learn that maneuver?"

"No way some bush-league rifle guys are going to mess with us, or my airplane." E declared, who had piloted U-10s in Viet Nam and had plenty of experience with 'unfriendlies'. "Screw them and the horse they rode in on," he said as he dipped his right wing so all could see the truck roll over below them and the spilled human contents on the tarmac.

"Big Joe is going to be missing a few of his guys," Coop said. "He'll be pissed."

"As if he isn't already pissed," said Jack.

"Better than us sleeping with the fishes in his aquifer," answered Coop.

CHAPTER TWENTY-ONE

That night Jack, Coop, Sara, and Veronica met at the R & D Kitchen on Montana avenue in Santa Monica. R & D experimented with some great dishes: stating on its website that it "brings sophisticated and fresh cuisine to a smart and convivial crowd." The restaurant also has a first class, friendly staff of servers. It is a favorite with the locals and does not take reservations. People start lining up at 4:30 pm in the afternoon for dinner. Fortunately, Jack had thought ahead and put his name in with a lovely young lady just inside the front door, so they didn't have to wait outside for a table.

Over some delicious starters, including a chip duo with guacamole and blended cheese, Jack summarized what they knew for their girlfriends.

"It's a tight operation," commented Coop. "We all know that water is essential to survival. Without it people, like my grandfather, either die, move, or live a very inconveniently shorten life."

"And if people move, they either vacate their premises or sell their property for rock bottom prices," added Jack.

"Those are the facts we uncovered, ladies," offered Jack.

"What he didn't tell you," added Coop calmly, "is that we almost got killed investigating Big Joe, his syndicate and his water works."

This startled Veronica and Sara, who simultaneously blurted out, "What!"

"Thanks, Coop," said Jack shaking his head.

"I think it is important for our ladies to know that Big Joe is not to be trusted and as we continue with this Star Ship adventure, we must be careful and they should keep an eye on our whereabouts," counseled Coop.

"OK," said Jack.

"So how did this 'almost got killed thing' happen?" asked Sara.

"We had been invited back to Big Joe's home to get more facts about his water operations, and he decided we were asking too many sensitive questions, so he asked his henchmen who were armed, to show us his 'special water features,' which turned out to be an underground aquifer," explained Jack.

"In we went and after swimming around for a while, Coop found a way out. We made it to the Tulare airport and our pilot flew us back to Santa Monica where we are delighted to have dinner with the two of you!" reported Jack.

After his explanation, Jack winked at Coop hoping that his omission of the airport shooting incident would not suddenly be shared by Coop.

Veronica said dismissively, "I sure hope that you boys know what you're doing."

"Veronica, we know more now than we did before," said Coop.

"And we have learned a lesson. To be particularly careful and on high alert with Big Joe and his syndicate," said Jack. Big Joe will stop at nothing to accomplish his goal."

"The big question is, what are his goals," posited Coop.

"Before they shoved us into the pit, one of the armed guards told me that Big Joe wanted me to know that it is unfortunate that we will not be around to see the full effect of 'Operation Watered down'," said Jack.

"Operation Watered down"? repeated Coop "What does he mean by that?"

Quiet took over the group as they picked at their dinner and gave the question further thought. A couple of beers and a glass or two of wine helped too. There was a football game on TV over the nearby restaurant bar. Jack and Coop could see the game reflected in the mirror behind Sara's and Veronica's shoulders while the two ladies could see the game directly on the bar TV in front of them. Forty Niners versus the Rams, the classic Northern/ Southern California rivalry. The game gave them a chance to cogitate.

"He could simply expand the theft, drilling and allocation of water a farm at a time," speculated Jack.

"Isn't California agriculture a multi billion-dollar business?" asked Veronica.

"Yes, still, I think he is up to something bigger," thought Jack aloud.

"Bigger?" questioned Coop. "He already has thousands of acres under his control."

"Yes, but he is ambitious," said Jack.

"And he doesn't want anyone to know what he is up to," added Coop.

"Do we know who is calling the shots? asked Sara.

"What do you mean?" asked Coop.

"Big Joe may be answering to a higher authority," answered Sara. "The word syndicate implies more than one. Who is the other one or ones? Who composes the syndicate, what interest do they have in water, and how active are the members in managing its direction?"

"Right on Sara," said Jack. "We have to find out who is a member of Big Joe's Syndicate and try to reverse engineer Operation Watered down."

"How are you going to figure that out?" questioned Sara.

"Maybe you could figure out who would benefit most from controlling Southern California water," suggested Veronica.

"What did you say?" asked Coop.

In answer, Veronica said, "It's Southern California water that is potentially controllable, Northern California water is self-sufficient. Through rain, rivers and snow melt, Northern California has sufficient water to meet its foreseeable needs."

"We all know," said Jack, "through that famous movie, Chinatown, Los Angeles is built in a desert-like climate with unpredictable rainfall. In the movie, a character portraying the Los Angeles Department of Water superintendent and chief engineer, William Mulholland, states during a hearing: 'If you don't get the water, you won't need it.' There is insufficient water self-generated in Southern California to sustain its population. Water must be imported from the North and the Colorado."

"So presumably, without water, Southern California as we know it, doesn't exist," said Sara.

"Correct, Mulholland was an avid proponent of Los Angeles growth, and he knew that to grow, water had to be added," said Jack.

"I guess one could say, 'just add water'," said Sara.

Jack continued, "So, the movie explains that Mulholland

was the principal advocate for construction of the Los Angeles Aqueduct in 1913, a 200-mile man made, gravity driven river, enabling the transportation of water from the Eastern and Northern Sierra foothills of the Owens Valley to the San Fernando Valley which had to be annexed to Los Angeles for LA to claim ownership of the water. Today, it is such an important source of water for Los Angeles, that a companion aqueduct was built in 1970. Without that water, Los Angeles could not grow, and, arguably, may not exist today. With the taking of that water, the farmers of the Owens Valley became dust farmers resulting in the long running Water Wars with Los Angeles."

"Like the movie Chinatown, to find Big Joe's Watered down game, let's start with the Owens Valley Los Angeles Aqueduct," recommended Jack. "In the morning, I think Coop and I should take a ride with E and visit the headwaters. As they say in the movie, one never knows what goes on in Chinatown."

CHAPTER TWENTY-TWO

"Your choice," said Jack. "Starbucks or Peets? They are both a few blocks away on Montana Avenue. "I prefer Peets," responded Coop. "You look rather drippy this morning. Late night?"

"Yes, Sam called last night and said that she was prepared to join us as her article was being reviewed by the editor," said Jack. "I told her to meet us at the Lone Pine airport in the Owens Valley which would save her several hours of additional driving if she met us in Santa Monica. I also did some late-night research on the Owens Valley and LA Aqueduct."

After a large cup of coffee, the boys headed to the Santa Monica Airport to meet E. After a quick preflight check, E said, "Let's mount up!"

About twenty minutes into their flight to the Owens Valley, Coop looked down and asked, "What's that?" as he pointed to water running down some steps mounted on a hillside North of I-5.

Jack explained, "Those must be the Los Angeles Aqueduct Cascades, I read about them last night. The Aqueduct runs over 200 miles from the Owens Valley and ends here at its Western point."

"Where did you pick that up?" asked Coop.

"In anticipation of our field trip, late last night I down-loaded 'A Self-Guided Tour of the Los Angeles Aqueduct' by Elson Trinidad. Here, take a look," as Jack offered Coop the downloaded pages. "Both the century old LA Aqueduct and the Second 1970 LA Aqueduct, terminate at the Cascades. It is there," said Jack pointing out the plane's window to the Cascades, "where over one hundred years ago, the Aqueduct's chief engineer, William Mulholland told then LA Mayor Henry Rose, 'There it is, take it'!" added Jack referring to the water.

Continuing their flight along the LA Aqueduct, Jack and Coop flew over the St. Francis dam site. Reading from the Guide, Jack explained that "The dam was conceived by William Mulholland to create a reservoir which together with over 10 others would provide water for LA in the event the aqueduct failed. Shortly after blessing the St. Francis dam as safe, Mulholland received an early morning call in 1928 informing him that the dam had collapsed and sent a 140-foot wall of water rushing to the Pacific Ocean near Oxnard 50 miles away. The dam failure killed over 400 people. It was the largest dam disaster in US history and ended Mulholland's career."

"Have there been more recent dam disasters?" asked Coop.

"There's been a near miss," said Jack.

"A recent near miss?" repeated Coop.

"A few years ago, the Oroville dam, the tallest in the United States, came close to failing," explained Jack. "Oroville is an earth-fill embankment dam. Although these structures are resilient, especially to earthquakes, once water overwhelms the spillway and starts flowing over an embankment dam, it can melt away with astonishing speed. This was reported by Christopher Cox for the New York Times Magazine in an article entitled, 'The Trillion Gallon Question: Extreme weather is threatening California's dams. What happens if they fail?'

"If the Oroville dam failed, it would send a wave nearly two hundred feet high sweeping into the valley below," explained Jack. "As experts assessed the possible path of water, as many as 200,000 people ended up having to leave their homes. Fortunately, the severe weather abated, and the dam did not fail, even though the spillway was destroyed and has since been rebuilt."

Jack and Coop touched down at the Lone Pine airport in the middle of the Owens Valley and were mesmerized by the Valley's 75-mile length, the height of the nearby mountains around which they flew and the dryness of the valley floor. Jack recited from his homework that the "Owens Valley used to be called the place of 'flowing water', located on the edge of the Great Basin which extends into and beyond Nevada and is sandwiched between the Sierra Nevada's on the West and the White and Inyo Mountains to the East."

Jack asked E not to tie down the plane as they would likely be using it again in the afternoon.

One mountain interested Coop who pointed and asked its name.

Out of nowhere a familiar voice replied, "That's Mount Whitney, the tallest mountain in the lower 48 at 14,500 feet. It is also the end of the John Muir trail which begins in Yosemite Valley over 200 miles away."

Jack and Coop spun around and to see Sam. "Hi Sam, fancy meeting you in the middle of this fabulous valley!" said Jack.

Coop added, great to see you Sam, "we missed your company and water knowledge."

"I missed you guys too," said Sam.

Then, mimicking Jerry Maguire, Coop shouted, "Show me the water!"

"LA has siphoned and diverted most of it," said Sam, leaving only a small body of water which she pointed at and called "Owens Lake". "That lake used to be the second largest lake in California after Tulare Lake," she said. "Instead of water, LA left the valley and its inhabitants with a dust bowl caused by the wind blowing across the Great Basin from the East over the dry former lake bed."

"So much for the 'flowing water'," Coop thought aloud."

Sam continued to explain, "The Owens River provides water to the Los Angeles Aqueduct, which carries as much as one-third of the imported water consumed by Los Angeles. The taking of Owens water under what some call 'false pretenses' was the basis for the long running California Water Wars which were the inspiration for the movie Chinatown. A century ago, Mulholland agents from Los Angeles converged on the Valley on a secret mission: to quietly purchase land, posing as ranchers and farmers, for purposes of acquiring water rights for Los Angeles.

"Soon, residents of the Valley realized much of the water rights they had owned were now owned by Los Angeles interests. L.A. proceeded to drain the valley, taking the water via the LA Aqueduct to fuel the explosive growth of Los Angeles.

"As a result of the diversion of water from the Valley and

Owens Lake to the Aqueduct, Owens Lake was virtually emptied by 1926, only 13 years after the Great Diversion of Water to Los Angeles had begun."

"I can understand why the folks have a bit of disdain for LA," said Jack.

"As we know," continued Sam, "The Los Angeles Aqueduct was built by William Mulholland. It was Mulholland and Los Angeles Mayor Frederick Eaton who envisioned the need for water to fuel the growth of Los Angeles. Without water, Los Angeles may never have existed, which led to that famous Mulholland line, 'If you don't get the water, you won't need it'."

"I wonder what he would think today?" asked Coop. "Look what his vision and effort have created? Fifteen million people and one of the largest and most prosperous cities in the World, and it was created atop a desert!"

Jack said, "Let's look around Lone Pine and get some local flavor."

CHAPTER TWENTY-THREE

Twenty minutes later they were meandering through Lone Pine and its 1500 inhabitants in Sam's car, a rental, as she explained that hers would not have made it all the way to the Owens Valley and back home. They were looking for a local watering hole, when they found Jake's Saloon.

"Perfect," said Jack as they pulled up in front. In they went and found a vintage small-town bar complete with a pool table and a sign that said,

"We distrust camels and anyone
that can go a week without a Drink."

"Well, let's see if we can get over the Camel syndrome," said Coop as he ordered a Bud from Mindy the bartender. Jack followed Coop's lead. Adorning the walls were dollar bills, often with cryptic messages written on them. Seeing Jack eyed the bills, Mindy said, "Those kept us alive through Covid."

"What do you mean?" asked Jack.

"We peeled many of them off the walls to pay the bills," she responded. "It worked. We're still here!" she said triumphantly.

"We understand that the Owens Valley is famous for the Water Wars. Can you tell us something about them?" asked Jack.

"Those bastards from Los Angeles." Mindy stopped mid-sentence, "You're not from LA, are you?" she asked with an embarrassed look on her face.

"No, we're from Northern California and the Central Valley," responded Jack to the relief of Mindy. He then introduced himself, Samantha, and Coop.

"Ok, otherwise, I would have to kick you out!" she exclaimed. "Why are you here?"

"We'd like to know how someone could significantly interrupt the flow of water to LA," Jack said.

"Well, someone did, once. A group of armed ranchers seized the Alabama Gates and dynamited part of the system, letting water return to the Owens River," said Mindy.

"When was that?" asked Coop.

"If my memory serves me correctly, around the early 1920s," answered Mindy.

"Nothing more recent?" asked Jack.

"Sure, in the mid 70s, after the new LA aqueduct was built, a couple of teenagers got drunk, stole some dynamite and blew apart a gate that regulated the flow of water to the aqueduct," she said. "In fact, an LA Times reporter interviewed one of the guys in this very saloon. I am told that they sat right over there," she said pointing to a table. "A copy of the article is plastered to the wall behind the table."

Jack stepped closer to the table and an LA Times article entitled: "The Man Who Bombed Los Angeles Aqueduct Reveals His Story." After taking a moment to read it, Jack said "That's fascinating Mindy," said Jack. "We were wondering if you might have heard anything more recently that might affect the flow of water toward LA."

"Well, nothing as dramatic as dynamite sabotage. There is something percolating; however, that could be more significant in terms of consequences to LA water," offered Mindy.

"What's that?" questioned Coop.

Mindy looked around the dozen or so patrons in the saloon to make sure that others weren't listening then leaned forward over the bar to whisper, "eminent domain".

"Eminent domain? Jack said in a hushed tone. "How would that affect LA water?" asked Sam.

"As I understand it, the concept is for Inyo County to sue LA for eminent domain over land that has water rights which will control the diversion of water to LA," said Mindy.

"Whose idea is this?" asked Jack.

"I don't know who thought it up, but I have heard that an outsider is funding the litigation and purchase of land if the suit is successful," she said.

"Can you tell us who the outsider is?" asked Coop.

"I'm not sure I should but it is a guy called Big Joe Thornley," she answered.

"Big Joe Thornley?" repeated Jack in a surprised fashion.

"Yes, he is someone from the Central Valley near Tulare and apparently, he resents or wants to do damage to LA through its water system," explained Mindy.

"How do you know this?" asked Coop.

"My boyfriend is the Inyo county counsel, and he told me," she said.

Jack responded, "We have reason to believe that Big Joe runs a syndicate that is involved in questionable water dealings. We are trying to figure out the long-term purpose of his syndicate. Have you ever heard anyone use the phrase, "Operation Watered down"?

"No, I don't recall hearing that phrase," she responded.

"If we knew the members of Big Joe's Syndicate, we may be able to figure out its purpose. Can your boyfriend help us? asked Jack. We would truly appreciate it."

"I'll ask him," she said.

"Mindy, please join us for a beer so we can continue our discussion," Coop suggested.

Intrigued, Sam asked, "Mindy, correct me if I am wrong. This eminent domain tactic is new and has not before been employed by the people in the Valley and their political leaders."

"That's what I have heard," said Mindy.

"Is the goal to retake the property acquired by Los Angeles in the early 1900s?" asked Sam.

"Correct," answered Mindy.

"What will that do with the much-needed water for Los Angeles?" asked Coop.

"Most likely, it will increase the cost of water and reduce some of its availability for LA as the water needs of the Valley residents will at long last be addressed and given priority," responded Mindy.

"How would this advance Big Joe's long agenda, what may be his so-called Operation Watered down?" asked Jack.

"It reiterates that water is the bed rock for survivability and growth," said Coop. "He who possesses it will survive and grow while he who seeks it will be part of a Great Migration like my Grandpa Walker."

Sam added, "All we need to do is look at Phoenix, a few hundred miles away, and see the impact of the lack of foreseeable water is having on the growth of that city. According to a recent Phoenix regulation, unless a developer can prove that there exists 100 years of sustainable water for a real estate development, no development permit will be issued. As a result, growth will likely stop."

"Or look at Mexico City which is running out of water for 22 million people. The LA Times reports that official indifference, faulty infrastructure, rising temperatures and reduced rainfall has led the city to rely principally on expensive bottled water," Sam added.

"Big Joe's Syndicate is attempting to control the allocation of water to enhance or detract from the value of some areas. Theoretically, he could control as much as one-third of the water LA imports through the assertion of water rights acquired by eminent domain," explained Jack.

"Wouldn't Inyo County hold those water rights?" asked Coop

"Yes, the county would, but given Big Joe's cleverness', he may have arranged through the county's political leaders to exercise those rights in a manner untoward to LA. God knows people of the Valley continue to be furious about LA 'stealing' their water even though LA has attempted to make reparations," said Jack.

"I'm still trying to figure out the long game," said Coop. "What if he diverted water from an area, or threatened to do so, then bought property in the affected area at rock bottom prices, then relented and did not cause the diversion?"

"That could lead to a significant fluctuation in property prices and if one bought at the 'right' time, that person could make a killing," speculated Jack. "Let's noodle on it some more. Here, Mindy, is my cell number," as Jack handed her a napkin on which he had written his cell. "Please call if your boyfriend comes through for us with a list of syndicate members."

"What's next?" asked Coop.

"Well, we have a feel for the Central Valley and the Owens Valley as sources of So Cal water," said Sam. "If Big Joe really is serious about controlling or at least significantly inhibiting the flow of L.A. water, the Colorado cannot be overlooked."

"Sam, you are welcome to join us if you wish," said Jack.

"I think I had better get back to my desk and work on the story I am trying to complete. My editor only has so much patience for me being out of the office," responded Sam. "Hopefully, we can catch up later."

CHAPTER TWENTY-FOUR

Sam dropped Jack and Coop at the Lone Pine airport, where they met up with E and headed South toward Parker Arizona, located at the southern end of Lake Havasu and the beginning of the Colorado Los Angeles Aqueduct. Rather than make the flight longer and arrive late at night, they decided to land about halfway for the evening in Victorville.

"Do you know what Victorville is famous for?" asked Coop.

"No, what?" responded Jack.

"Roy Roger's horse, Trigger, was housed in a museum there!" said Coop.

"How in the heck did you know that?" asked Jack.

"I told you that my mother loved Westerns," said Coop. Hence, she named me after Gary Cooper and she thought Roy Rogers and Dale Evans, were terrific singing together."

"Do you know that else Victorville is noted for?" asked E.

"Oh no, not you too," said Jack "Is this a Trivial Pursuit question?"

"Herman Mankiewicz," said E answering his own question.

"Who the heck is Herman Mankiewicz and what does he have to do with Victorville?" asked Jack.

E answered, "Mankiewicz wrote Citizen Kane, one of the greatest movies ever made staring Orson Wells. He had a drinking problem and the producers decided to get him out of L.A. without the booze so he could finish writing Citizen Kane. They decided to seclude him in Victorville."

"Well, I guess we picked the right place to spend the night," said Coop.

That evening the trio had dinner at a local diner. Nothing fancy, just good food at Molly Brown's Country Café. While relaxing over dinner, Coop asked Jack about Sam's 'hit' piece on Big Joe.

"Where do you think her article stands, Jack?" asked Coop.

"She says it is on her editor's desk, Jack," replied Jack.

"I think she mentioned that several days ago. How long does editorial review take?" asked Coop.

"It can take a while as this involves a subject sensitive to the Central Valley water and a controversial political figure, Big Joe," answered Jack. They want to make sure the facts and stats are buttoned up. They know that the newspaper will suffer blow back from Big Joe and want to be on firm ground."

"Understood," said Coop. "I assume that they also want to make sure the road map for prosecution, regulatory intervention or legislative reform is laid out in clear terms."

"Makes sense to me," said Jack.

"Still, it seems like a long time to finish the article," thought Coop aloud.

The next morning, they flew the remaining miles to Parker Arizona, where the Colorado Los Angeles Aqueduct begins. As they touched down, Jack read from the Metropolitan Water District of Southern California website that said, "the Colorado River Aqueduct is a 200-mile system of open canals, tunnels and siphons that carry millions of gallons of water each day to the people of Southern California. There are five pumping plants with multiple pumps at each plant, along the river. The pumps lift water hundreds of feet on the way to Los Angeles."

"I think the river provides as much as a third of Southern California imported water," said Jack "Between the Owens Valley and Colorado River, nearly two-thirds of Southern California's imported water needs are met."

Focusing on the Colorado River, Jack summarized his understanding gained from his late-night review of some LA Times articles which mentioned that "There are seven states and Mexico that take water from the Colorado. It is 1400 miles long and serves about 40 million people. Although California is but one of the seven, it has priority rights over the other states including Arizona."

Jack added, "Arizona is somewhat late to the party because the state was a late bloomer in terms of industrial developments and attraction of residents in the early 1920s when water priority between states was initially established. That pecking order, commonly referred to as the Law of the River, has been upheld by the Supreme Court.

"I understand that recently the President has negotiated a water saving plan agreed by the participating states which was necessitated by the years of drought and the depletion of the river through its overuse by the participating states," he said. It also did not hurt that the president tempted Colorado river states by offering them as much as $1 billion to modify their water usage. As I recall, California, Nevada and Arizona committed to a 25% reduction in water usage over the next three years."

Returning to the Metropolitan Water District website, Jack noted that "Parker dam houses major hydroelectric generating facilities. Four hydro units can each produce 30,000 kilowatts of non-polluting hydroelectric power."

"Whoa," said Coop. "This one dam can create 120,000 kilowatts of energy?" he said rhetorically. "So, if Big Joe wanted to do real damage to So Cal and parts of the Western United States, in addition to meddling with its water, he can disrupt a major source of its energy located at the beginning of the Colorado Los Angeles Aqueduct."

"I had no idea how vulnerable, So Cal is to the availability of imported water and a significant portion of its energy," Jack thought aloud. "It still begs the question of who would benefit most from a significant disruption."

"And how it would be accomplished," added Coop.

Jack's cell rang. "Hi, this is Jack," he said into the phone. "He does. We just landed near Parker Arizona. Can't we simply speak with him by phone? No? Ok, then, we will be there this afternoon." As he closed the phone, he looked Coop in the eye.

"That was Mindy," he said. "Her boyfriend, the Inyo county counsel, got back to her and wants to meet with us this afternoon at Jake's Saloon. Ominously, she does not feel comfortable giving us any information over the phone," Jack said. "E, how long to Lone Pine?"

"About 2 hours," he responded.

"Let's head back," directed Jack.

"Agreed, there is no sightseeing to be done here in Parker Arizona anyway," E said comically looking at the barren landscape as far as the eye can see. Let's load up and I'll show you 'Water Dogs' a thing or two from the air that might interest you."

Within a short time after refueling and take-off, Coop pointed ahead to a distant massive object and asked, "What's that?"

"That, my 'Aquamen' friends, is the 700-foot-high Hoover Dam. The dam impounds the water of Lake Mead, the largest reservoir in the United States when full," commented E. "It also generates electricity for Nevada, Arizona and California. Lately, with the multi decade drought, Lake Mead is approaching dead pool status at which level the flow of water will not be sufficient to generate electricity. The lack of hydroelectric generation will affect millions negatively," said E.

"The dam was constructed during the FDR administration with thousands of workers. It was deemed so important to national interests that during WW 11 guards were placed on the dam and the public was excluded from it."

Flying over Lake Meade, E pointed out that, "The lake took a big hit with the two-decade drought. It declined nearly 200 feet from its full level. Although recent rain, melting snow and conservation efforts are beginning to refill the lake, you can see the 'bathtub ring' around the edge of the lake showing the significant decline of water from its full level. "There is no assurance that it will return to 'normal'."

"Remarkable," said Jack.

"On to Lone Pine!" shouted E, as he dipped the left wing, pointed the plane West, slapped his thigh and said, "Giddy up."

As the plane approached the Lone Pine airport, E suddenly swerved to the right. "What was that?" asked Jack.

"I don't know what it is, but some object is dangling from a balloon in our flight path, and I almost ran into it. Why anyone is messing with balloons near an airport is a mystery to me and they ought to be prosecuted for interfering with airspace."

"Just look at the thing," said Jack. "It looks like a small bus hanging from a huge balloon."

"What is the purpose of that?" asked Coop.

"Beats me," answered E. "Let's land this baby before something else happens." E brought the plane to a stop near a hangar at the Lone Pine airport.

"Our meeting shouldn't be too long, E. Will you wait for us here?" asked Jack.

"Sure, I will see if someone has a coke nearby and some information about the balloon," he responded.

"We'll call a cab, or Uber and head to Jake's Saloon," said Jack.

CHAPTER TWENTY-FIVE

"**H**i Mindy, we are pleased to see you," said Jack. Mindy introduced Jack and Coop to her boyfriend, Dave Hughes, the Inyo county counsel. They each shook hands. "Pleased to meet you Mr. Hughes," greeted Jack.

"Please call me Dave."

"I'm Jack and this is my colleague Gary Cooper, we call him Coop," announced Jack. Dave eyed Coop oddly as he digested the disassociation between Coop's name and the famed Western character. "Can we buy you a beer and sit for a while?" asked Jack.

"None for me" said Dave, expressing an all-business attitude.

Jack turned to Dave and said, "Mindy volunteered that you are familiar with Big Joe Thornley."

"Yes, he came to us several months ago and expressed interest in our water needs. More specifically, the lack thereof because of Los Angeles sucking us dry," said Dave.

"What did Big Joe offer the county?" asked Jack.

"He offered to help fund the eminent domain litigation and purchase of land acquired by eminent domain," responded Dave.

"How much?" asked Jack.

"Whatever it takes," answered Dave.

"That's rather generous," commented Coop.

"And once eminent domain is exercised, what will happen?" asked Jack.

"The county will own prime land and the water rights associated therewith," answered Dave.

"So, with the ownership of land the county can control the water allocation to Los Angeles," summarized Jack.

"That's right. We will control our water destiny as it was before Mulholland stepped in and stole our water rights," said Dave.

"Good luck with your suit," said Jack. "We have some suspicions about Big Joe and his syndicate. We think he and his syndicate participates in water theft and diversion as well as control of water drilling rights in California's Central Valley," offered Jack.

"I'm surprised by those allegations although he seems very well connected and determined," commented Dave.

"What do you think his goal is in helping the Owens Valley?" asked Coop.

"When we met with him, I had the impression that his desire was not so much to enhance the water supply for Owens Valley as it was to reduce significantly water flowing to Los Angeles," said Dave.

"What would Big Joe and his syndicate gain by depriving Los Angeles of water?" asked Coop.

"Your guess is as good as mine," answered Dave.

"Perhaps we can gain some insight by learning who is a member of his syndicate. Mindy led us to believe that you have a membership list," stated Jack.

"Before the county does business with or accepts a sizable gratuity from someone, it does some due diligence." answered Dave.

"What did your diligence show for Big Joe Thornley?" asked Jack.

"We saw that he was a sizable farmer in the Central Valley and had business associates who appeared to be reputable," answered Dave.

"Who are those business associates? Are they members of his syndicate?" asked Jack.

"We are unaware of a formal syndicate in which he or his business associates participate," said Dave.

"Who are they, irrespective who how they are labeled?" asked Coop.

"In anticipation of our meeting, Jack, I looked for the list of associates Mr. Thornley gave to us for our background check, and it was missing," announced Dave.

"Missing?" repeated Coop.

"Yes, missing," responded Dave.

"Are you sure?" asked Jack.

"We have searched high and low, and the list is nowhere to be found. In fact, we notice that one of the locks on my office door had been jimmied," added Dave.

"Was anything else missing, Dave," asked Coop.

"No, nothing," said Dave.

"Can you remember any of the names?" asked Coop.

"Other than Big Joe, no," he responded hurriedly.

"What do they have in common?"

"That I couldn't tell you either," answered a non-committal, Dave. "To us they appear to be substantial businesspeople who had not exhibited a propensity to violate the law. At least there is no public record of them doing so."

"Not yet, at least," offered Jack.

"Who could have been interested in the list?" asked Coop.

"My question exactly," said Dave. At which time a police officer stepped from a room behind the bar and approached the table.

"Gentlemen, please place your hands on the table. You are under arrest," the officer said.

"Whoa, wait a minute," said Jack.

"You will have a minute and much more as we discuss this further at the station," instructed the officer. "Hands behind your back please."

Jack and Coop were handcuffed and taken out of the Jake's and toward two waiting patrol cars. Seeing that they would be split up, Coop told Jack "This is a set up. We each get a call, you call E for bail, and I will call Murph to put in a word for us."

"Got it," said Jack as they were separated and disappeared into the two patrol cars.

CHAPTER TWENTY-SIX

Big Joe called his contact and asked if the syndicate list had been secured.

"Yes," was the response.

"Destroy it," commanded Big Joe.

"Consider it done," was the response as a flame was lit and the list became history.

Next Big Joe texted the person tailing Jack and Coop. "Did you follow my plan to have them arrested?"

"Yes," was the response. "I left an anonymous tip with the county counsel's office and the police station telling them where they could find 'the culprits who stole your list of business associates'."

"Good," said Big Joe and disconnected.

At the Police Station, each Jack and Coop were asked if they wished to have an attorney present for the B and E and 459 PC charges. Each responded "no", contingent upon one request, that they each be allowed to make a phone call before questioning. Their request was granted, and the calls were made.

Each was taken to a separate room for interrogation. "Mr. Armstrong why were you interested in obtaining the list of names provided to the County by Mr. Thornley? We have an anonymous tip that you stole the list from the county counsel's office. We also have you on tape inquiring about the list of names with Mr. Hughes, our county counsel," said a police detective. "You asked a lot of questions about the list and showed a genuine interest in obtain a copy of it."

"We have reason to believe that Big Joe is running a syndicate that profits off the control of water in the Central Valley through theft, drilling and diversion of surface water." answered Jack.

"What facts lead you to believe that?" asked the detective.

"Coop and I witnessed the theft of water from Coop's grandfather's ranch. The stolen water was taken by10 tanker trucks into the surrounding hills to an abandoned gold rush town where the thieves have created a hidden farm to grow illegal marijuana. We confronted the thieves and Big Joe's name was mentioned. We also learned from a well driller that permission from Big Joe must be sought to drill wells in the Central Valley or adverse consequences will occur.

"What kind of adverse consequences were alleged to have occurred, Mr. Armstrong?"

"Spiking the wells and equipment of the 'unauthorized' well drillers as well as harassment of the drillers themselves," answered Jack. "We saw the diversion of water from the California aqueduct when we flew over Big Joe's ranch. We confronted Big Joe with these facts. He didn't deny them and instead try to kill us by having his henchmen throw Coop and me into an aquifer and sealing the well head. And why would we steal the list if we were seeking it from the county counsel? That enough 'facts' for you? We have been set up."

"We need to collaborate what you are saying Mr. Armstrong," said the officer.

"Fine, please collaborate away to your heart's content. In the meantime, why don't you 849 B 2 Coop and me and release us on our own recognizance? I am a California licensed attorney and licensed private investigator, and Coop is a former Navy Seal and Berkeley Cop. I believe that Coop's former police captain is calling right about now to alert you guys of Coop's background and mine. Should you decline to release us on our own recognizance, my financial advisor is on his way with bail; however, we would prefer not waiting for a judge to set bail. So, what do you say?"

"I will speak with our police captain and let you know," the detective said.

"And while you are at it, perhaps you can explain why a giant balloon with what looks like a small bus dangling from it is interfering with air space around Lone Pine airport," questioned Jack.

The detective then left the interrogation room and closed the locked door.

Thirty minutes later, he returned and said, "You are free to go, Mr. Armstrong. We will release you and your colleague on your own recognizance. Please leave us your contact information and be available should the need arise. We will check on the balloon sighting. Have a nice day," the detective said smiling.

"Thank you, detective," responded Jack who left the room and met Coop in the police station lobby. "You have a nice visit?" asked Jack.

"Yep," responded Coop. "You?"

"Yep," repeated Jack. "Let's get out of here and compare thoughts."

CHAPTER TWENTY-SEVEN

"What do you think?" Jack asked Coop.

"Someone is onto us and our every move," answered Coop.

"There aren't too many people who knew we wanted the syndicate list," said Jack.

"I agree. It's as if someone is spying on us, said Coop.

"My thoughts exactly," nodded Jack. "Big Joe somehow has our number and is causing us a bit of inconvenience."

"Perhaps they have our tail number from the plane," suggested Coop. "Inconvenience is one thing, but the attempt on our lives is another," stated Coop. "One thing is for sure: Big Joe's Syndicate doesn't like anyone checking them out and will kill to prevent it," he said. "As we continue our investigation, we need to keep our eyes open, heads on swivels and ears clear."

About then, E arrived and said, "Fancy meeting yous guys here at the town police station. How nice!"

"Someone doesn't like us, E," said Jack.

"I gather that," responded E.

"Let's get outta here," said Coop as they hopped in a waiting taxi that E had arranged for a ride back to the airport.

At the airport, E asked, "Where to Fellas?"

"Santa Monica airport, E," said Jack as he and Coop needed a nap and some fresh ideas.

About two hours later, they touched down in Santa Monica. "Let's head to Sara's, get a bite and figure out where we are," said Jack to Coop. Coop nodded his agreement.

Jack asked, "E, can you hang around for another day or two? We may need you again. I'll make sure you will be rewarded for your great service and effort."

"Sure, flying beats financial advising," E responded.

Twenty minutes later, Coop and Jack arrived at Sara's apartment, knocked on the door and when Sara answered, she said, "You guys looked like yesterday's wet newspaper. What did you do, spend time in jail?"

"As a matter of fact, we did!" answered Jack.

"What? You guys must explain. "First why don't you have a drink. I'll fix dinner. We can eat on the deck this evening. The sunset should be as fabulous as the story you are about to tell us."

"Love it," said Jack as he looked lovingly into Sara's eyes before he and Coop headed to the deck. Just then, Sara's dog Charlotte, a labradoodle, jumped up and said 'Hi'. Where did Charlotte come from? asked Jack. I thought you left her in a kennel in San Francisco."

"I did. Since our stay continued, I thought it appropriate to have the whole family here and arranged for her to be bussed to Santa Monica.

Jack scratched Charlotte's ears and she tamed down to enjoy the ear rub.

Veronica heard the commotion and stepped on the deck, "Tell us the latest," she said.

"Coop, your turn," said Jack.

"Before we do, I have some unfinished business," Coop said while he approached Veronica swept her up in his arms and gave her a passionate kiss. After finishing his 'business', Coop announced, "We were arrested in Lone Pine."

"Arrested? For what?" questioned and incredulous Veronica.

"For Breaking and Entering the Inyo county counsel's office and stealing a list of Joe Thornley's syndicate names."

"What a dumb thing to do," she said.

Then Veronica followed by asking, "Did you?"

"Of course not. It was a set up and after our explanation, we were released. But it raises a bigger question. Who knew we were interested in the list and how did they know we would be in Long Pine asking about it?" asked Coop.

"And" said Jack, "who alerted the police?"

"The answers to those questions will materialize over time, I expect. In the meantime, let's call it a long couple of days, take the night off and enjoy each other's company and this beautiful view. All in favor?" questioned Jack as he looked at everyone's raised hand, then said, "It's unanimous!"

CHAPTER TWENTY-EIGHT

The next morning, Jack was able to round up some coffee and pastries from La La Land, a coffee house on Montana Ave, for all to enjoy. "Ladies, he said to Veronica and Sara, would you mind if I borrowed Coop for a while to brainstorm some ideas we have been kicking around?" They nodded their agreement and were content to go for a walk and some shopping while the boys headed to the apartment's terrace table for a chat.

Jack initiated the conversation by expressing the need for more information about Big Joe's associates to solve the Operation Water down riddle."

"What is the common denominator between them?" asked Coop.

"Clearly, water is what the syndicate members have in common," said Jack. "For example, a real estate developer needs water to develop future real estate. Look at what is happening in Arizona where 100 year guarantees of water are required to obtain permits for future real estate development."

"A rancher needs water for his crops," said Coop.

"So, their control of water is a valuable asset," said Jack.

"If water is depleted people and business suffer," said Coop. "Initially, people like my grandfather suffer inconvenience and attempt to cope with the shortage through conservation and use of existing water sources, such as reservoirs and bottled water."

"Thereafter," added Jack, "People realize that there is little or no end in sight for alleviating the water crisis and they move, or migrate, causing real estate values to plummet, and businesses to close, as is the situation with your grandpa Walker."

Jake Bittle in his book: 'The Great Displacement', comes to the same conclusion," said Coop.

"What if it is not the end result, but the threat of the end result that holds value?" posited Jack.

"You mean that the concern raised about what might happen could motivate people to act without the need to suffer the actual consequences?" said Coop.

"So, if a credible threat to one or more of the principal water ways leading to Southern California is demonstrated, the threat of disruption may be all that is needed to achieve the desired goal," opined Jack.

"And if the consequences of enforcement are minimal under state and federal law...", Jack said.

"You, got it," agreed Coop. "Heck, if you were a home buyer, a businessperson, a rancher, or a real estate developer, would you move into Southern California and risk having little or no water?" asked Coop rhetorically.

"And if you were any of those people with a presence in So Cal, you wouldn't want to be left 'holding the bag' and would act to sell before the bottom fell out of the market. In effect, So Cal would be shut down!" exclaimed Jack.

"Now, we have to figure out where this so-called credible threat could occur, and how Big Joe's syndicate can capitalize on it," said Coop.

"And what if the depletion of water is caused legally?" questioned Jack.

"What do you mean?" asked Coop.

"We know that water is a finite resource that is being over-drafted by farmers. There is less water because its consumption is not offset by its replacement through rain and snow melt. So, there is less of it, not only in California, but in other states like Arizona and throughout the world. Heck, the LA Times recently reported that groundwater levels are dropping around the world in a multipage article citing research performed by the journal Nature. Some users may be drawing water legally from California to offset or preserve the limited supply of water they possess elsewhere," said Jack.

"What do you mean 'elsewhere'?" asked Coop.

"By a sovereign state other than the US," answered Jack.

"I still don't get it," said Coop.

"Water cannot easily be exported to countries in need. It would create a flashing yellow or red light to the US and the rest of the world that water in some countries is in short supply," explained Jack.

"And if water can't be exported, what can?" said Coop. "Crops and agricultural produce can be grown here with our water and exported," he said answering his own question.

"You got it!" exclaimed Jack. "The Washington Post recently reported that a Middle Eastern Country is leasing property in Arizona to grow alfalfa for its cattle back home. Better to use American water to grow food for its cattle industry than use its own water."

"If crops are grown legally here, what can be done to preserve our water?" asked Coop.

"Contracts can be terminated, and laws and regulations

can be changed to prohibit the depletion of a state's limited supply of water," offered Jack.

"On the other hand," said Coop, "the state, and the US, may be reluctant to terminate the contract or implement restrictive laws if adverse consequences might occur."

"So, we need to figure out what those adverse consequences might be, and, otherwise, what credible threats there may be to disrupt So Cal's water," said Jack aloud. "Are you ready for another road trip?"

"Always," said Coop. "What do you have in mind?"

"I have a friend in NY who deals in stock market futures, including water. I expect that he would have a bunch to say about who is investing in water futures and the basis therefore," answered Jack.

"If we are headed East, we could also hit DC and a guy I know may have some ideas about who and how water can be disrupted," offered Coop.

"Sound like a plan. Tomorrow?" asked Jack.

"I'm in. We need to be sure our ladies know what we are up to," said Coop.

CHAPTER TWENTY-NINE

"E, can this plane of yours get us to NYC and DC?" asked Jack.

"Sure, but it will take a while. How much bladder capacity do you fellas have?"

"I guess we will find out," said Jack as he boarded the plane and grabbed an empty milk carton, 'just in case'.

As they settled in Coop asked Jack what he could share about the friend they were going to visit in New York City.

"Johnny K is a longtime friend who I met through E. He is a stockbroker who hit investment home runs with Facebook, Apple, and Google. Now he plays the futures market and is very knowledgeable. If anyone knows what is going on with water futures, it will be Johnny K," said Jack.

After several stops for refueling, bladder depletion and food along the way, they made it to Teterboro Airport in New Jersey, FBO to tri-state area private planes. Once the plane had been tied down, the trio hired a car and headed to the Lincoln Tunnel and the West Side Highway in Manhattan which led them to the Wall Street area and One Chase Manhattan Plaza, as Jack recalled the building, now known as 28 Liberty Street after Chase moved out.

Jack was familiar with Manhattan as he interned at the UN Legal Department while in law school and started as a young lawyer in a Wall Street firm located at One Chase. He was always impressed with the location of the 60-story building near the fortress like Federal Reserve Bank, overlooking NY harbor and the Statute of Liberty. He also smiled when he saw and pointed to the familiar Dubuffet "Group of Four Trees" sculpture on the building's plaza.

"They look more like mushrooms to me," commented Coop. "Isn't this the building where scenes from the HBO show Billions was filmed?"

"Sure is," said Jack. Let's head to the 48th floor and Johnny K's office. Upon exiting the elevator, they saw a prominent sign for The Indian Ridge Financial Group and entered the office. Met by a lovely receptionist who the boys eyed carefully, then Jack asked for Johnny K. Within minutes, he appeared.

CHAPTER THIRTY

"Hi Johnny," Jack said as he extended his hand and introduced Coop and E, who Johnny already knew from the financial world.

"What have you guys been up to?" Johnny asked.

"We've been up to our ears in California water issues," Jack related.

"Let's sit in the Board Room and learn more about your water issues," said Johnny motioning the way with his hands.

As they entered the Board Room, they were taken with the floor to ceiling windows and the spectacular view of the surrounding buildings and New York Harbor. Each was mesmerized by the breath-taking view. From nearly 50 floors up, the view was like flying over lower Manhattan and the Harbor. "I am always blown away by the view of the Harbor," said Jack.

"It is impressive," agreed Johnny, "I never tire of it either."

"Where did the Indian Ridge Financial Group come from?" asked E.

"I have a home in the California Desert in an area called Palm Desert and a development named Indian Ridge near Palm Springs. I like to evacuate from the East Coast cold in the winter and play some golf. My private plane can reach the Desert without refueling and fits nicely in the Palm Springs airport. My Desert home is only 20 minutes away. I can be on the golf course within an hour after I land. Shall we have some coffee and discuss your 'water issues'?"

"Yes, more precisely the disruption of Southern California imported water caused by an organized crime syndicate," explained Jack.

"How can I help, my friend?" asked Johnny.

"You trade in water futures, don't you?"

"You bet I do, Jack."

"Doesn't that require you to be mindful of the water market?" asked Jack.

"Sure does," said Johnny K. "And more precisely, the weather. If there is a lack of rain, or diminished snowpack, it affects the amount of water which will be available."

"Have you noticed any recent volatility in the market?" asked Jack.

"Nothing dramatic. As water becomes scarcer, prices rise." responded Johnny. "I watch the new Nasdaq Velez's California Water Index. It seeks to track the spot price of water rights in California. The goal of the index is to show the current valuation of water as determined by water entitlement transactions from California's surface water market and selected groundwater basins. The prices reflect the commodity value of water at the source. The data are limited to transactions resulting from market negotiations and exclude transactions involving non-financial consideration. The index is priced in USD per acre foot."

"That's helpful," said Jack. "Have you detected any trends on the Velez?"

"Only, the obvious," responded Johnny. "Futures have been increasing in value as the long-term drought in California persists. The Velez Index has risen 87% this year to over $923 per acre-foot and has recently declined given the sizable rain and snowpack which have occurred."

"What would happen if there was a cataclysmic event which affected the availability of water for Southern California?" asked Coop.

"You mean like an earthquake causing aqueduct damage or pipeline breach?" asked Johnny K.

"Or a man-made event, causing the same?" questioned Coop.

"As with any cause affecting the availability of a commodity like water, the market assesses how long it will take to return to normal conditions in a particular geographic area. The longer it takes, the higher the price." answered Johnny K. "The futures contract will do nothing to increase the supply of water. Nor will it facilitate moving water from one place to another. Holders of the contract upon expiration can't take delivery of water, and sellers of the contract won't provide any."

"Water is a heavy commodity with lots of restrictions on how it can be moved," explained Johnny. "In California, some water rights date to the 19th century where water users such as miners were located far from water sources. The dominant doctrine in the state became 'prior appropriation'—those who first draw water for any reason can continue using it indefinitely for the same purpose. The state constitution requires water to be used 'reasonably' for a 'beneficial use' but those terms are not defined and have not been court tested," he added. "Furthermore, there is a legal question whether these water rights are 'property' rights rather than 'use' rights. "So, if you don't use the water, can it be sold? A question to be resolved."

"Even if water cannot be sold," said Jack, "the produce created by water can be sold and moved."

"Yes, it can and is being done," said Johnny. "A critical issue for states and even our country is whether we allow investors, even sovereign funds, to grow crops in the US and export the produce overseas. In effect, mining our water saves the use of water elsewhere. Initially, this may not be viewed as problematic and enhances free trade and capitalism, but as global water declines and people in urban areas begin to suffer a lack of water, water insecurity is fostered. And water insecurity makes the world less stable.

"According to the UN, about 2 billion people live in countries where water supplies are under high stress. Even in this county, it is estimated that 90 million Americans are living under drought conditions. And in a few years, it is estimated that almost half of the world's population will struggle to meet their water needs."

"So, a significant interference with water destined for Southern California could have a devastating effect on that region and even the country," thought Jack aloud.

"Absolutely," replied Johnny. "Just think of the dependence of real estate, industrial business, and life itself upon the need for water, particularly in a semi-arid region. Real estate alone in Los Angeles' 4,000 square miles is assessed at $2 Trillion," he added. "Lord only knows how LA business is valued. Just think of the immense value of Hollywood including the entertainment and music industries, the Aerospace industry,

Bioscience, Transportation and Fashion! What leads you to think So Cal is at risk?" Johnny asked.

"We have evidence that a syndicate is attempting to control water in California's Central and Owens Valleys," said Jack. "We don't think it is far-fetched to think that the crime syndicate to which I allude and whose members are a secret, may have plans to extend their control of water over Los Angeles."

"That would mean control of imported water from the Owens Valley, the Colorado River, and the State Water Project?" asked Johnny.

"Yes, without them, LA would suffer immediately and immensely," said Jack.

"And the elimination of significant hydro electricity generated by several of those sources would add to the havoc," said Coop.

"What is the end game?" asked Johnny.

"Good question and one with which we have been struggling," offered Coop.

"There has to be a quid pro quo if LA is to be strangled by turning off its water," queried Jack.

"And there has to be a prime mover," asserted Coop. "We should check with some contacts I have in DC."

CHAPTER THIRTY-ONE

"We can fly into Signature Aviation an FBO located at Reagan, but need to be careful about White House airspace," commented E. "That will put us within 20 minutes of the FBI HQ, Coop."

"Forget HQ. My contact has agreed to meet Jack and me away from the office," said Coop.

"Where?" asked Jack.

"The Newseum in DC," answered Coop.

"The Newseum? I thought they closed because of financial difficulties," said Jack.

"They did close, but I happen to like the roof top garden and the surrounding views," commented Coop. "I also like the privacy afforded by a closed building."

"How are you going to get into a closed building?" asked Jack.

"Are you kidding me? Can of corn," said Coop.

"If you say so," murmured Jack.

The short flight to Reagan National Airport was uneventful as was the 20-minute taxi ride that Coop and Jack took to the Newseum. As they exited the cab, they entered a service alley on the side of the building and quickly found a fire escape ladder which was reachable by Coop getting a leg up with an assist from Jack's hand hold. Once Coop was safely attached to the ladder, he reached down and grabbed Jack's hand to give him an assist. Jack grabbed the ladder with his free hand and with some effort wiggled his way up the steps. Since the

Newseum was closed and night had fallen, there was little chance that the pair would be seen or heard as they climbed to the top of the building and over the roof parapet.

As Jack caught his breath and stood upright, he observed the surrounding view, "Wow, I see what you mean." Located halfway between the Capital and the White House, Jack agreed with Coop: "The view is outstanding! I can see why you like this location."

From behind the elevator engine room, appeared an individual who immediately walked toward Coop. "Hi buddy, how you doin ?" the unnamed person said to Coop.

"Jack meet Hank Svoboda, my brother in protecting America."

"Glad to meet you, Hank. Thanks for agreeing to meet with us. I hope you can help us get to the bottom of a mystery that has perplexed us," responded Jack.

"What's that?" asked Hank.

"We have reason to believe a criminal syndicate wants to cut off Southern California from its supply of imported water from Northern California. Does the FBI have any intelligence supporting our suspicion?" said Jack.

"What makes you suspicious of a criminal syndicate trying to interfere with US water supplies?" asked Hank.

"We have bumped into a syndicate in the Central Valley of California that is diverting, allocating and stealing water in California's fertile Central Valley. The syndicate is controlled by a fellow named Big Joe Thornley. Remember the movie Chinatown?"

"Yeah, sure," responded Hank.

"Like the movie Chinatown, Big Joe and his syndicate are implementing plans through land right acquisitions to control the water flowing from the Owens Valley to LA which provides about one third of L.A.'s imported water." responded Jack.

"We also think the Owens Valley water diversion is part of what Big Joe calls Operation Watered down. Watered down could be part of a bigger play to shut off water being imported by Southern California from its prime sources: the Owens Valley, the State Water Project, and the Colorado River."

"Why would the syndicate attempt to interfere with the water flow to Southern California?" asked Hank.

"We are not sure," answered Coop. "It would be helpful if we knew who comprised the membership of Big Joe Thornley's Syndicate Can you, or the FBI, help with that?"

"I'll take a look. Let's plan to meet back here the night after tomorrow," Hank offered.

"Time for a beer?" Coop asked.

"Not tonight, brother," Hank responded as he headed back behind the elevator shaft.

CHAPTER THIRTY-TWO

Two nights later the threesome met again, this time at the W Hotel (aka The Hotel Washington). Hank explained to Jack that the hotel was established in 1915. From the top floor it was easy to see across the street at least two snipers patrolling the White House roof top. There was also speculation that the roof top contained false chimneys which housed missiles or anti-aircraft guns.

Hank imparted what he had learned. "We checked into Big Joe Thornley's syndicate and found evidence supporting your suspicious. In the immortal words of Joe Pesci in the movie My Cousin Vinny, your theory 'holds water'."

"What leads you to believe that?" asked Coop.

"The syndicate is composed of two prominent Southern California real estate developers, another large rancher in addition to Big Joe, two politicians and a possible foreign interest,' said Hank. "Let's simply say that we have reason to believe that there is money laundering and other possible criminal activates involved."

"How did you find the syndicate membership list?" asked Coop.

"If I told you, I'd have to shoot you," responded Hank. "Let's just say that we have our ways of tracing people and their associates through many channels."

"Can you tell us who the foreign interest is?" asked Jack.

"The name is still a mystery." answered Hank. "Do you have any clues?"

"Not really," said Jack.

"And if you catch the name of the politicians, we would be interested in that too," said Coop. "In the immortal words of Forty Niner Jerry Rice, shall we try for a 'threepeat' and meet in another day or two here?" asked Coop.

"No need for another meeting," said Hank. "I'll give you a call with what I find."

"Good," said Jack. "We are heading back West to scope-out how Big Joe's Syndicate will try to convert Los Angeles into a Giant Dust Bowl. Now for that beer we skipped at the end of our last meeting."

CHAPTER THIRTY-THREE

After the beer and some light hearted conservation with Hank, Coop and Jack headed to Signature Aviation at Reagan. "Take us home, Great Wizard of the Sky," Jack said to E. They boarded the trusty U-10 Helio Courier and settled. Soon after receiving flight instructions, they were in the air heading West. "Any particular destination in the West?" asked E, adding, "I filed a flight plan for Santa Monica."

"After giving it some thought, Jack suddenly said, "E, let's take our Magic Carpet Ride to the fabulous Tulare International Airport." We can meet Sam there. Then facing Coop, he explained, "She can help us understand the water infrastructure and possible targets. Besides, I'd like to catch up with her and figure out where her reporting stands, and, more importantly, I have a suspicion that she is the leak who is causing all our problems with Big Joe."

"I share your suspicion," agreed Coop.

"I'll give her a call and arrange to have her meet us at the airport," said Jack.

"Good idea," responded Coop, now I like to get some rest and quickly closed his eyes.

Hours later they landed in Tulare where they met Sam and invited her onto the plane. "Sam, great to see you again. It seems like weeks but has been only a few days since we parted in the Owens Valley," said Jack. "Have a seat."

"Yeah, after you departed, we were arrested," said Coop.

"Arrested?" she asked quizzically.

"Yep, someone misinformed the local police that we were up to no good and they brought us in for interrogation," said Coop. "You wouldn't know who that might be?"

After a brief hesitation and some thought, Sam answered, "Not a clue. Are you guys, OK?"

"Yes, Sam," said Jack. "But we have reason to believe someone is watching us and whatever moves we make. How could they know that we were meeting with the county counsel responsible for the Owens Valley without keeping an eye on us? And who could have tipped off the police about our interest in the syndicate list?"

"I don't know," answered Sam, looking away from Jack's stare. "How about Mindy?"

"Mindy? Mindy is the person who connected us with her boyfriend, the county counsel and told us about Big Joe's plan to assist the county in asserting eminent domain over Owens Valley water. I doubt that she had planned a sting operation the moment we walked in the door to Jake's Saloon," said Jack.

"Give it some thought Sam as to who the leaker is," said Coop.

"And while you are at it, tell us what's the latest on your water article for your newspaper," Coop said.

"It is still under consideration and editing by the editor," responded Sam.

"We've heard that repeatedly, Sam. Is he trying to make sure it doesn't run?" asked Jack.

"I can't imagine why he would try to do that," she responded.

"I can," said Coop. "Big Joe may have done a Catch and Kill of your article, paying off your publisher not to print the article. It's an old trick used to bury unwanted attention. The publisher of the National Enquirer is alleged to have done that for a certain Presidential candidate."

"I may have to give a call to a friend of mine at the California Attorney General's office. He may see enough evidence to look into it," said Jack.

Agitated Sam began to squirm in her seat and said, "Fellas, I don't think law enforcement focus is justified yet. Let's give the editor a bit more time before that trigger is pulled. I could lose my job if your suspicions are off-base and legal action is commenced. And my daughter and I don't have deep pockets."

"You have a daughter, Sam?" asked Jack with surprise. "I saw no wedding ring and thought you were single."

"Yes, I am single, Jack: a single mom. My daughter, Megan, is the apple of my eye. I don't know what I would do without her," she said.

"Can her dad help with the support? asked Jack.

"Dad took a hike as soon as she was born," Sam said sheepishly. "That was 10 years ago. He's a flake. We haven't heard from him since. Now my mother, Megan's grandmother, pitches in to help when I need a hand."

Coop looked at Jack and raised an eyebrow.

"Ok, we'll back off, Sam. We just think something smells fishy with the delay in publishing your article and our arrest in Owens Valley. Someone doesn't want to call attention to the manipulation of California water and our investigation of the same," said Jack.

"Thanks," said a relieved Sam.

"Sam, please excuse us for a moment," said Jack. He put his arm around the shoulder of Coop and guided him toward the back of the plane and out of her earshot. "Do you trust her?" asked Jack.

"You mean sufficiently to share the crown jewels of what we have being working?" said Coop. "Frankly, no! There is something fishy going on as you have suggested. Her inability to publish the article timely, and more importantly, the prospect that she is the someone who was tailing us and sharing that information with Big Joe is compelling."

"Still, she provides value in terms of her knowledge of the state's water system as well as Big Joe and his dealings in the Central Valley," thought Jack aloud. And she may know something about his syndicate as well as Operation Watered down. So, I don't trust her, but we need her."

"Ok, let's get to the bottom of this," Coop said as he turned and walked back to face Sam. "Sam, we would like to spill the beans with you, and we value your help, but simply put we don't trust you! Your inability to publish an article critical of Big Joe for two weeks. Your introduction of us to Big Joe and subsequent conflict which allowed you to not join us when Big Joe pushed us down his aquifer Rabbit Hole to experience his 'Special Water Feature'. And, the inexplicable way that Owens Valley police were tipped off about our interest in the LA aqueduct after you left us, are simply not believable without your involvement. What have you to say?"

Sam hesitated for a full 30 seconds staring at the floor and avoiding eye contact, then she blurted out: "guilty," to the surprise of Coop and Jack. After a few silent moments which allowed the shock of her admission to set in, she added, "But with some background that may return your trust in me."

"It had better be a show stopper," said Coop.

"Big Joe has threatened to kidnap my daughter and my mother, if I did not cooperate with him and set you up," she said.

Jack and Coop were stunned. They looked at each other with slack jaws.

She continued to explain, "Big Joe wanted to be aware of any investigations into his Operation Watered down, and he figured a good way to do so was to have an investigative reporter from the local newspaper research and write about the California water crisis and possible manipulation thereof. He knew that at some point, his activities would draw scrutiny as people began to feel the pain of less water like Coop's grandfather has felt. He needed a heads-up about any investigations, and he used me as a pigeon, bait, if you will. It worked to draw you guys out and thus, the introduction to him. I had to report your interest to him or suffer the consequences. If Big Joe knew that I confided in you two, my daughter, mother and I would all be dead."

"Where is your daughter now?" asked Jack.

"She is with my mother here in town," answered Sam.

"You have a decision to make," explained Jack. "We can part here, and you can resume your life under Big Joe's thumb and never see us again, or you can help us complete the investigation we are pursuing. If you choose to come with us, we will make sure that your daughter and mother are taken out of harm's way."

Coop warned, "If after agreeing to partner with us, we learn that you are two timing us, feeding information to Big Joe, we will burn you by telling him that you have been cooperating with us. Big Joe does not suffer liars or people he cannot trust. What is your answer?"

"If you can assure the safety of my daughter and mother, I'm with you!" Sam declared.

"You made the right decision," said Jack. "Please call your mother and tell her that you, she and your daughter will be going on a plane ride. Ask her to pack a few things for a few days stay in a place that will be a surprise. Also, tell her that Coop and I will pick her up within the hour and take her and Megan to the airport. Let her know that the flight leaves shortly, and it is important that she be ready to leave when we arrive," instructed Jack.

Sam questioned, "There is a chance that Big Joe has some of his men watching the apartment which could make the pick-up problematic."

Jack responded, "Coop will call some contacts he has with law enforcement who will alert the police and run interference for us." In jest, Jack turned to Coop and declared, "If you are captured, Mr. Phelps, the Secretary will disavow any knowledge of you!" then he began humming the Mission Impossible theme.

"I will call Sara," said Jack while addressing Sam, "and make sure that arrangements are made to welcome you, your mother and daughter. I think she said that some friends of hers, Rick and Kathy, had moved in next door to her Santa Monica apartment and will be away for a while. Perhaps she can arrange to have the three of you stay there."

"Wow, I'm impressed, and relieved. You made those arrangements so quickly," said Sam as she smiled for the first time since they met that day. They departed the plane and Sam walked Jack and Coop to her car and the boys stopped abruptly when they saw it. It was a 1956 International pickup truck originally painted yellow and which had faded predictably over its nearly 70 years of age. Clearly no one had enhanced the truck's cosmetic beauty in the intervening years. Still, it looked solid, not rusted, a tribute to the Central Valley dry climate.

"Where did you find that?" asked Jack.

"From a concrete construction company," said Sam.

"Why?" asked Coop.

"Because I need to travel over the back roads of the Valley and don't want a vehicle what can't operate unless the road is velvet smooth. Besides, I kinda like driving my truck. Gives me a sense of freedom and style, and it was cheap," said Sam.

"Style?" said Jack. "Woman, you had style when we met you at the Hacienda Bar and Grill. You were dripping with style in the clothes you were wearing."

"Thank you, kind sir! I was dressing like bait on the end of a Big Joe fishing hook and look what I caught: a couple of jumbo fish, or pigeons" she responded.

"Enough," said Coop. "Let's get moving before Megan and mom disappear."

"Keys please," said Jack as he faced a smiling Sam. She offered them to him, and he climbed into her truck, started it without hesitation, then ground a couple of gears taking off down the road to her north-side apartment.

CHAPTER THIRTY-FOUR

While Jack drove to Sam's apartment, Coop phoned the County Sheriff's Department to run interference and provide some law enforcement protection if needed. Twenty minutes later they approached Sam's apartment. It was a modest building in a multi-use neighborhood. They noticed a car parked in front of the building with two burly men seated inside. Without looking to Coop, Jack asked, "How do you want to play this?"

Coop quickly scanned the area, slumped down in his seat below the windowsill and suggested that they drive around the block and approach the building from the backside. Jack passed the parked car without looking at it. The lookouts in the car did not associate the old faded yellow pick-up truck with Jack as he drove by them with Coop hidden below window level.

They reached the end of the block, turned right, and suddenly Jack saw flashing red and yellow lights in his rear-view mirror. A loudspeaker directed them to pull over. Before the sheriff's deputy exited his car, Jack got out and approached him with his hands away from his sides offering no threat. The officer approached Jack and asked him to explain what he was doing in the neighborhood. Jack noticed the name badge above the officer's shirt pocket which said "Adams". "Deputy Adams, I'm here to take some individuals to the airport."

"Are you a taxi or an Uber driver?" asked officer Adams.

"No," of course not, responded Jack, "Not in that old

truck," pointing to the rusted International. "We are just friends."

"Who are you picking up?" Adams asked.

Jack did not wish to identify specifically who they were to pick up as no doubt this sheriff's deputy was not party of the interference Coop had ordered, so he said, "A mother and her daughter."

"Do they have names?" Adams asked.

"I am not sure as the person whom we are assisting simply said that they will be at her apartment," said Jack.

"What is the address?" Adams asked.

"It is located around the block," Jack responded vaguely.

"Didn't you pass it?" asked Adams.

"Yes, I mistakenly passed the apartment and am circling the block to return to it," said Jack.

"Just a minute," said the officer. "Wait here," he instructed Jack. Then he returned to his car to receive instructions from his headquarters. Coop, who was in the passenger seat out of sight, heard where this was leading and quietly opened the truck door, couched low and crept alongside the truck to its tailgate while Jack remained near the truck's driver's door. Coop overheard the deputy say, "What does Big Joe want done? Shall I turn him over to Brown and Struggles who are in a nearby car, or bring him in? Ok, will do, 10-4."

As he replaced the radio and turned around, he was confronted by Coop who was holding a gun and instructed, "Please turn around and hand me your handcuffs with your left hand." Coop then handcuffed the deputy's right wrist to the steering wheel of his patrol car and raised the driver's side window while the deputy stood aside the driver's door, making it difficult, if not impossible for him to reach his car radio or the horn. Then Coop unplugged the radio mounted on the deputy's shoulder and put it in his pocket. Coop said to him, "Sorry Pal, we have to be going now as we have a flight to catch in Tulare. Tell Big Joe, we look forward to having tea with him next visit."

They hustled back to the truck, hopped in, and kept driving around the block stopping opposite the backside of Sam's apartment building. Coop told Jack to stay in the truck with the engine running and keep an eye open for any of Big Joe's henchmen or the sheriff's deputy while he brought Sam's mother and daughter out.

Coop located the back stairway to Sam's apartment and climbed the stairs two at a time. He located the back of Sam's apartment and knocked softly on the door. Sam's mother opened the door and answered. Coop quickly pushed the back door open and entered the apartment holding his finger to his lips. He huddled Sam's mother and daughter together, put his arms around them and said that there were some bad guys outside in front of the apartment who had to be avoided. He was here to help them join Sam. He explained that Sam's truck was waiting in the back of the apartment house and the threesome should proceed quietly down the back stairs to the waiting car for a trip to the airport where they would meet Sam. They began to gather their bags. Instead, he said that "someone would pick them up later and deliver the bags to them," which Coop knew was not going to happen as speed was of the essence. They could always buy what they needed at their destination.

Just then, they heard someone pounding on the apartment front door. Megan let out a scream. Coop gabbed her arm and lead her to the apartment's back door with grandma following. The three exited the apartment, proceeded down the back stairs quietly and ran for the waiting truck. Jack had opened the truck passenger door to allow for quick entry of Sam's mother and her daughter. Coop jumped into the bed of the truck and motioned for Jack to get moving.

Once the door was closed, Jack shifted into first gear, gunned the truck and it took off like a jack rabbit and leaped forward in a comical sprint. Shifting feverishly, Jack had the truck rolling as he saw two muscle men running up the street after them. Just as he shifted into second, one of the men grabbed for the door handle and barley missed. The other guy reached for his gun and took aim.

Seeing what was happening, Coop took out his Glock and fired three quick shots from the truck bed which sent the gunman diving for the ground. Still struggling to build up speed, the old International was now going 30 miles an hour. Today's cars easily hit 60 in less that 5 seconds. The truck would take 20 seconds, or more to gain the same speed. Hopefully, they would have some distance by the time the heavies ran around the block or back through the apartment, got in their car and took off after them.

Jack called E on his cell phone, "E, listen carefully and do what I say, OK?" Then Jack explained what his plan was. Jack drove to the end of the block and turned left and around the next block, heading North instead of South to the airport. Coop knocked on the rear window of the truck, pointed to the rear of the truck and shouted, "Hold on brother, we are heading away from the airport."

"Yes, we are," Jack shouted back.

As they left, the embarrassed sheriff's officer stood beside his patrol car and the two associates of Big Joe came roaring around the corner in their car. They stopped to release the deputy with a pair of bolt cutters kept in the trunk of their car. All crowded into the deputy's patrol car and took chase with red light flashing and siren screaming.

"Yippee Kayo Kaiyay" shouted Jack as he floored the truck and headed right around the end of the block and headed toward the freeway in a northerly direction away from the airport. The deputy with Big Joe's two men headed south toward the airport following what Coop had told him about "having a flight to catch."

Next, Jack called Coop with his cell phone and briefed him: "Coop, I called E, and told him to lift off asap with Sam. Also, I told him to file a false flight plan showing us heading to Austin, Texas. He will tell Sam that we have the valuable packages on board her truck."

Coop responded, "We had better hurry."

"Not to fear," said Jack. "Big Joe and the Sheriff's Department will be attempting to head us off at the airport, while we head in the opposite direction and E has taken off."

Meanwhile, the sheriff's deputy radioed the Department. "This is car 40," he said. "I have been held up and am in pursuit of two WMs with two WFs in an old yellow International truck headed to the Tulare airport. Call Big Joe and tell him two of his men are with me in pursuit."

Coop sat against the back of the truck cab and wrapped his arms around his knees. Then he smiled as they headed away from the Tulare airport and thought to himself, "What is that boy up to now?" He quickly closed his eyes and fell asleep.

About 20 minutes later, Coop awoke as the road was very rough, and he was being jostled about. He looked around and saw that they were in the middle of a large field. Nearby he noticed the back side of Big Joe's house mounted atop a nearby hill. A few minutes later the truck came to a stop. Coop hopped out of the truck bed and approached the driver's door. Jack wound down the window and said, "Hi, miss me?"

"What going on, Jack?" Coop asked. "That was a close call with the snatch and grab of the grandmother and daughter."

"Turn around and tell me what you see," said Jack.

Coop did so and saw an earthen runway. Jack said, "Did you remember when we did the fly over of Big Joe's property there was a runway. Presumably it was used for small planes and crop dusters. Well, guess where we are?"

At about that time, they both heard an airplane engine and looked up to see E's plane approaching the runway. "Good move," said Coop realizing that Jack had instructed E to take off in a Southern misdirection from the Tulare airport and then circle back to Big Joe's property which was North of Tulare. No doubt Big Joe's goons and the dirty sheriff's deputy would head to the airport with red lights flashing and siren blaring while E and Sam flew North and now were landing at Big Joe's airport. The Courier was particularly fitted to make landings on rough runways and E did so with great ease. He quickly brought the plane about after landing and positioned it to take off in the opposite direction from which it landed. Jack drove Sam's truck to the side of the plane. Sam's mother and daughter ran to the plane as Sam exited it to greet them with open arms and big hugs.

Jack and Coop approached the plane and encouraged all to climb aboard quickly while E kept the engine running and prop turning. Once all were aboard and seated, E gave the plane full throttle and in a little more than 300 feet it was airborne again.

"Nice touch, Jack, and in Big Joe's backyard, while his men are looking for us 20 miles away!" said Coop.

"E a flyby of Big Joe's is in order." No sooner had he said it, than E dipped his wing and aimed the plane at Big Joe's home coming within 5 feet of its atrium, then reaching for the stars. "That will give him something to think about," said Jack. "Sam, I hope you don't mind 'donating' the 56 International to Big Joe if he can find the key I threw into the field. No doubt he will view it as a memento of our visit. You deserve better!"

"And his men and that sheriff's deputy might suffer a bit once Big Joe finds out that we evaded them," said Coop.

"Let's head West and follow the California coast to Santa Monica," said Jack.

CHAPTER THIRTY-FIVE

"What the F—k happened, Cedrick? I pay you guys to watch her mother and daughter and they are snatched right out from under your noses. No doubt you and Fred were asleep at the switch. And the cop we brought off is handcuffed to his car! Does it get any better than this?"

After listening to Cedrick, Big Joe responded, "You are sorry? Sorry? Do you realize that Operation Watered down is now jeopardized? How are we going to fix that big guy? I want solutions, not rhetoric! I want a plan from you and Fred to Solve the Problem, not just talk about it. Do you hear me? You have 24 hours to develop and present a plan to me."

Once back in Santa Monica with Sam's mother and daughter housed in the apartment next to Sara's apartment, Jack took a crack at exploring with Sam what their suspicions are. He thought aloud, "If I were advising a client who wishes to significantly disrupt the flow of water to So Cal, where would I begin? Envelope please. And the answer is…", questioned Jack.

"The State Water Project," answered Sam, "It's long, vulnerable in multiple places and carries a significant amount of water to So Cal providing water for 27 million people, 750,000 acres of farmland and hydroelectric power to many. Besides, I once saw some plans spread on a table at Big Joe's highlighting the State Water Project. Clearly, he has an interest in it."

"You saw a State Water Project map on a table at Big Joe's?" asked Jack.

"Yes," answered Sam.

"Where do you think Big Joe would attack the State Water Project to cause the most disruption, Sam?"

"Well, there were red circles around four areas of the State Project on the map: in the North, Clifton Court Forebay and another area around Sacramento. In the South, an area around the Grapevine, and one around Pyramid and Castaic Lakes," responded Sam. "Maybe we should focus on these four areas."

"Let's start at the top of Water World, where it all begins?"

"Of course," said Sam, "The State Water Project and Central Valley Project begin at a place in Northern California near Tracy called Clifton Court Forebay.

"So that is the Garden of Eden for California water," said Jack.

"Almost," responded Sam, "California water really originates at Shasta Lake and the Sierras. Water from those sources travels to Oroville Dam where as much as a trillion gallons are stored. When released from the dam it travels down the Sacramento River and enters the San Francisco Delta, the wetlands, where it either heads to the Bay and Pacific Ocean, never to be seen again, or is drawn into Clifton Court Forebay by huge pumps which lift the water 200 feet into the California Aqueduct and the Delta-Mendota Canal. The California State Aqueduct travels 400 miles to LA while the Federal Delta-Mendota Canal travels nearly 120 miles to California's Central Valley ending in Bakersfield."

"What is this business I hear about a Peripheral Canal or Delta Tunnel Project?" asked Jack.

"The Canal was never approved by the voters. Instead, a Tunnel under the Delta will connect directly with Clifton Court Forebay and avoid dumping millions of gallons of water into the ocean. Hopefully, regulatory approvals and funding will enable this sensible solution for transporting much needed water South."

"Eventually, this has to be done," said Jack. "The need for an efficient water transportation system to sustain one of the most productive and economic regions of the state, require it."

"Yes," said Sam, "The Delta Tunnel Project would do that. In the face of heavy opposition from environmental groups, the Governor is pushing forward with a controversial plan to build a 45-mile water tunnel beneath the Sacramento-San Joaquin River Delta. The tunnel would be 36 feet wide and run 140 to 170 feet underground and connect to a new pumping plant that would send water into the California Aqueduct. Costs are estimated to be in the $16 Billion range.

Sam continued, "The Tunnel Project would allow for the system to capture and transport more water during wet periods. The current infrastructure makes for missed opportunities when large quantities of stormwater are allowed to flow through the delta and into the Pacific Ocean during rainy periods.

"The state estimates that had the Tunnel been in place during the past rainy season, an additional 228,000 acre-feet of water, enough to supply about 2.3 million Californians for a year would exist. The Tunnel also would mitigate against the potential catastrophic losses expected from earthquakes.

A size able earthquake could make the water system unusable for up to a year or more and would be the largest catastrophe in any water system in America. Southern California residents will pay for nearly all the Tunnel Conveyance project," Sam explained.

"So, without the Tunnel, today, California water that is inefficiently captured, is pumped from Clifton Court Forebay into the two principal aqueducts heading South?" questioned Coop.

"Yes, and the pumps are some of the most powerful in the world. The Bill Jones Pumping Station pushes over 5,000 cubic feet of water per second into the Central Valley canal and the Harvey Banks Pumping Station pushes twice as much into the State Water Project canal. This is accomplished by six Central Valley pumps and 11 State Water pumps. Combined, the 17 water pumps consume more electricity than any other location in California."

"If someone were to interrupt electricity to the pumps, pull the plug so-to- speak, what would happen, Sam?" asked Coop.

"Clearly, water would not flow South," said Sam.

"Two of the four sources of water imported by the Central Valley and So Cal would be decapitated," thought Coop aloud.

"Moving south, what significant State Water Project water features are near the Grapevine," asked Jack.

"Before we move south to the Grapevine, Jack, it is worth noting that another pipeline/ tunnel project is being cleverly conceived: the Columbia River proposed water infrastructure project (WIP)," explained Sam. "It would transport 12,000 acre-feet of water daily to California and the Southwest. This initiative reduces the need for Colorado River water for California."

Sam continued describing the Columbia River WIP, "An intake structure would be created to extract and treat Columbia River water at Columbia City, Oregon, 31 miles downstream from the Port of Portland. The water then would be moved 166 miles through pipes buried under the riverbed and ultimately to a 600 foot depth in the Pacific Ocean (about 14 miles offshore). This water would be transported south though a pipe tethered under water off the Oregon and California coasts to deliver needed water to four Oregon coastal water treatment plants, and in California: the San Luis's Reservoir; Castaic Lake in Southern California; and San Diego. To make this attractive to Oregon, the water users will make annual payments to Oregon of $440 million dedicated to improving the Columbia River ecosystem."

"Both the Delta Tunnel Project and the Columbia River WIP are creative ways to 'mine' water resources which are essential to the sustainability and growth of California," proclaimed Sam.

"I hear you Sam," said Jack."I am pleased that bright minds are creating new solutions to the state's water problems. While we work on future solutions, we have the immediate threat of Operation Watered down. What else can you share with us about Big Joe's attack on the State Water Project?"

"Near the Grapevine, there are the Chrisman Windgap Pumps and the Edmonston Pumping Station," responded

Sam. "You may recall when you drove Interstate 5 to Santa Monica a few days ago, you passed four huge pipes climbing the hillside to the right of your car as you headed South. Those pipes and their pumps, lift California Aqueduct water 800 feet up the hillside as it begins its climb over the Tehachapi Mountains."

"Yes, they stick out like a sore thumb," said Jack.

"Thereafter," she continued "A few miles away, the Edmonston Pumping Station lifts water another 2,000 feet further up the mountain and across the top into Southern California. Edmonston is considered one of the most powerful water lifting systems in the world. It is mostly comprised of underground tunnels," said Sam.

Looking at her iPhone, Sam continued, Wikipedia, says that "Edmonston has 14 four-stage 80,000-horsepower centrifugal pumps that push water up to the top of the mountain. Each pump stands 65-feet high and weighs 420 tons. The pumps extend downward six floors. At full capacity the pumps can push nearly two million gallons a minute up the Tehachapi's. At the top of the mountain the water is divided into two aqueducts: one serving the West of Los Angeles which is stored in Pyramid and Castaic Lakes for distribution to Los Angeles and the surrounding area; and one dedicated to the East of Los Angeles which passes through Palmdale and Lancaster and stores water in Silverwood Lake."

"According to the Water Education Foundation," Sam noted, "the California Department of Water Resources has determined that a breach of the California Aqueduct between the Bay Delta and the Edmonston Pumping Plant lasting for

4 and a half months would result in structural damage of $1 billion, in addition to cutting off water supplies to a large population."

"That is one target rich environment," said Coop. "I think we will zero in on a plan of hypothetical attack and we recon Chrisman at the Grapevine. Always easier to attack above ground than below ground at Edmonston," advised Coop.

CHAPTER THIRTY-SIX

Near the Grapevine, the trio saw a road leading to the Chrisman Pipes. The Chrisman Pipes take California Aqueduct water from the West side of the freeway 800 hundred feet up the mountain, then back under Interstate 5 and on to the Edmonston Pumping Plant located several miles to the East of the Interstate at the foot of the Tehachapi's. As they proceeded along the road toward the Pipes, Jack received a call:

"Hi Hank," announced Jack. "You do? OK, I'm ready," he said and then began listening. After 10 minutes, Jack thanked Hank and hung-up pledging to keep him informed.

"Well?" said Coop. "Name that tune."

"Hank called to follow up on the political connection to Big Joe's syndicate. He said that there are two: a Congressman from Bakersfield and a California Senator," said Jack.

"That must be Congressman McNitt," said Coop. "Mike McNitt."

"You Named that Tune," said Jack. "What do you know about him?"

"He is very clever, ambitious and totally untrustworthy," said Coop.

"Untrustworthy?" Jack repeated.

"Yep, he tells anyone what they want to hear in an effort to please them even if they have opposing views and he is unable to deliver Da Goods because no one trusts him!" explained Coop.

"Sounds like his days are numbered in political office," concluded Jack.

"Where does he get his campaign contributions?" asked Jack.

"About 90% of his campaign funding comes from CV ranchers. Where the money flows, he goes," said Coop. "McNitt has always favored the Big Guy vs the Little Guy: sort of an anti 'Jack and the Bean Stock' kinda guy," explained Coop. "Regulations or laws that interfere with a rancher's ability to thrive, irrespective of the consequences to smaller ranchers or sustainability, are to be disregarded or discarded."

"As a member of the syndicate," Coop explained, "he can be useful in alerting the group to what's going on in DC. Because of his seniority, he is on several key committees. He can also help head off legislation that may be troublesome to ranchers, including efforts to regulate water. Once he is out of politics, for whatever reason," said Coop, "the syndicate will pay him back nicely."

"And there is also a California Senator Nunley in the syndicate according to Hank," said Jack. "Do we have a book on him?"

"He is heavily involved in Federal water infrastructure projects," said Sam.

"Well, I guess that fills any holes in the Congressional lineup," said Jack. "After this brief 'commercial' interruption, we will now return you to your favorite radio station," quipped Jack.

As they drove toward the Chrisman Pipes, they quickly saw that they would not be allowed to see them up close because of signs and gates preventing public access. They pulled off the road in a nearby vineyard and visually inspected the Pipes.

There are four huge water pipes each of which is divided in six sections up the mountain. Coop took out a pair of Swarovski EL 8.5 x 42mm binoculars from his backpack. He scanned the pipes imagining the flow of California Aqueduct water from the valley floor to the top of the first 800-foot rise of the mountain. Slowly, he next panned the ground level at the base of the pipes where water from the California Aqueduct began its journey over the Tehachapi's. After several minutes without speaking, he carefully viewed the sides of the pipes going up the mountain, then down. "What do you think?" Jack asked.

"A couple of questions," he answered. "Sam, if there were a breach of these pipes, would the flow of water up the mountain cease to reach the Edmonston Pumping Station and thereafter, Los Angeles?"

"Yes, a breach would disrupt the flow of water up and over the Tehachapi's," answered Sam. "In fact, it would likely flood the valley and the Interstate, cutting off traffic along a very heavily traveled highway.

"So, we can ignore Edmonston because a breach of Chrisman would effectively eliminate one of the three sources of water imported by Los Angeles?" concluded Jack.

"Yes," said Sam. "Roughly one-third of L.A.'s water comes through the Chrisman Pipes before it travels to Edmonston and then over the hill," summarized Sam.

"Give me another minute." Whereupon, Coop pulled 'Tinkerbell' out of his backpack. He launched Tinkerbell and off she went toward the pipelines about a mile away. Jack asked what the range of Tinkerbell was, and Coop said, "about 5 miles."

Peering over Coop's shoulder, Jack and Sam saw the flight of the drone, along the base of the pipeline, then up one side of the six-section pipeline and along the top. The drone crisscrossed the pipes as it descended the pipes and returned to Coop. "Nothing unusual," Coop reported.

"Which means?" Jack rhetorically questioned.

"Which means, I don't see any significant impediments to planting explosives by hand or by drone on each of the four pipes and causing catastrophic breaches in each," said Coop, as a simple matter of fact.

"Ouch," said Jack.

CHAPTER THIRTY-SEVEN

"Next stop, Sam?"asked Jack.

"Let's head toward Pyramid and Castaic Lakes, a few miles past the Chrisman Pipes. The lakes are reservoirs and pump storage hydro facilities creating nearly 1,500 megawatts of LA electrical generation. The Los Angeles Department of Water and Power has turned the two lakes into a monster battery to store energy. They source their water from the West branch of the California Aqueduct as part of the State Water Project after it tops the Tehachapi Mountains." The trio pulled into the Vista Del Lago Visitor's Center parking lot overlooking beautiful Pyramid Lake.

"If there were a breach before water is diverted into Pyramid Lake, there would still be water in the lake, correct?" asked Jack.

"Yes, and quite a bit of it. Pyramid Lake has a volume of 180,000-acre feet of water and is the deepest lake in the State water system with a depth of 700 feet," said Sam. It is contained by a nearly 400-foot dam. Castaic Lake is nearly twice as large with 320,000-acre feet of water.

"The Lakes are connected by the Angeles tunnel which is about 7 miles long. The tunnel's flow is bidirectional," Sam explained. "During peak energy demand hours, water flows downhill through the tunnel, starting at an elevation of over 2,500 feet and falling over 1,000 feet to the turbines of the Castaic Power Plant. The water is then pumped uphill back to Pyramid Lake during non-peak energy hours using alternate energy sources such as wind and solar," said Sam.

"Quite a remarkably creative operation," commented Jack.

"Yes, the operation is an engineering marvel. There are six 30-foot diameter pipes in which water flows from Pyramid Lake down to Castaic Lake," described Sam. "The six pipes connect to 550-ton turbines lodged in a chamber four stories high. Their combined output is enough to power 83,000 homes over the course of a day."

"If one were to attack the set-up, where is it most vulnerable?" asked Coop.

"Why don't we park here and rent a recreational boat and tour the lake to make that assessment," suggested Sam.

"Good idea," agreed Jack as they headed to the public boat launch.

"I assume a breach of the Pyramid Lake dam would not be feasible," said Coop as they meandered around the lake.

"I think you are correct, Coop," said Sam. "Breaching the dam would create monumental havoc, much like when the St. Francis dam was breached. Water would follow Interstate 5 into and onto the 405 which would create a traffic nightmare while leading into LA and Santa Monica. The likelihood of a significant breach would be challenging. The earthen dam is high and wide at its base. Any significant breach would have to take out much of the bottom of the dam, a challenging task, as you can see from here," said Sam pointing to the dam at the end of the lake. The three powered their boat around the lake looking for vulnerable points of entry and exit.

After thinking quietly while they toured the lake, Coop smiled and said, "Maybe we are looking at it all wrong.'

"Wrong?" questioned Jack.

"The Pyramid Lake dam has already been breached," said Coop.

"What are you taking about?" asked Jack as they floated atop 700 feet of water.

"The Angeles Tunnel already penetrates Pyramid Lake and allows a high volume of water to flow out of the Pyramid Lake daily," answered Coop.

"Isn't that what Sam said?" responded Jack.

"What if someone left the spigot 'on' when the water rushed to Castaic Lake? Would the 'bathtub' overflow? Would Pyramid Lake empty?" posited Coop.

"Whoa, you may have something there," said Jack. "Override the shut off valve and flood Castaic Lake with as much as 180,000-acre feet of Pyramid Lake water!"

"If the Chrisman Pipes were breached, Pyramid Lake would not refill," added Sam. "And if Castaic Lake overflowed, the water would head down Interstate 5 to the 405 and eventually the ocean, snarling traffic on the most heavily traveled highway in America and creating a disaster like the collapse of the St. Francis dam!" said Sam with alarm.

"It would further cut off water and hydroelectricity to much of Los Angeles," added Coop.

CHAPTER THIRTY-EIGHT

As the trio headed back to Santa Monica, Jack thought aloud, "Two down and one to go. Sam what can you tell us about the Colorado River as a source of imported water for Los Angeles and Souther California?" asked Jack.

"We know," she explained, "that it is a significant water contributor, providing about a third of imported water. The Colorado River Aqueduct is a 240-mile system of canals, tunnels and pumping stations used to deliver water. In the East, the flow of Colorado River water begins at the Parker Dam which you saw in your fly over. The dam holds back the Lake Havasu Reservoir which is 45 miles long and stores as much as 210 billion gallons of water.

"Four hydro units at Parker can produce 30,000 kilowatts of power. Four 22-foot-pipes each push more than 40,000 gallons per second to feed the generators. After Parker, there are five pumping stations to lift the water to high points where gravity can take over.

Near the Western terminal for the Colorado River Aqueduct is the San Jacinto Tunnel which runs through Mt. San Jacinto, Southern California's second tallest peak at 10,800 feet. The tunnel is 13-miles long and delivers half a billion gallons of water to Los Angeles and San Diego every day.

"Lake Mathews is the Western terminal reservoir for the aqueduct and is located at the upper end of the Los Angeles service area at an elevation of nearly 1400 feet which allows water to flow by gravity through much of the area. Lake Mathews' capacity is nearly the same as Pyramid Lake. Two-thirds of the Colorado River Aqueduct winds up in Lake Mathews while one-third heads South to Riverside and San Diego," said Sam.

"That was a mouth full, young lady," commented Jack. "Now if we could only find a weak point along the canals, pumps or tunnels."

Coop thought for a while, then asked, "You said that there are five pump stations?"

"Yes," Sam answered.

"What happens if the stations don't pump?"

"Then the water doesn't flow," said Sam.

Coop quietly thought some more. Jack asked, "What are you thinking?"

"We keep toying with old fashion physical destruction of facilities. There may be an easier way to be a major disruptor. What is the common denominator for the flow of water through virtually any aqueduct?" asked Coop.

"Gravity?" responded Jack.

"Electricity," said Coop. "Without electricity, pumps stop pumping and water doesn't move to where gravity takes over. Or, valves stay open, and water cannot be stopped which creates a flood. I think we need to look closer at how electricity, which is critical to the system, can be interrupted. What is the source of power for each of the imported water systems?"

"I may have a short cut that can significantly affect the State Water Project and ties into the Northern California portion of Big Joe's map circled in red," said Sam. "Have you ever heard of Joan Didion?" Just as she was about to describe her thoughts, her phone rang. "Hello," she said.

"You have been a bad girl, Samantha," the voice said.

Suddenly, she began to quake with fear. "Who is this?" she demanded.

"You know who this is, Samantha," the voice said.

Coop and Jack looked at her and saw fear etched across her face. They asked who was calling and what was it about. She could not respond. Instead, they heard her simply say, "Yes." Then she screamed and threw her phone down. Coop steered the car on the side of the road and stopped.

Jack reached for her phone and picked it up. He said, "Who is this and what do you want."

The voice spoke clearly and authoritatively without emotion. "This must be Mr. Armstrong. Correct?"

"Yes, this is Jack Armstrong. You scared Samantha half to death. Who is this and what do you want, Jack repeated?"

"This is Joe Thornley, Mr. Armstrong. And I want you, your partner, Mr. Cooper, and Samantha to stay out of my business. Do you understand?"

"Why should we do that?" Jack challenged him.

"Because I have Samantha's mother and daughter, and I won't hesitate to harm them if any of the three of you continue to interfere with my business, Mr. Armstrong. Do I make myself perfectly clear?"

Jack was dumbfounded. They had just extracted Sam's mother and daughter from the watchful eye of Big Joe's muscle men in Tulare and deposited them in a safe house in

Santa Monica next to Sara's apartment. How did they find them? How did they kidnap them? Were they OK?

For want of a little water for Coop' grandpa, they had been shot at three times (with Red's Well Service, in E's plane and on the Tulare airport tarmac), nearly drown in Big Joe's aquifer, arrested in the Owens Valley and now the loves of Sam's life had been kidnapped. These guys mean business, Jack thought, then answered, "Yes, you have made yourself clear, Mr. Thornley. When can we know that Miss Curtis' mother and daughter are alive and have not been harmed?"

"You will receive a call on Samantha's cell phone at 6pm tomorrow and both her mother and daughter will speak briefly to her," Big Joe said. "In the meantime and thereafter, stay out of my business and don't call law enforcement!" Big Joe then hung up.

Jack looked at Coop, then at Sam. He said to Sam. "Sam, Coop and I will get your mother and daughter back unharmed. You have to trust us."

Sam exploded, "You said that before when I agreed to work with you and look what has happened. Trust you? You have got to be kidding. I want nothing to do with you or Mr. Cooper. And you had better stop interfering with Big Joe's Operation Watered down, or you will have Hell to pay from me, Mr. Armstrong! Do I make myself perfectly clear?

CHAPTER THIRTY-NINE

"Sara," Jack asked, upon returning to Santa Monica, "Can you tell us what went down, what happened?"

Veronica and I were walking Sam's mother and daughter through the Palisades Park to Montana Avenue. We had just crossed Ocean avenue at Montana and were walking to the Starbuck's at 7th when a black van pulled up. The sliding side door opened, and a burly man jumped out, grabbed Sam's mother and her daughter each by the wrist, said that Sam needed to see them right away, it was an 'emergency' and pushed them into the van, closed the door, and the van took off down Ocean avenue toward the PCH. We did not even see a license plate," she said. "We were horrified. I tried calling Sam and her line was busy. Then I tried you, Jack, and the call went into voicemail."

"I know, I got your message as we were consoling Sam and heading back here. Big Joe has threatened to harm Sam's mother and daughter if we interfere with his Operation Watered down, or call law enforcement. Sam understandably wishes for us to stand-down and not do anything that could jeopardize her mother or daughter. While Sam rests next door at Kathy and Rick's, Coop and I must come up with a plan to rescue Helen and Meagan and trip up Big Joe's Operation without placing them in harm's way. Coop let's take a walk on the beach and sort this out. Sara and Veronica, please comfort Sam if she awakes before we return." The boys left the apartment and headed down the back stairway to the beach.

"Seems to me," said Jack, "Our first, priority is to get Sam's mother and daughter back unharmed, then we can try to blow up Operation Watered down."

"Agree," said Coop. "Didn't Big Joe say that Helen and Megan would be calling Sam's cell at 6 pm tomorrow?" asked Coop.

"Yes, he did," Jack replied.

"It's 8 pm now. We have 22 hours to solve this riddle."

"Well, then, I have some calls to make," said Coop.

"Calls?" asked Jack.

"I figure that with the technology we have today, we can pinpoint where the call emanates from and, if we are on the ball, we will know where Helen and Megan are," said Coop.

"Is telephone tech that good?" asked Jack.

"Why do you think terrorists like Al-Qaeda and Hamas are relegated to delivering messages person to person? Kind of like the caveman days," opined Coop. "Big Joe is probably ignoring tech. Let's see if we can give him a tech lesson."

"So, what's next?" asked Jack.

"I need to hook up quickly with some of my buddies at the CIA. They may speak to some of their contacts at the NSA and FBI," said Coop.

"Isn't the CIA and the NSA focused on foreign terrorism? They aren't supposed to focus internally on the US, are they?" asked Jack. "I thought the FBI was responsible for internal terror threats."

"I kinda play with the letters interchangeably (CIA, FBI, NSA) depending on what is needed to do the job," said Coop. "It all adds up on how to defeat the bad guys. "

"Have at it and let me know what the plan is," said Jack. "Incidentally, we should keep this quiet with Sam and the Ladies."

CHAPTER FORTY

"How are we doing?" asked Jack of Coop, "We only have an hour until the call from Big Joe and the hostages."

"Making progress," answered Coop. "I'll explain. Big Joe most likely will be using a cell phone. A mobile phone needs to connect to a nearby base station to send its message. Each base station can serve many users in parallel and has a limited reach, which is even more limited in cities because of urban buildings. If one knows which of the base stations the phone is connected, we can identify the area where the phone is located. Accuracy is within 50 meters in cities. The operator of the network does know which mobile phone is connected to which base station. It will also store this information for a while and will provide law enforcement with this information. Alternatively, triangulation from 3 or more towers in a cell phone network can pinpoint the location of a phone."

"So, the bottom line is that pinpointing a cell phone can be done?" asked Jack.

"Yes. Through the help of my buddies, they are connecting with network operators in the Southern California area to be alert once we receive a call from Big Joe and disclose it to them through law enforcement. We also will be plugged into satellite interception of Big Joe's call. I have given the operators Sam's cell number and the time at which we expect to receive the call from Big Joe. They will be monitoring Sam's phone for incoming calls and will immediately begin tracing the call when it commences."

"How long will it take them to trace Big Joe's call?" asked Jack.

"With today's electronic and satellite equipment, a call can be traced very quickly by law enforcement," said Coop. "So, soon after the call, we should know where Helen and Heather are being held as they will be using the cell phone we are tracing. Then the challenge is to get to them before they are moved."

"What else should we be doing?" asked Jack.

"Listen in on the call for any distinguishing noises. Hold the caller on the line as long as possible to get a good fix on location and be ready to run once the call is complete and the location known. Also, you might call E and have his plane ready, if needed," recommended Coop.

"Let's meet with Sam and brief her on the plan," said Jack. We may wish to have her join us once the call concluded."

"You do so, while I outfit the BMW," suggested Coop. "I will join you at 5:50 pm."

CHAPTER FORTY-ONE

Precisely at 6 pm, Sam's phone rang, "Hello," she said in a hesitating voice.

"Samantha, have you behaved?" asked Big Joe without announcing his name.

"Yes," answered Sam. "We have stayed away from your business." With the phone on speaker setting, Jack and Coop silently listen.

"OK, I promised that you would speak with your mother and daughter if you behaved. You will hear that they have been treated well," said Big Joe.

"Let me speak with them!" Sam cried.

"Mommy, it's me," said Megan.

"Oh darling, are you OK?" asked Sam.

"Yes, except I want to be with you!" Megan cried.

"Have they hurt or touched you, dear." Sam asked.

"No, I am fine, but I miss you. When are we going …?" suddenly Megan's voice was cut off.

Next, Sam heard her mother say, "I too am fine, dear. They have not harmed us. Please follow their instructions, and we will be fine." Then the call was terminated.

Sam was in anguish having heard her daughter and mother without the ability to help them. Jack asked Coop if he had "heard any distinguishing sounds in the background of the call."

Coop said he thought he had heard "waves breaking" in the background and began heading to his car. Jack asked

Sam if she wanted to accompany them. "Absolutely!" she said. When they caught up with Coop in his car, he was already on his phone. "You did? Good. Ok, give it to me," as he wrote on a slip of paper, he had brought with him. "We may need back up and should be there in within thirty minutes. Let's coordinate as we get closer."

"Where too?" asked Jack.

"Malibu Colony," answered Coop as he began to head North on the PCH. As the sun was beginning to set, Jack and Coop noticed the beauty of the Palisades. Gently sloping mountains which disappear into the Pacific Ocean. "So this is what paradise is all about," said Coop.

"You can imagine the spectacular views from either the ocean front homes, or those located high up on the side of the hill," answered Jack.

"I can picture the sun dropping into the ocean nearly every evening and celebrating the event with a beer or glass of wine," offered Coop.

When they reached the Malibu Colony, "Nice high-end area," commented Jack. "Lots of celebrities and a gated, guarded community. One road in and out and on the water. Do you have an address?"

"I am told the location is in or near 70 Malibu Colony Road," replied Coop then thinking aloud he added, "I wonder how Big Joe wrangled a house on Malibu Colony Road?"

"Good question," Jack nodded in agreement. "Maybe one of those real estate developers who are members of his syndicate have connections to homeowners or realtors there. Sam, please google 70 Malibu Colony Road and let us know what you find."

A few minutes later, Sam said, "Bingo! That house is for sale. A mere $14 plus million. I'll check out the listing and any advertised floor plan."

"Great, now we are 'logging', as my father used to say," commented Jack. "Coop, depending on what Sam finds, what is our likely plan of attack?"

"One if by land and two if by sea," responded Coop.

"And I bet that you will take two, the sea," bet Jack.

"You and Sam take the Guard Gate," said Coop. "I am a Seal by nature and training," added Coop. "So, I packed some of my water gear, 'just in case'. Like the Boy Scouts motto: be prepared!"

"Sam, perhaps you can put on your best female presentation and distract the guard long enough for me to sneak by and under the gate on foot," suggested Jack.

"Sure, anything to get my daughter and mother back. I will be very, shall we say, 'charming' to the guard," said Sam.

"Have you found anything about the listing online that may be useful, to us?" asked Jack.

"It is a four-bed, three-bath 3300 square foot home on a third of an acre. It is set on 60 feet of prime Malibu Colony beach frontage. It has a two-bedroom guest house and a large deck surrounding the main house with stairs leading to the ocean," reported Sam.

"Likely that your daughter and mother are being held in the two-bedroom guest house. Let me see the pictures you have found," asked Jack. After glancing at them, he told Coop that he should take a look once they parked, to acquaint himself with the layout.

The PCH was a traffic nightmare as usual at "rush hour". Jack thought to himself, when is it not "rush hour" with LA traffic? It took them over an hour to travel the 10 miles to the Malibu Lagoon State Beach. Too many straws in California water and too many cars on Los Angeles roads.

They pulled over on the side of the PCH near the Cross Creek Shops. Coop got out and headed to the back of the car for some equipment. First, he pulled out Tinker Bell, his trusty dragon fly-sized drone. With Jack and Sam by his side, he launched it over the Malibu Lagoon. Directing it and watching what it flew over allowed Coop to size up the Lagoon and where it exited to Malibu Bay, which was his likely route of travel. From there he flew Tinker Bell along the Malibu Colony waterfront then along the single road that split the Colony into the ocean and the Lagoon sides. While over the road, he viewed the front of each home and located one label 70 on the Ocean side of the road. "Found you!" he exclaimed. Both Jack and Sam peer over his shoulder.

Next, Coop was able to fly Tinker Bell around the target home including the deck in the back, its stairway to the beach and the nearby ocean. He saw no impediments obstructing an approach from the water. Then he flew her to and around the cottage adjacent to the Main house. Because of the quickly approaching darkness he was able to direct Tinker Bell to "look" into the windows of the cottage with little risk of her being noticed by anyone inside. He saw Cedrick and Fred, on the first floor watching TV. On the second floor, he located Helen and Megan in a bedroom in the back of the cottage. "Got them," he exclaimed.

"Let me see," asked Sam as she looked over his shoulder. She began to sob.

Coop did a final fly by around the Main house to see if Big Joe or others were present after the call to Sam. He saw none. "I guess the Big Guy evacuated after making the call to Sam half an hour ago. If not, he will enjoy a big surprise in a few minutes" said Coop.

Coop wiggled into his wet suit and donned his sea equipment and his Glock 19. He spoke to Jack. "I will enter the Malibu Lagoon over there," pointing to the nearby Malibu Creek and the beginning of the Lagoon. "And swim through the Lagoon out to the Bay then follow Malibu Point North until I find number 7 Zero. I estimate 30 minutes to reach the vicinity of the target house from the ocean. Hopefully, there is signage on the side of the houses facing the water, but that is unlikely. So, take a flashlight with you and one of my weapons of your choosing from the back of the SUV. When you find the target house, go to the back, and use your flashlight to signal me with three flashes from your light. When I see your signal, I will return a flash. I plan to exit the water near the cottage. Looking at the online photos of the house, Coop said, "I see the stairway leading to the back deck of the house. I also see the cottage is a separate building and to the South of the main house. We should focus on the cottage first as that is where the hostages are being held."

"After you receive my return flash give me 5 minutes to exit the water and approach the cottage. You will hear a loud explosion as I enter the dwelling. Keep an eye out for anyone exiting the main house once you hear the explosion and cover my back if someone exits the house.

"After I secure Big Joe's muscle men, I will head to the second floor and lead Helen and Heather down the stairs and out the backdoor of the cottage. Meet me there so we can reacquaint them with Sam who will be standing in the street. Then lead them out the community gate asap and to my car. You can provide cover for them as they leave and anticipate a police response as someone in the neighborhood will call 911 once they hear the explosion. I will head to the main house to make sure that there are no 'odds and ends' left about. Questions?" asked Coop.

"Nope," said Jack. "Off you go into the Wild Blue Lagoon!"

After Coop took off for the Lagoon, Jack and Sam drove the remaining mile to the road leading to the Community Gate. To break the tension, Jack said, "I see a Starbucks across the road, time for a coffee?" Sam looked at him with disdain for his ill-timed joke.

They parked the car out of sight from the Gate house and began walking to the Gate. Fifty yards before the Gate Sam began to saunter suggestively while Jack split off into the bushes paralleling the road leading to the Gate. Jack was frequently amused at how security gates worked to stop cars and not people as he walked by the gatehouse hidden by a decorative hedge. He glanced at Sam and noticed that she has engaged an elderly male gate attendant who was taking in a friendly fashion to her. Fifteen minutes down, fifteen to go, Jack thought to himself. Once around the gate he reentered the only road leading into the Colony and walked quickly in search of 70 Malibu Colony Road. Thankfully, he managed to avoid bumping into any neighbors walking their dog as he might have trouble explaining why he was in the Colony. Ten minutes later he spotted it, 7 Zero, a stately home as advertised online. He looked in the windows of the house, and he saw no movement. He drifted around the side of the building and took out his flashlight, one minute to go as he checked his watch. He flashed his light at the ocean, once, twice, three times. A moment later 25 yards out to sea there was the return flash from Coop. So far, so good, said Jack to himself, now the "fun" begins. Jack spun quickly around, took a step toward the front of the house and faced a Walther PDP C 9mm inches from his forehead.

CHAPTER FORTY TWO

The Walther was held by a large man who said, "Fancy meeting you here, Mr. Armstrong. To what do we owe this honor?"

Recovering quickly, Jack said, "Just checking out the scenery, Cedrick. Apparently, you are intrigued by it too!"

"I think someone will want a more detailed explanation, hot shot. Inside the house," said Cedrick motioning to the side door of the main house.

Jack stepped inside and was greeted by Big Joe. "Mr. Armstrong," said Big Joe. "That didn't take you long. We've been expecting you. Where's your partner, the Black cowboy?"

"Oh, you mean Gary Cooper?" responded Jack.

"Yes, the Western named guy," said Big Joe.

"I'm not sure. He is floating around here somewhere," said Jack.

"Very funny, Mr. Armstrong, have a seat," said Big Joe pointing to an empty chair. "We have some catching up to do. What part of not interfering with my business did you not understand?"

"I was just checking on real estate in the area. This is such a nice development, and the house is advertised for sale," answered Jack.

"It will be nice to rid ourselves of you two," commented Big Joe. "Then we should have smooth sailing for Operation Watered down."

Jack saw movement out of the corner of his eye and the

door through which he entered began to move. He saw a grenade shaped object roll into the room. He fell backward away from the object, using the chair as a shield and covered his ears with his hands and opened his mouth to help absorb the expected blast. Just then a flash bang exploded in the room.

Coop quickly pushed the door open stepped inside and gave a powerful round house kick to Cedrick hitting him in his lower back and sending him flying across the living room and over a coffee table. The gun Cedrick had been holding fell to the ground. Jack, leapt up from the floor found Cedrick's gun and held him at gun point.

Hearing the explosion, Fred Brown rushed from the cottage and charged blindly into the main house through a door opposite the one that Coop had entered. Expecting Cedrick's companion to come to his aid with the explosion, Coop took three quick steps across the room in time to give Fred Brown a well-planted, powerful roundhouse kick to his left knee as he stepped inside the living room. Brown went sprawling and quickly grabbed his injured left knee likely suffering a torn ACL.

Coop then pirouetted across the room and planted a well-placed sharp elbow to the back of Cedrick's neck as he laid sprawled over the coffee table putting him under. Coop zipped tied his limp hands behind his back. Then he returned to zip tie Fred who was roiling on the floor holding his injured knee. Coop shouted to Jack, "Where's Big Joe?"

Jack still could not hear from the explosion and cupped his hand behind his ear. Coop understood and ran outside to see a car speeding away toward the guardhouse gate. No doubt Big Joe was getting away. With no car available to chase after him, Coop headed to the cottage to check on Helen and Meagan. The two of them were huddled together on the second floor when Coop found them. They recognized him and rushed to him with open arms. He took Megan in his arms and led Helen down the stairs and out of the cottage. He found Sam and let Meagan down so she could rush to her mother screaming "Mommy." Sam hugged her and her mother and began to cry.

"Well done," Jack said to Coop, marveling at how quickly Coop had attacked, disabled and zip tied Big Joe's two muscle-men. "Thanks for the backup, change in plans and quick action. I had no idea that Cedrick would be patrolling around the big house, or that Big Joe was inside."

"I guess Tinker Bell doesn't see everything," said Jack.

Checking his watch, Coop said, "In a couple of minutes this place will be crawling with police reacting to the explosion and no doubt, calls from neighbors. So, we sit for a minute, catch our breath, and when the police arrive, turn Cedrick and Fred over to them as kidnappers." As if on cue, they could hear sirens in the background.

"As for Big Joe, he continues to be on the loose and very dangerous to us and apparently to Los Angeles if our suspicions about Operation Watered down are correct," said Jack. "Once we complete our cooperation with the police, let's take Helen and Meagan back to Sara's next-door apartment and add a couple of guards this time."

"Good idea," said Coop. "I know a couple of guys who would be happy to provide that service."

CHAPTER FORTY-THREE

Jack knocked on Sam's apartment door. "Who's there?" When Jack announced himself, Sam cautiously opened the door even though two of Coop's men were posted outside. "How are they doing?" he asked quietly.

"They are resting calmly," responded Sam.

"Can Coop and I borrow you for a few minutes?"

She responded, "OK, let me check again on them, and I will join you."

A few moments later Sam entered Sara's apartment. Jack said "This will only take a couple of minutes." Then he asked, "Before we were so rudely interrupted by the phone call from Big Joe announcing the kidnapping of your mother and daughter, you were saying something about a short cut to the water disruption situation. Can you explain what you were thinking?" asked Jack.

"That's right, Jack," answered Sam and catching her breath and jogging her memory. "Have you ever heard of the author, Joan Didion?"

"No, I haven't," said Jack.

"Joan was a writer and journalist who passed away recently. She is considered one of America's great journalists, pioneering so-called, New Journalism. She was an inspiration to an aspiring journalist like me," commented Sam. "She wrote thought provoking essays for many notable magazines and published several books one of which won the National Book award for Non-Fiction. She grew up in Sacramento and later in life, lived in New York City until her recent death."

"That's nice to hear Sam. What has it got to do with So Cal water?" asked Jack.

"In the late 70s she wrote an essay as part of her White Album, a copy of which I have read and is on Kindle. It addressed her interest in water and tellingly she described what we have been researching. Let me see if I can pull up my Kindle copy on my iPhone. Ok, here it is."

"Enough, Sam," interrupted Jack. "I am sure it professes what we have been thinking in an eloquent tone. How does it advance our investigation?"

"Sorry, Jack," said Sam. "The foregoing is a prelude to what Joan discovered which may be of significant interest to us. The Operations Control Center for the California State Water Project and the Central Valley Water Project is located as the Sacramento Bee says, in 'an unmarked Sacramento office building next to a Costco.' That is likely the Sacramento area circled on Big Joe's water map."

"Whoa, you may have hit on something!" exclaimed Jack.

"Joan was one of the few visitors to see the Operations Control Center in action," recounted Sam. As she observed:

"They collect this water up in the granite keeps of the Sierra Nevada and they store roughly a trillion gallons of it behind the Oroville Dam and every morning, down at the Project's headquarters in Sacramento, they decide how much of their water they want to move the next day. They make this morning decision according to supply and demand.'

"She described the project as a 'three-billion-dollar hydraulic toy.' It occurred to me," said Sam thoughtfully, "If someone took over the Operations Control Center, they could command the State Water System and the flow of much needed water to Southern California."

"You are onto something, Sam. Coop, what do you think?" asked Jack.

"Does a bear do what where?" answered Coop rhetorically. "If the Operation Control Center were taken over or destroyed, So Cal would be without a significant amount of the water it imports. Kind of like hijacking a plane: difficult to do, but once done, the hijacker is in control!"

"Add to that the possible sabotage or electrical short circuit of the Owens and Colorado River water and So Cal will be up a creek without a paddle!" added Jack.

CHAPTER FORTY-FOUR

"Let's consider another option for disrupting the flow of water South," said Coop. "The water infrastructure in California is old. As such it has not been modernized to defeat the latest hi tech cyber incursions. I doubt that passwords have been updated or layers of cyber security have been added."

Jack recalled reading about "A recent Florida case where someone hacked into a water treatment plant's computer and began moving the mouse around on the screen. The hacker increased the amount of lye from 100 parts per million to over 11,000 parts per million. The plant operator reversed the change almost immediately and there was never a public threat, but...". said Jack.

"The plant had been hacked!" exclaimed Coop.

Sam counseled that, "Many systems in California are still operating with outdated software, poor passwords, aging infrastructure and other weaknesses that could lead to great public risk. You can see any number of critical infrastructures, like dams and water diversions, even pump storage hydro projects like the Pyramid and Castaic Lakes that may not be well protected in terms of passwords.

Sam added, "The Department of Homeland Security runs national security drills for dams and other critical infrastructure projects every couple of years, but even with the best protocols there still is going to be a risk of a cyber or physical attack. Compounding the problem is a lack of central regulations or uniform protocols. Many of the day-to-day decisions are left up to individual operators. Fortunately, the Metropolitan Water District of Southern California which supplies 26 agencies and serves 19 million people, including the Los Angeles Department of Water and Power, constantly takes steps to ensure the security of water supplies against physical and cybersecurity threats."

"Perhaps they are prepared for the disgruntled employee. What about the sophisticated hacker?" asked Jack.

"Let's glue this all together," said Coop. "Water is imported to sustain the Central Valley, our Nation's breadbasket, and So Cal, one of the most lucrative regions of California and the US. Two of the sources, the California Aqueduct, and the Delta-Mendota Canal, representing most of the water imported by CV and So Cal are controlled by the Sacramento Operations Control Center. The other two sources: the Owens Valley, and the Colorado River, are operable only if electricity is supplied. Seems to me, if I were interested in doing major disruption to imported water, I would be looking to disable the Ops Control Center in Sacramento and the transmission of electricity needed to operate Owens Valley and Colorado River water."

"And Great Foreign Strategist, how would you accomplish that?" asked Jack.

"I would turn loose an army of hackers on an aging infrastructure," answered Coop.

CHAPTER FORTY-FOUR

Leaving Sam to comfort her daughter and mother, Coop and Jack decided to head to the Golden Bull on West Channel Road for a burger or steak and a bottle of red. As they entered the neighborhood bar and restaurant, Jack asked Coop what he knew about hacking.

"The Russians are good at it," responded Coop. "But by far the Chinese have the largest hacking program. The FBI is on top of domestic hacking."

"Perhaps we can speak to someone at the FBI to get a better handle on how hacking and Operation Watered down fit," recommended Jack.

"I think I know just the person, a former Navy Seal brother of mine, Bill Lang, who is with the FBI cyber division in DC. We can give him a call when we finish up here. He is a night owl," said Coop as the boys continued to enjoy their food and good wine.

Returning to Sara's apartment, Jack said, "Shall we give Bill a call." They found comfortable seats on the deck. Ignoring the view, Coop dialed his cell phone and soon a "Hello" came over his speaker.

"Hey, buddy, its Coop."

"No! Not the Gary Cooper of Western fame," Bill said.

"Sure is, how you doin?" asked Coop.

"Can't get any better than this," responded Bill.

"Bill, I am with a very good buddy of mine, Jack Armstrong. He and I have run into some bad guys who we think have a plan to significantly disrupt the Southern California water system. We think a California crime syndicate with foreign ties may be behind this. What can you tell us about hacking?"

"Interesting," Bill said as he thought for a moment. "I doubt that the crime syndicate itself has the capability to inflict significant damage to public infrastructure. And for what purpose would they have? More likely, it is a foreign state that has ransom or a grudge to bear as the motivation and has the capability to pull it off."

"If so, who are the likely culprits in your opinion?" asked Coop

"The Usual Suspects," quoted Bill from the movie title. They are the North Koreans, the Iranians, the Russians, and the Chinese. They are the big players in state hacking, Coop," responded Bill.

"Can you give us an overview of these bad boys?" asked Jack.

"Sure," said Bill. "The North Koreans, seem fixated on money and targeted state secrets. They are after ransom and play with crypto currency trying to convert it to cash. As for targeted state secrets, they have attempted to penetrate some nuclear secrets likely in an attempt to up their nuclear game. To date, Pyongyang has not shown any interest in disruption of US infrastructure."

"How about Iran," asked Jack.

"Unlike North Korea, Iran is a likely suspect," opined Bill. "Recently, the US has warned that Iranian government-sponsored hackers are targeting key US infrastructure. In one instance, they targeted a small Pennsylvania water authority operating in multiple states. Their focus is on water and water treatment facilities and have included four other utilities to their list of hacks."

Jack looked at Coop and smiled. "What is their angle in targeting US water infrastructure?" asked Coop.

"It isn't about the water per se," said Bill. "They have declared "illegal" all Israeli made equipment used to regulate pressure, temperature and fluid flow because of the Israeli-Hamas war. So, if your water system uses Israeli equipment, be careful and be on the lookout for a group called Cyber Av3ngers. I should also add that cyber experts say that water utilities have paid insufficient attention to cybersecurity and are particularly vulnerable to hacks."

"Good advice, Bill. We knew we were onto something," said Jack. "How about Russia?"

"Russians are a sophisticated hacking force, as most people know, because of the recent Presidential election where one candidate invited the Russians to distribute information derived from their hack of thousands of documents from the opposing candidate," said Bill. The prime hacking unit is Turla which is an elite cyber espionage unit embedded in Russian intelligent services. They even breached US Central Command several times, so they are to be taken very seriously. Sandworm is a malware installed by Cyclops Blink which targets firewall devices and helps achieve DOS (denial of service) attacks. They are genuine pros and should be respected."

"And China?" asked Coop.

"China presents the broadest, most active and persistent

cyber espionage threat to the US government and private sector networks, according to our US Intelligence agencies annual report. Chinese hackers are increasingly implanting sophisticated, disruptive malware in critical US infrastructure that's difficult to uncover."

Bill continued, "You may have heard that the DOJ has indicted four Chinese nationals for coordinating the hacking of trade secrets from companies in aviation, defense, biopharmaceuticals and other industries. We worked with the DOJ in bringing the indictments. We found that Chinese nationals operated from front companies that the Ministry of State Security in China set up to give Chinese intelligence agencies plausible deniability. The DOJ also accused Chinese universities of playing a critical role, recruiting students to the front companies, and running their key business operations. The indictment pointed to Chinese 'government-affiliated' hackers for conducting ransomware attacks that extorted millions of dollars. We have reason to believe that a state-sponsored Chinese hacking group has been spying on a wide range of US critical infrastructure projects and organizations."

"What kind of infrastructure projects?" asked Coop.

"Recently, over a six-month period, Chinese hackers targeted an Asian country's national electric utility to disrupt power generation or transmission within the country," related Bill. "We also have evidence that another Chinese hacking group penetrated some US electric utilities, perhaps laying the groundwork for cyber attacks in the event of a future conflict with the US." Bill continued, "The New York Times reported that government officials were particularly concerned that malware had been placed in the power networks to create the ability to cut power to US military bases."

"Thanks for that," Coop said to Bill. "As we get closer to figuring this thing out, we will keep you apprised."

"This sounds like a matter to be considered by the CISA (Cyber Security Infrastructure Agency)," said Bill. "I will give them a heads up."

CHAPTER FORTY-FIVE

"What country would benefit the most?" Coop asked Jack.

"Not the Saudis, who appear to rely on our water to grow their crops and raise their beef," answered Jack.

"Perhaps another country wants something in return for not interfering with Los Angeles water," responded Coop.

"Who could that be?" asked Jack.

"A country that wants the US to stand down from interference in their affairs,' said Coop.

"Russia?" suggested Jack. "Russia wants the US to quit supporting the Ukraine."

"True but isn't their focus and preoccupation with the war sufficient to preclude attacking US water?" suggested Coop. "Besides even if the US backs off, its NATO allies who are under direct Russian threat, likely would not."

"And a Russian attack on US water would likely result in us doubling down and possibly taking direct action in the Ukraine/ Russia war," said Coop coldly.

"Which, in turn, could result in a nuclear war," thought Jack aloud.

"How about Iran?" posited Coop.

"To encourage the US not to side with Israel or use Israeli devices?" questioned Jack. "We are so committed to Israel that I don't think that an attempt to pry us apart will ever happen."

"Nor do I think North Korea has a beef to pick currently with the US," commented Coop.

"That leaves China," concluded Jack. "We know that China receives almonds and other water intensive crops from California. But what threat does the US pose toward China?" he asked.

Coop thought aloud, "Let's back up a bit. Big Joe derives revenue from the allocation of water, through theft, drilling access and diversion of water. If China was a member of Big Joe's syndicate, what would benefit China other than receiving a portion of Big Joe's purse? There must be strategic value to their participation. What is it?" Coop asked rhetorically. "What if China, were able to significantly control the allocation of water to Southern California in exchange for something?" Coop thought aloud.

"In exchange for what? What does China value and California can deliver?" asked Jack.

"Let's rephrase the question," said Coop. "What does China value and the US can deliver? In effect, holding So Cal hostage."

"What does China need?" asked Jack. "Hold on," after thinking a moment, he added, "China needs to sustain an economic growth rate and likely cannot achieve that goal without marketable technology through advanced semiconductor chips. Although China produces some chips, they are not of the sophisticated variety that are most useful, valuable, and marketable, according to Peter Zeihan, geopolitical analyst and author of The End of the World is Just the Beginning: Mapping the Collapse of Globalization."

"Where are the advanced chips produced?" asked Coop.

"According to Zeihan, the principal sources for advanced

chips are made, for example, in the US, Belgium and Taiwan," answered Jack.

"What are we saying here?" asked Coop rhetorically. "That the Chinese will cut off water needed by Southern California in exchange for chips? I think that's extortion," said Coop.

"There is probably more to it than a chip exchange," offered Jack. "To be sustainable, they need to be able to manufacture advanced chips. There happens to be a place within 90 miles of mainland China with that capability: Taiwan."

"What makes Taiwan so special?" asked Coop.

"Taiwan has chip manufacturers like TSMC which are at the top of the food chain in advance chip manufacturing," declared Jack. "The technology and an educated workforce are all located within 90 miles of mainland China."

"You've got to be kidding," said Coop.

"Exchange So Cal water for Taiwan?"

"Not exactly, Coop," said Jack. "Instead, what if China simply said: 'Like Hong Kong, Taiwan is part of Mainland China. US stay away from Chinese 'family matters' if we seek to occupy Taiwan and take over its chip making enterprises, or else So Cal water will be significantly disrupted?"

"Recently, you may have heard that several of our senior political leaders have visited Taiwan to emphasize that the US will aid Taiwan if China asserts itself," said Jack.

"And the Chinese Premier responded with war games in the China Taiwan Strait and has announced his desire to take over Taiwan soon," said Coop.

"The invasion threat won't be illusory when Taiwanese voters elect their new president. The two major political parties, the Democratic Progressive Party (DPP) and the Kuomintang (KMT) differ in their relations with Beijing," said Jack. "The DPP has strived for Taiwanese independence from the Big Dog, while the KMT has sought greater relations with Beijing."

"China doesn't want to start an action without a clearly winnable result unlike what Putin did with Russia's invasion of the Ukraine," thought Coop aloud. "They would rather have a Hong Kong type handover. If the US quietly agreed not to aid Taiwan in exchange for China staying the hell out of our water, China would have a fighting chance to grow economically and survive."

"You may be on to something," said Jack.

"We need to find a there, there, before we jump to geopolitical conclusions, Jack," admonished Coop. "All we have is some intelligence that Big Joe's syndicate has a foreign rep as a member. We need proof that the rep is Chinese and is doing China's bidding."

"Of course," said Jack. "All of this is speculation. How do we nail down what the syndicate's long game is, who is a member and what are their intentions?

"And, how they would pull it off," said Coop.

"Good question," said Jack then he added, "You may not have noticed when we met with Big Joe the first time, the wedding picture on the piano outside his office. The picture was of Big Joe and his now deceased wife, a woman who appeared to be Chinese. Besides the marital ties to China, Big Joe realizes size able annual profits from his export of almonds to China. Thus, there is superficially at least, a strong connection to China."

"I didn't consider Big Joe's family ties to China," agreed Coop.

To obtain a US agreement, we think that China needs to threaten some catastrophic event in the US. Ergo the disruption of water to a vital area of the US economy, aka, Los Angeles, which as we know, is built on a desert."

Coop agreed nodding his head.

"Big Joe Thornley is a master at knowing and manipulating water in Southern California though diversion, theft and allocation. As further evidence of his intent to disrupt the state water system, consider the water map Sam witnessed with the areas circled in red."

Coop's phone rang, "Hello," he said. "Yes, Bill, I can hear you." Motioning to Jack and pointing to his phone, Coop continued his discussion with Bill Lang. He repeated some of what Bill said so Jack could get the jest of the conversation, "You and your colleagues have researched Big Joe's connections and the membership of his syndicate. What have you found?" he paused. "Really?" he said. "Interesting," he commented. "Please explain further," he asked. "Ok, I think I got it. Now how about Big Joe and his connection?" asked Coop. "You've got to be kidding me," Coop quipped. "Anything else, I should know?" Coop asked. "OK, thanks, Bill. We will keep you advised of our progress."

"What did you learn?" asked Jack.

"Bill confirmed that Big Joe's syndicate is composed of a couple of prominent ranchers, two big real estate developers, two politicians and a representative from a foreign country," said Coop.

"Ah ha, just like we thought," said Jack. "Which country?" he asked.

"China," responded Coop.

"How could they know who comprised the syndicate?" asked Jack.

"They are the FBI, and we were informed that they have many sources which can impart substantive information. Perhaps they consulted with counterparts in the CIA, CISA, and even the Treasury Department to examine Big Joe's tax records and discern what syndicate profits were shared and with whom," speculated Coop.

"Or more to the point," Jack offered, "Perhaps the NSA shared some incriminating phone conversations with the FBI between Big Joe and his syndicate colleagues."

"Whatever the methodology, we now have a working theory of who sits on the syndicate," offered Coop.

"What about Big Joe and his connections to China? asked Jack.

"That too is an interesting story according to Bill," answered Coop. "Apparently, Big Joe met his Chinese wife whose maiden name was Wong while traveling through Hunan Provence in Eastern China while on a business trip with an engineering firm. His soon to be bride rode on a tour bus as the Communist Party guide and apparently made a very favorable impression on Big Joe when she sat next to him and put her head on his shoulder. After returning to the States and corresponding for several months, at her request, he invited her to visit America and specifically his almond ranch in the Central Valley, Bill reported."

"So Big Joe married a Chinese Communist," observed Jack. "That supports Bill's comment about China's involvement in the syndicate."

"There's more," said Coop. "Bill said that the brother of Big Joe's wife is high up in the Chinese military and reports directly to the Premier. Apparently, before she died, she persuaded Big Joe to place him in the syndicate as a member. So, he is the Chinese designated member of the syndicate."

"Does he have a name?" asked Jack.

"Simon Wong," replied Coop.

"Now isn't that nice, tidy, and convenient," said Jack smiling.

"Big Joe thought that it couldn't hurt him to have his brother-in-law as a syndicate member with the sale annually of 50,000 acres of almonds to China," said Coop.

"Apparently, it hasn't," commented Jack.

CHAPTER FORTY-SIX

The next evening, Sara suggested that the group head for dinner at the Ivy on Ocean near the Santa Monica Pier. By the time they arrived, the brightly lit Ferris Wheel was in full bloom with its array of brilliant colors mesmerizing onlookers for miles around. Sara commented that she often walked her dog Charlotte through Palisades Park near sunrise and loved looking at the colorful Ferris Wheel two miles from her apartment as the sun was beginning to appear, and the moon was retiring after a night's work.

The Ivy was noted for its fish, great BBQ ribs, generous salads, and full pour drinks. They sat in the indoor patio aligning Ocean Avenue which gave great views of the Pacific Ocean sunset, Palisades Park and the Santa Monica Pier complete with rotating Ferris Wheel.

Helen and Meagan were showing no signs of trauma after their ordeal. Everyone was in a celebratory mood. Orders were taken, Jack and Coop went for the BBQed ribs, while Sara, Veronica, Sam and Helen ordered the Petrale Sole and Meagan decided to try the fried chicken. Several bottles of celebratory, top notch California wine were requested and a Shirley Temple for Meagan. After dinner, Meagan's eyes grew big when she saw that Jack had ordered a $25 strawberry, chocolate and vanilla banana split with chocolate sauce, whipped cream, nuts, and a cherry on top! "Wow," she exclaimed. "I've never seen so much ice cream. Is it all mine?"

Jack and Sam said simultaneously, "It is all yours!" As

Meagan began to devour her banana split, Sam asked Jack, "what the next steps are?"

"Good question, Sam."

"We know we are on to something real which can be highly destructive to the So Cal infrastructure and sustainable living conditions. We also know that Big Joe's syndicate and his Chinese connections may be behind the effort. What we don't know is the vulnerability of the water system to disruption and when it might be triggered."

"Would it help if you spoke to someone at the MWD?" asked Sam.

"The MWD?" questioned Jack.

"Sorry, yes, the Metropolitan Water District of Southern California," clarified Sam. "In my researching articles about water for the Tulare Telegraph, I developed an investigative news relationship with Erin Quinn, who is Chief Engineer for the MWD, the largest supplier of treated water in the United States. It services 26 water related authorities, and provides water to 19 million people over a 5,300 square-mile service area. Erin is the modern-day William Mulholland of the MWD, and she liaises with the FBI about water vulnerabilities. She is the person with whom you should speak about your theories and concerns," offered Sam.

"Could you connect us with her?" asked Coop.

"Sure," answered Sam. "I will give her a call tomorrow. I have her cell."

The next morning, Sam called. "Hi Erin, it is Samantha from the Tulare Telegraph, how are you?" asked Sam.

"Samantha, great to hear from you. You still writing California water stories?" Erin asked.

"Yes, and I have associated with a couple of water aficionados, Jack Armstrong and, believe it or not, Gary Cooper," she said. "I would like you to meet them. They have some information and theories that would likely be of interest to you and MWD."

"Ok," said Erin cautiously. "I will take your good word for it."

"How about tomorrow at 1 pm at your office?" asked Sam.

"Let me check my schedule," said Erin. "Let's see, if it is important, I can move a couple of things around for you."

"You won't regret it. See you then with my friends," concluded Sam. Turning to Jack and Coop, she said, "Fellas, we are 'on': tomorrow at 1 pm at her Los Angeles office."

CHAPTER FORTY-SEVEN

"Hi Erin, please meet Jack and Coop. They have some interesting information that could significantly disrupt the MWD," claimed Sam.

Erin said, "Enlighten me."

Jack explained what the group thought.

"How and why?" asked Erin.

"Much is still a mystery," said Jack.

"Tell me what you have," said Erin borrowing from the Beverly Hills police captain's interview of Eddie Murphy in Beverly Hills Cop.

Jack explained what the group had learned about possible attacks on sources of imported water destined for the Central Valley and Southern California.

"What evidence to you have?" asked Erin.

"We have more suspicion than evidence, however, our lives have been threaten several times by the syndicate boss, and he and his henchmen have kidnapped Samantha's mother and daughter who we were able to free," recounted Jack.

"You believe that these attacks could be done simultaneously?" said Erin.

"Have you ever seen the movie the Italian Job?" asked Jack.

"Yes, it was a fascinating film," answered Erin.

"Remember, the hacking of the LA traffic light system which controlled the flow of traffic to enhance the robbery get away?" asked Jack. "That is what could happen here if the Operations Control Center and other water and electrical infrastructure are hacked. We suspect that much of the system is antiquated and susceptible to hacking."

"Why would anyone do this? What is the end game?" asked Erin.

"We don't think it is a single person," said Jack. "Instead, it is likely a foreign state with sufficient hacking capability and an interest in having the US refrain from some conduct in which it is participating. Three countries stand out: Iran, Russia and China are the most prevalent choices."

"We believe that China has the most to gain realistically if the US backs off its defense of Taiwan," said Coop. Thus, the threat of a Southern California water disruption, or an actual water shutdown, could be most effective to deterrent future US action involving Taiwan. Furthermore, we know that the Chinese have been involved in hacking foreign utilities."

Jack added, "We have reason to believe that a member of the Central Valley crime syndicate is a Chinese representative and the brother of the syndicate boss's deceased wife who also was Chinese. Besides, the syndicate boss does an enormous amount of agricultural business with China."

Erin exclaimed, "These fit with what the FBI Director testified in Congress yesterday! CNN reports he warned that Chinese hackers are preparing to 'wreak havoc' on US critical infrastructure. They are targeting things like water treatment plants, electrical infrastructure and oil and gas pipelines and transportation systems. Frightening. When is this supposed to go down?" asked Erin.

"We don't know," responded Jack. "Although it could be soon as the kidnap of Samantha's mother and daughter a couple of days ago, were intended to prevent us from interfering with the plan, and we doubt that the kidnapping was intended to last long. We suspect that the Chinese rep on the syndicate knows of the timing because he has connections high up in the State Security Ministry. If we can find him, we may be able to gain some insight as to timing, targets, and methods," speculated Jack.

Erin suddenly remembered that "A couple of weeks ago a Chinese fellow who said that he was an official with the Chinese government on a water fact-finding tour, stopped by and talked to several of us."

"Did you get his name?" asked Coop.

"Yes, he said that his name is Simon Wong," said Erin.

"Bingo," responded Jack. "That's the name of Big Joe's syndicate rep and is the boss's brother-in-law. What did he want?"

"He asked about our water infrastructure, electrical power generation and water conservation efforts," said Erin. "Apparently, because of climate change, China is very much interested in preserving water and maximizing its use in generating power. He was particularly intrigued by the Pyramid Lake pump storage hydro project and how the Parker Dam is used to generate and deploy power throughout the system."

"Did he leave a card?" asked Coop. Erin shuffled through her desk drawer and, magically, came up with a card which she offered to Coop. Coop looked at it and asked if he could keep it. Erin nodded her agreement.

Jack read the card: "Simon Wong, President of the Chinese

American Almond Growers Association, 2335 Haidian District, Beijing, China, or 821 N. Spring Street, Los Angeles."

After a moment, Coop said, "In my phone conversation with Bill Lang, I think he mentioned that the Haidian District is where the Chinese Ministry of Security is located. We should check with Bill and Hank to confirm the location of the Ministry of Security," said Jack.

"The N. Spring Street address is Chinatown in LA," offered Samantha.

"The Beijing address should confirm our suspicions that Simon is tied into the State Security system and the Chinatown address gives us a target in the US to locate the needle in the haystack," said Coop.

"I have a better idea," offered Erin.

"Which is…", said Jack.

"Mr. Wong has made an appointment for another visit. We expect him to be here tomorrow at 10 am to view some of our facilities," said Erin.

"Our luck continues," said Jack while looking at Coop and Sam.

CHAPTER FORTY-EIGHT

The next day, Erin introduced Jack, Coop and Sam, "Mr. Wong, I have some colleagues who have a few questions for you. Please meet Jack Armstrong, Gary Cooper and Samantha Curtis who are assisting the MWD."

"Questions?" answered Wong, "what type of questions?"

"We would like to know for whom you work, Mr. Wong, and what is your interest in Southern California water," asked Jack.

"I work for the Chinese American Almond Growers Association, and we are interested in the water needs of almonds and water conservation," he responded.

"Are you sure that you don't work for the Chinese State Security Ministry?" asked Coop.

"The State Security Ministry? No, I don't," answered Wong.

"If you are not employed by the State Security Ministry, do you have connections with that organization?"asked Jack.

"Connections, what do you mean by connections, Mr. Armstrong. I am a businessman who knows lots of people," responded Wong.

"Your business card shows an address for the Chinese State Security Ministry, Mr. Wong. How do you explain that?" asked Coop.

"That address is where I have a Chinese Mainland apartment. I don't know anything about the State Security Ministry's address," he answered.

"How about a syndicate composed of Big Joe Thornley, your brother-in-law?" asked Jack.

"Of course, I know Joseph Thornley, my deceased sister's husband. My commercial dealings with Mr. Thornley only involve the almonds he sells to China. I am President of the Chinese American Almond Growers Association," repeated Mr. Wong.

"Yes, that is what your business card says, Mr. Wong," repeated Jack, eyeing his business card. However, we would like to know what your interest is in California water."

"Like the U.S., China is very concerned about climate change, Mr. Armstrong. As part of the California Almond Growers Association and the Chinese Premier's interest in controlling the adverse effects of climate change, we are interested in learning about water conservation and the multiple uses of water in generating power. We are also intrigued by the MWD, and Ms. Quinn has graciously offered to show me the progress they have made in this regard."

"Well, then, we wish you well, Mr. Wong. We may have a few more questions for you about reciprocal arrangements between our two countries before you leave for China. Please let us know when you plan to depart and where we can reach you," asked Jack.

"I would be pleased to do so Mr. Armstrong," replied Simon. They each shook hands, then Jack and his team departed.

"Well, that was a nonevent," said Sam.

"Not so," said Jack. "He knows that we are onto him. He will report that to Big Joe and to his Premier."

"That may accelerate their plans," said Coop.

"Or, gum them up," speculated Jack. "Perhaps we should call our plan Operation Bubble Gum!"

"And I bet that there will be some phone calls immediately following Simon's meeting with Erin and us," said Jack.

As if on cue, Simon prematurely left the MWD offices and headed to his car a block away. The trio discretely followed him and were close enough to see him enter his car and hold his cell phone to his ear. "Oh, to be the fly on the window of his car," said Jack.

"Big Joe, this is Simon."

"Yes, Simon, how are you today?" asked Big Joe.

"Not well," was his reply.

"And why is that my friend," asked Big Joe.

"Because I ran into your problem unresolved problem: Jack Armstrong and Gary Cooper with Samantha Curtis while visiting the MWD offices!" he screamed. "I thought you had gotten rid of those people as well as Samantha's mother and daughter."

"Not exactly," replied Big Joe sheepishly.

"Not exactly, is right," shouted Simon. "More accurately, 'Not at All!' You have failed to eliminate the biggest threat to Operation Watered down. What are you going to do now before we trigger the Operation?"

"I will take care of it, Simon!" exclaimed Big Joe. "Trust me."

"That's what you said last time after multiple chances, Joe ! I'm not sure I can trust you and hold off a change in personnel," said Simon. "I prefer to have my body parts left intact." Simon then abruptly hung up.

Big Joe thought to himself, I should have simply drilled a well for Cooper's grandfather when we first met. None of this would have happened. And with Fred and Cedrick incarcerated I will have to rely on other, less capable operatives. I better keep moving to avoid the law for the failed kidnapping. More importantly, I have to get rid of the Armstrong / Cooper gang for once and for all and quickly before some one get the bright idea that I am expendable. He placed a call.

"Well, that didn't take long," said Coop watching Simon remove his cell phone from his ear and drive away. "Since it is in the middle of the night in Beijing, I doubt that the call was to the Premier. We should be on the lookout for action by Big Joe to make up for his previous screw ups in eliminating us."

"And we should alert the FBI to help keep an eye on Simon. If he rabbits to China, that could be a signal that the trigger is about to be pulled on Operation Watered down," said Jack.

CHAPTER FORTY-NINE

As luck would have it, Jack's phone rang. It was Johnny K. "What's the latest Johnny?" asked Jack.

"I'm in the Desert and came across some financial news that you should be interested to know. Let's meet at my home and I will brief you," recommended Johnny.

They pointed Coop's X3 east past downtown LA toward the Desert, a two-hour ride away. Jack noticed a white van with blacked out windows following them across the Colorado Los Angeles Aqueduct which would find its way through the San Jacinto Mountains that towered above them. Jack studied the van and kept scratching his head. "What's up?" asked Coop.

"See that van behind us?" asked Jack. "I think they are following us. I saw them when we left L.A."

"Is this another attempt by Big Joe to derail our investigation of Operation Water-Down?" asked Coop rhetorically.

"Could be," responded Jack.

Jack's phone rang. It was Johnny K. "Have you arrived?" he asked.

"Yes, Coop and I are staying at the Ingleside Inn in Palm Springs," answered Jack.

"I know it well," said Johnny K. "Let's meet in half an hour at my home."

"Perfect," said Jack as he took down the directions.

As they drove to Johnny's Desert home, Jack called Bill Lang as to the whereabouts of Simon Wong. "Bill, it's Jack.

Any word on Simon Wong's whereabouts?" He listened for a moment and said, "Keep on top of it, he portends bad things about to happen."

"They lost him?" asked Coop.

"Or, they never found him," responded Jack.

"Great, so we have the two masterminds running around lose: Simon Wong and Big Joe," said Coop.

"They pulled into Johnny K's Desert residence at Indian Ridge, a development featuring two first class golf courses surrounded by well-maintained homes surrounding the courses. As they entered the home, they were greeted by Johnny K and his lovely wife, Vicki. They were immediately taken by the spectacular view of the fairway and green in front of them, which was framed by picturesque mountains in the distance. Steps outside floor to ceiling sliding glass doors were a pool, hot tub, patio with BBQ and a nearby pond in which waterfowl landed and played.

"You have captured a bit of Paradise," commented Jack. "I don't think it gets much better than this, especially if you are a golfer."

"Thanks, Jack. Fortunately, I am a golfer and love spending time here to unwind," said Johnny. Let's sit outside where we can quietly discuss what I have learned. They proceeded through the sliding doors, and each took up a barrel style chair which rotated and rocked. Johnny offered them a cup of coffee which they gladly accepted.

"Moody's has downgraded China," Johnny blurted out. "It lowered its outlook for China's credit rating from stable to negative."

"Thanks, but why?" asked Jack.

"China's financial outlook change reflects how risks from China's local government debts have become too big to ignore," said Johnny. "China's central government said last month that it places great importance on preventing and resolving the risks of these hidden debts."

"Hidden debt?" questioned Jack.

"Chinese cities and provinces have as much as $11trillion in off-balance-sheet-debt, according to some estimates," said Johnny. "Many economists have warned that a large chunk of the debt is at an elevated risk of default. So, a broad effort is underway to refinance some of the problematic hidden debt. Moody's said that without imminent financial support, there are significant risks to China's fiscal, economic, and institutional strength."

"This should accelerate China's interest in Taiwan," said Jack.

"You bet," said Johnny.

Coop agreed with the assessment that Beijing now had more motivation to make a move on Taiwan to take over the lucrative chip manufacturing businesses. That in turn should speed up the need to threaten or disrupt California water in an effort to keep the U.S. on the sidelines.

On an oft chance, Coop asked, "Johnny, have you ever heard of a fellow named Simon Wong?"

"As a matter of fact, I have," answered Johnny. "He discussed investing in Water futures and said he had access to some proprietary information about mapping water reserves in the U.S."

"Mapping water reserves?" asked Jack rhetorically. What did he mean by that?"

"He said that he was working with someone who mapped water reserves by collecting information from a hot air balloon which collected data as it swept regions of the US. Hanging from the balloon was a large bus-like sized data collection device that could measure aquifer, river, aqueduct and snow depths, providing valuable information for predicting water futures. You guys have been flying around California, perhaps you have seen the balloon," asked Johnny.

"We have," responded Jack, "near the Owens Valley airport."

"So that's what that thing was," said Coop. "We almost flew into it."

"Lots of people have seen it and the U.S. government was tracking it as a possible hostile act by a foreign country. China admitted launching it and said it was blown off course when it entered U.S. airspace. Instead, it was a well-organized plan to quantify U.S. water reserves," said Johnny.

"Did you ever do business with Simon?" asked Jack.

"No, his story sounded too fishy to me and when news reports began following the hot air balloon across country, I knew that whatever information was being mined about U.S. water supplies, they would not be shared with me for investment purposes," related Johnny.

"What is your connection to Mr. Wong?" asked Johnny.

"He is a member of an organized crime syndicate organized by a fellow named Big Joe Thornley. The syndicate deals in water diversion, allocation and theft in the Central

Valley. Wong recently made an appearance at the Los Angeles Metropolitan Water District where we were introduced to him."

"What was he doing at MWD?" asked Johnny.

"Allegedly, he was researching conservation and environmental techniques on behalf of the California Almond Growers Association," answered Jack. "However, on behalf of the Chinese government, he was gaining intelligence on methods by which water was imported into Southern California with an eye toward threatening, or massively disrupting the water system."

"That connects with some information that I received from a long-time friend and former MIT classmate of mine. Have you guys heard of CISA, the Cybersecurity and Infrastructure Security Agency?" asked Johnny K.

"Yes, we have," answered Jack.

"Good," said Johnny. "My friend is high up at CISA. On occasion he shares public intel with me. He knows that I am very interested in anything that can affect U.S. infrastructure and how it might affect future trading. My friend tells me that the Chinese military is increasing its ability to disrupt key American infrastructure, including power and water as well as communications and transportation systems. The Washington Post and the FBI Director recently disclosed this publicly, so my CISA friend did not feel he was restricted in sharing the information with me.

Johnny then handed Jack and Coop copies of a Washington Post article, the substance of which had been reaffirmed by the FBI during Congressional hearings. They read the following:

"Chinese hackers affiliated with the People's Liberation Army have entered the computer systems of about two dozen infrastructure entities over the past year. The goal is to lay the foundation for causing panic and chaos as well as disrupt logistics in the event of a US-China conflict in the Pacific (i.e. Taiwan)."

"That ties nicely with our suspicions, Johnny," said Jack. "Thanks for the briefing."

"You had better keep your eyes peeled!" said Johnny.

CHAPTER FIFTY

As they left Johnny's residence, they noticed the white van which had been following them, parked next to the exit of the Indian Ridge guard house.

"Who are those guys," asked Coop recalling the line in the movie, Butch Cassidy and the Sundance Kid.

"You don't think those guys are 'messengers' from Big Joe, do you?" asked Jack of Coop.

"He is tenacious," responded Coop. "He never seems to give up".

"And he has a lot to lose if we continue to investigate and call attention to his Operation Watered down," commented Jack.

"Although he lost 'our buddies' Cedrick and Fred, I am sure that he could find others to do his bidding," said Coop.

"Maybe so, but how did he or they find us?" asked Jack.

"Simon Wong probably told him about meeting us at MWD, and, once found, Big Joe put a tail on us," said Coop.

As they headed back to the Ingleside Inn, they noticed the van with the blacked-out windows behind them. "You see what I see?" asked Jack.

"Sure do," responded Coop who was driving his BMW. "Let's goose it a bit." With that he hit 100 mph in no time in a 50 mile zone. The van fell behind not able to keep pace and caught a traffic light.

Once at the Inn, they decided to try the famous Melvyn's for a steak and some wine. Not only was the food good, but there was some terrific live music. After dinner and some relaxation, they decided their next move was to return to LA in the morning and search for Simon Wong. He seemed to be the likely trigger man for the implementation of Operation Water down. As they began walking outside the restaurant to their rooms, the two tattooed guys from the blacked-out van, quietly came out of nowhere, walked up behind the boys and shot each of them in the back.

Both went down and withered violently on the ground, then they each passed out. The two men quickly looked around and saw no one. One brought the van onto the Inn's driveway, opened the sliding door and helped his partner throw Jack in the van. Then they did the same with Coop. While one of the men climbed in the back of the van and closed the sliding door, the other took the driver's seat. As the driver of the van began to drive, he again scanned the surrounding area and saw no one. The fellow in the back of the van took some duct tape from a bag and began tapping Jack's, then Coop's mouths shut. He next taped their hands behind their backs and, finally, he taped their legs together at their ankles. Then he placed a black bag over each of their heads. About then, Jack began to moan softly followed by Coop.

They had been shot in the back with tasers. Coop had been tasered before in Navy Seal training and remembered it well. Basically, taser weapons send a signal to the muscles telling them to flex, to seize-up. This induces a state of neuromuscular incapacitation, which hijacks the communication link between one's body, Coop remembered, and the brain, making it difficult to make any voluntary movements.

Because the strikes from stun guns cause severe, uncontrollable contractions of the muscles, they are very painful. His muscles suffered from their charley-horselike conditions, which was breathtakingly painful. He tried to retract his toes to loosen his muscles, but the pain did not subside. If only he could stand and place weight upon his legs, the muscles would loosen, and the pain would subside. But trussed up like a turkey, he had no hope of standing.

Coop kept asking himself, "Why", as his short-term memory was erased and he had no knowledge of how this happened, why it happened or where it happened. The fact that he was surrounded by blackness, and he was unable to move mouth, hands, or legs, also added to the confusion.

He began to hear some Spanish spoken between two people and heard Mexican music. He felt strong vibrations caused by the platform upon which he laid. His guess was that he was being moved in a vehicle. Something rolled into him as the vehicle turned. "What is that?" he thought aloud. Whatever rolled into him was warm. "Another body," he thought. "Who?" His mind was still hazy. His muscles began to loosen, and that charley-horse type pain began to subside, thankfully.

Then another turn and he rolled into the other body. It grunted. "Who is that?" he questioned, unable to speak. He began to recall that he had been with Jack, somewhere, so he figured the other body must be Jack's. But where, when, and why?

Coop continued to count the turns as he and presumably Jack rolled around on the floor of the vehicle. The first roll into him suggested that the vehicle, likely a van, because he was stretched on the floor, had turned left, a right turn as the other body rolled into him. The road was relatively smooth, so it was likely a city street. Then he remembered the Ingleside Inn and the dinner at Melvyn's. About then, the vehicle began to pick up speed and Coop assumed that they had entered a highway, perhaps I-10. He had no way of knowing the direction in which they were traveling. He did remember Jack rolling into him before they hit the Interstate, if they were on the Interstate. So, they must be heading East, away from Palm Springs and Los Angeles. He could hear the van cruising but straining a bit presumably to keep up with the flow of traffic.

How far will they go on the Interstate, Coop wondered? Where were they being taken? What plans did the kidnappers have for them? No doubt Big Joe was behind this and had given instructions to the Mexican fill ins for his usual muscle men, Cedrick and Fred. How would Big Joe attempt to dispose of them this time? Can they escape?

CHAPTER FIFTY-ONE

As a former Navy Seal, Coop had a reasonably accurate internal clock. He had learned it from years of deep-sea diving and underwater swimming. How long could he hold his breath? How far could he swim underwater? How far was it to a particular distance? All these questions resulted in a sense of time and movement for him. So, as the van headed East, Coop kept track internally of the time that had elapsed. After about an hour from when he became conscious, he began to roll into Jack, who was making some noises through his tapped mouth. The roll indicated to Coop that they were presumably turning off the Interstate. No sooner had he rolled into Jack, then Jack began to roll into him. So, they were no longer headed East. They were exiting the Interstate and were likely headed North. Also, the road speed was significantly reduced leading him to believe that he was on a state road.

The road was undulating as they would feel a rise, then a decline in the road. Yet, he sensed that they were on an incline and concluded that they were headed up a hill or mountain. After what seemed like 15 or more minutes, they slowed, and felt their departure from the paved road. The ride was bumpy and he heard gravel hitting the van.

Coop guessed that he and Jack were being driven somewhere in the wilderness where the kidnappers would do what had to be done with them. No doubt in his mind this all was the result of Big Joe Thornley. Big Joe had tried unsuccessfully multiple times to get rid of the two of them.

The failure of Big Joe to eliminate them had caused agita for Simon Wong who envisioned Operation Watered down now to be in jeopardy. This, of course, would not play well back home in China. And not playing well back home means that Simon would suffer consequences. If Simon was going to suffer consequences, so was Big Joe. Thus, the agita for both men.

If Coop and Jack were finally eliminated, then matters may settle down and all would be forgotten. Forgive and forget, wasn't that the phrase? And with Jack and Coop eliminated, who would know what was about to transpire?

That may be fine for them, what about us, thought Coop? He was not keen on being eliminated for once and for all. So, he would be alert for escape opportunities.

Then, the van turned sharply to the right and continued to bump along over an uneven road. This continued for what seemed like several miles. Suddenly, the van stopped and began to turn around. Then, it stopped again. The sliding door opened, and someone grabbed Coop's arms with his hands tied behind his back and someone else grabbed his legs. He was swung back and forth, then hurled in the air. While flying, blindfolded, and trussed like a turkey, it is always nice to guess when the ground will abruptly stop one's fall. Is it a few feet? Or was the throw off a cliff? Are there rocks on which you will land? Will your bones be broken, or your skull be cracked? Then suddenly it is over as he crashed hard on the ground, rolled once or twice and had the wind knocked out of him. He checked for broken bones, or other infirmaries and found none. Congratulations! And what about Jack he thought.

Suddenly, a body landed on top of him, knocking the breath out of him a second time. No doubt the body was Jack's, he thought. Since he cushioned Jack's fall, he doubted that Jack had been injured. Still, Jack was heavy, and Coop could barely regain his breath. There was laughter from the Mexicans who had kidnapped them and thrown them to the ground somewhere.

Now if they chose not to shoot us, or throw boulders on us, or douse us with gasoline and light us afire, as Black Markets often do, Coop thought cheerfully, not knowing what was to come next, we might have a chance to survive. Instead of an unforeseen end of life, he heard the van sliding door close, followed by two cab doors closing and the wheels beginning to spit rocks on the two of them as the van sped away.

Then silence. Thank God, thought Coop. So much for that. We are alive. But where are we, and how are we going to get free and out of wherever we are? He suddenly heard some sniffing and a growl. What the heck is that? Should he lie still and hope whatever it was would leave, or make some frantic motion even though tied up with Jack on top of him to scare it away?

First, I need to get this body off me, thought Coop. He rolled over and Jack slide off. In the immortal words of Martin Luther King, "Free at last, free at last. Thank the Lord above that I am free at last." Coop being a man of action, decided to try wiggling around on the ground as best he could and grunting as loud as he could, rather than playing dead. After 30 seconds of intense movement. He stopped and listened. Nothing. Only silence. After a minute of hearing nothing, he decided that the 'thing' had retreated.

He was not exactly Free at Last, as he was still duct taped and hooded. I simply had removed that extra sack of sh__t that was on top of me, he thought. At least I can breathe. Now what? Yoga teaches the "downward dog" position. Tough to do with your arms tied behind your back, thought Coop. At least I could try it from my knees and facing the ground I may be able to shake this f_cking bag from my head. Shake, shake, shake, thar she Blows! Off it goes. Much better now seeing where we're at. Or is it?

Where are we? Coop looked around on his knees as night enveloped them and the temperature rapidly declined with the sun out of sight. It looks like desert to me he thought. Nothing but rocks, boulders, cactus, scrawny trees. Whoa, that's it, those scrawny trees are Joshua trees. We must be somewhere in the Joshua National Park, thought Coop. Which makes sense from the direction he innately sensed during their ride to this "resting spot."

Then he saw Jack wiggling on the ground with his hood still covering his head and a furry spider like thing crawling on him. Whoa, thought Coop. It looks like a tarantula. And it was a big one! Probably 3 and ½ inches long. And it had legs that appeared to extend 10 inches. I hope it does bite Jack as it crawled over him. Maybe I can help him get rid of it, thought Coop. He fell on his side and raised his legs over Jack then quickly kicked them at the tarantula. He connected with the furry varmint, and it went sailing off of Jack and into the brush. Success!

Next Coop attempted to free Jack from the hooded mess he was in. Coop rolled over so his back was to Jack. He wiggled his way past Jack to position his tied hands were at Jack head level and he grabbed a-hold of the hood and began to wiggle away from him. The hood came off in his hands and he rolled over to see his duct taped friend smiling at him. That's a start. Now for the hands to be freed.

Coop managed to rise to his knees and back into Jack. He grabbed Jack's shirt with his hands and pulled on it to communicate with Jack that he needs to get up on his knees too. Jack got the message. Next Coop pulled Jack shirt sideways with his hands to get him to turn around. He also rotated his head in a circle to reaffirm the same. Once Jack had turned with his back to Coop, Jack managed to rise on his knees, so he was aligned back-to-back but next to each other as their feet were tied together. Still, Coop was able to reach over to Jack's hands and take hold of the duct tape with his hands. Coop had trouble getting any leverage and kept re-balancing himself. Finally, he decided that they would be better off on the ground back-to-back with their hands aligned behind them, so he grabbed hold of Jack's hands tightly and simply fell sideways on his right shoulder pulling Jack with him.

Once on the ground, Coop continued to explore the duct tape around Jack's hands until he found the end. He was able to pry the corner with his fingernails while Jack held his hands perfectly still. Slowly he was able to widen the end of the tape to an inch in length. Then, he could grab hold of the tape and pull it against the direction in which it was wound until it was halfway around Jack's hands. Jack began to rotate his hands slowly in a motion against the tape and Coop held it firmly with his two hands. After several rotations, Jack's hands were free.

Once his hands were released, Jack immediately grabbed the duct tape covering his mouth and pulled quickly. "Mother f_cker," he yelled, that hurt! Next, he unwound the tape around his legs. He jumped to his feet and began to walk away from Coop. Coop thrashed wildly on the ground attempting to attract Jack's attention. Jack turned and said, "Oh, I forgot, would you like some assistance, sir?"

Once untapped, Coop said, "I should have left the tarantula on you!"

"Oh, is that what that creepy crawly thing was?" asked Jack.

"Or sicked the growling animal that kept sniffing me on you!" added Coop.

"How many lives does a cat have?" asked Jack.

"Nine, I think," said Coop.

"We must be part cat," thought Jack aloud.

"Don't be too premature," instructed Coop.

"We still don't know where we are or how we are going to get out of wherever we are," said Jack.

"See that tree over there?" asked Coop.

"Yes," answered Jack.

"It's a Joshua tree. We are likely in Joshua Tree National Park," as he explained to Jack his reasoning from length and direction of the ride. "I figure that we are North and East of Palm Springs, probably close to the Eastern end of Joshua Tree National Park."

"You any good at that star gazing stuff?" Jack asked.

"We learned some in Seal school," answered Coop. "The night sky is so vivid here. No ambient light from surrounding cities. Good for viewing the stars, bad for finding help." Coop looked up and spotted the Big Dipper. Aligning the two stars from the Dipper's handle, he followed them to the North Star. Pointing to the North Star, he told Jack that "My back is facing South, my left arm, West, and my right arm, East."

"Ok, hot shot, in which direction do we head?" asked Jack.

"Not North. There is nothing helpful to us in that direction for many miles. East will likely take us to the state highway that we road in on. West would take us deeper into the Park and South might lead us to the 10," answered Jack.

"Those idiots!" exclaimed Coop as he took something out of his back pocket and examined it.

"What?" asked Jack.

"They didn't check our pockets!" explained Coop.

"I doubt cash will do us much good here," said Jack.

"Not cash, our phones, dummy!" shouted Coop. "And I have 2 bars of reception. We can call for help!"

Jack said aloud, "Big Joe can never be accused of hiring the Best and the Brightest. Thank God for that!"

Coop dialed 911and a voice said, "This is 911 what is your emergency?"

An hour later they were at the Ingleside Inn. They decided to gather their things and return to LA. Their singular focus now was to track down Big Joe. It was pay back time for the trouble he had caused them.

Enough is enough: swimming with the fishes in an aquifer; being sniffed by a coyote and walked on by a tarantula while taped up and dumped in the Desert!"

"How about offering target practice multiple times for his goons and having people under our protection kidnapped," offered Jack.

"Let's not forget, he is committed to implementing Operation Watered down," said Coop.

"He will stop at nothing to get it done. Which is reason enough for us to track him down and put an end to it," agreed Jack. "Let's get it done!"

CHAPTER FIFTY-TWO

"We last saw Big Joe hightailing it out of the Malibu Colony," commented Coop. "He likely returned to home base in the Central Valley, or around there.

"Someplace with which he is familiar and can control things," said Jack.

"Still, he can hide in a million places," thought Coop aloud. "I think we need to bait him and draw him out," said Jack.

"Make him come to us?" asked Coop. "Kinda like fly fishing. One must select the proper fly to attract the fish."

I think I have just the right fly," said Jack. "Let it be known that Sam's article for the Tulare newspaper is about to be published and that it will alert the public and law enforcement of Big Joe's plan and involvement. Big Joe will want to stop that and will need to see his, I mean the newspaper's, editor. We can be lying in wait for him to arrive."

"Good plan let's alert Sam so she can cast the fly and head to Tulare," said Coop.

"Don't you find it ironic?" asked Jack.

"Ironic?" responded Coop.

"Ironic, that we are using Sam as bait for Big Joe, when Big Joe used Sam as bait for us!" thought Jack aloud.

The next morning, Sam approached the office of the Tulare newspaper editor, knocked on the open-door sill and asked if he had a moment. The editor was sitting at his desk with his back to the door. He turned, faced the open door and said, "yes".

Without entering, Sam said from the open door, "I have finished my article on the Central Valley water crisis, and it is ready to publish. I have entitled it, The Great Water Heist. It tells about Big Joe Thornley's plan to hold hostage water destined for the Central Valley and Southern California in exchange for the US agreeing not to come to the aid of Taiwan if China invades Taiwan," said Sam.

"That's quite an accusation against one of our prominent Central Valley citizens, another country and involves some serious speculation, Sam. Do you have the facts to backup your assertions?" the editor asked.

"I do," answered Sam as she proceeded to lay out her diligence behind the article in detail for them.

"The newspaper needs to consider this, Sam. We are sure you understand the far-reaching implications of publishing such an article," said the editor.

"I did meet with him and had an hour interview with Mr. Thornley," added Sam.

"As a good journalist, I am sure you did," commented the editor. "Someone will give you a call once we have made our decision, Sam."

"I hope you make the correct decision," said Sam, "I wouldn't want to publish elsewhere."

That left the editor stunned as Sam left the office. He immediately placed a call to Big Joe, explaining the situation. Big Joe responded, "I thought I paid you guys to catch and kill this thing. I'll be right over."

Sam called Jack on his cell and reported her meeting with the newspaper. In answer to Jack's question, she replied, "Yes, the bait is set. They will call Big Joe and Big Joe will not resist meeting with him to discuss the situation."

"Ok, Sam," give us a shout if you see him. Be careful, he is desperate," warned Jack

Jack briefed Coop, then switched gears and focused on Operation Watered down, "I think we need to move up the governmental food chain to make sure that the appropriate agencies are notified about the China threat," said Jack to Coop.

"You mean CISA?" asked Coop.

"No, I think the NSA should be notified, if they don't already know what's going on," answered Jack. "The NSA is responsible for global monitoring, collection, and processing of information and data for foreign and domestic intelligence. It is also alleged to have been involved in significantly damaging Iran's nuclear program."

"I recall a severe power outage in Russia after some international controversy," said Coop. "I wonder whether, the NSA, had a hand in that too?"

"Could be," said Jack. "I know that it has a first-class hacking division called TAO, the Tailored Access Operations division."

"Who do we know at NSA?" asked Coop.

"My former law partner is the GC of the NSA," said Jack.

"Bingo," said Coop.

"I will give him a call," responded Jack.

CHAPTER FIFTY-THREE

"Roger Clark, please," asked Jack over the phone.

"Who may I say is calling?" the assistant asked.

"Jack Armstrong," he answered. As Jack waited to be connected, he remembered Roger as a very bright attorney, who was by the book, ethical, a tireless worker and very personable.

"Jack, long time, no see or hear. How are you?" asked Roger.

"I am terrific, Roger and know that you must be too," answered Jack. "I have some information that my partner, Gary Cooper, and I have discovered in which we think you and your colleagues at the NSA would be interested. Coop and I would like briefly to discuss it with you. We think this has a lit fuse. Mind if I put Coop on the speaker?"

"Jack, I take you at your word which has always been good to me. Good to meet you Coop," said Roger.

"For the past couple of weeks, we have encountered, by accident, a criminal syndicate located in California's Central Valley," Jack began to explain.

After his explanation, Roger said "You have my attention, Jack," as he focused on Jack's every word. "I have several questions. First, who do you suspect to be responsible for this endeavor?"

"We believe, it to be a state actor," explained Jack, "China."

"Why would China wish to actively disrupt water imported to a United States region located thousands of miles away from its shores?" asked Roger.

"We have a one-word answer," said Coop. "Taiwan."

"Why Taiwan?" asked Roger.

"Because China needs Taiwan's advanced chip industry to help lead it economically out of the death spiral it finds itself," answered Jack.

"What you said, makes sense Jack. How is China going to accomplish or threaten the disruption of California water?"

"The most likely disruption will be by hacking: cyber interference with the water pumps, electrical systems and control centers which direct and can stop the flow of water through the state water projects," explained Jack. He then summarized the vulnerabilities of each of the state's four imported sources of water for the Central Valley and Southern California.

"To state the obvious, the California water infrastructure is a target rich environment for an enemy state with hacking capability," added Coop.

"Clearly so," said Roger. "Why bring this to the attention of the NSA? What about CISA?"

"Because a foreign state, China, is likely involved and the NSA has the ability to identify its hacking targets through its electronic eavesdropping and TAO Operations cyber monitoring," said Jack. "We are asking for the NSA to confirm our suspicions and involve other governmental agencies as appropriate."

"When is this supposed to go down?" asked Roger.

Jack answered, "We don't know. We think it is reasonable to conclude that if Simon Wong leaves the country, Operation Watered down is a 'go'. We met with him briefly once, and we expect that he reported our interest in his operation to the Premier."

"Thanks for the Who, Why, How and When answers, Jack," said Roger   We are keenly aware of China's interest in infrastructure disruption and your description is spot on, in my opinion. I will run it up the flagpole and alert other agencies which will have an interest. What's next for the two of you?"

"Since Simon may be the trigger for Operation Watered down, we thought we should locate him and have a lengthier talk," answered Jack. "We have asked the FBI to keep an eye on him."

"I have some information that would be useful once you have that chat with him. Let's extend our talk on my secure line."

The call continued another 30 minutes after which Jack and Coop smiled at each other.

CHAPTER FIFTY-FOUR

As they entered the apartment, they were greeted by Sara and Veronica who gave each of the boys a hug and big kiss. "Wow," that was nice, Jack said as he looked first at Sara, then to Coop who was still embraced with Veronica.

"How was your conference call?" asked Sara.

"Very beneficial, we think," said Jack. "Did you bring Sam up to speed with what happened in the Desert?"

"Yes, she couldn't believe what happened. Then she said that she always managed to miss the 'fun'."

"Well, she may get another chance. We need some help locating both Big Joe and Simon Wong, our friends who double for needles in the haystack. Simon gave the FBI the slip. He has a card stating his U.S. address as the Chinese American Almond Growers Association in Chinatown. I am familiar with San Francisco Chinatown, but I have no idea where the Los Angeles Chinatown is. We need some help."

"We also have set some bait for Big Joe by alerting the editor of the Tulare Telegraph that Sam is ready to publish her article either in the Telegraph or elsewhere naming Big Joe, China and describing the water scheme. It will be a dynamite article which will draw great public, media and government attention.

"Do you think, Sam knows someone who knows where we might find Simon?" asked Sara.

"She always does," answered Jack. "I'll give her a call."

"Hi Sam, Coop and I are trying to find Simon Wong and

figure that we may need some help from someone familiar with Chinatown. Any ideas?"

"Let me think," she said. "Try Henry Fong. He works at the LA Central Library in the Research Division. I met him while writing a story about Chinatown for my newspaper. He is very knowledgeable and speaks Mandarin."

"Can he be trusted?" asked Jack.

"Yes, absolutely," she responded. "I understand that you did some 'sightseeing' while in the Desert, Jack," said Sam.

"Yes, it was a self-guided tour of Joshua Tree National Park with a friend of ours named Duct Tape," answered Jack tongue in cheek.

The next morning, Coop and Jack were off to the LA Central Library. After questioning several people, they found Henry Fong, who greeted them by saying, "Welcome to the People's University, the Los Angeles Central Library. What can I do for you?"

Jack repeated, "The People's University?"

Yes, explained Henry. "The Central Library offers over 900 online courses. People may qualify to obtain a high school degree by taking appropriate courses. And we have just announced a new addition to the Library. We have acquired Angels publishing and will now be able to publish as well as collect and present books!"

"Congratulations," Jack said and then explained that Sam had recommended that they speak with Henry about trying to locate someone in Chinatown. "Happy to help anyone who is a friend of Sam's," Henry responded.

"He is the President of a group called the Chinese American Almond Growers Association," said Jack.

"Let's take a look," offered Henry as he typed into his computer. "Yes, I see that they have offices at 821 N. Spring Street. The offices are in the Dynasty Center, a group of shops. Is that helpful?"

It gives us a lead," said Jack. "Is there information about which we should be aware, he asked?"

Henry recounted that there is the Old Chinatown, which was raised to make room for the Union Station. "So, the Almond Growers offices are in the New Chinatown which was opened in June 1938. It is less than one square mile and fewer than 8,000 aging poor people, so you will not have too much area to search if he is not in his office," he said laughing. Chinatown is about 2 miles from the library and 2 and a half miles from Dodger Stadium: Go Blue!"

"Thanks, Henry," Jack said sarcastically as he and Coop headed out the door and toward Chinatown's Twin Dragon Gateway. Just then, Jack received a call from Sam. "He's here," she said.

"We are on our way. Keep an eye on him," directed Jack.

CHAPTER FIFTY-FIVE

Sam carefully watched the front door of the newspaper office from her car across the street. After 30 minutes, she saw the door open and Big Joe emerge. He did not look happy. Just then, a panel truck pulled up in front of the office, two men exited the sliding door, appeared to incapacitate Big Joe with a taser and muscle him into the panel truck. Off they went, heading north. Sam did a U turn and followed them from a two car distance. She called Jack and explained what had happened.

Jack said, "Stay with him. We are forty-five minutes behind you. Do you have any idea who grabbed him?"

"No, They appeared to be pros by the way they walked right up, tasered him and quickly put him in the van. They were all business: knew what they wanted and knew what they were doing," answered Sam.

Jack's phone was on speaker, Coop said, "Who wants Big Joe?"

"I can think of only one guy," said Jack. "Simon Wong!"

"Why?"

"Because Big Joe failed to eliminate us, and we are viewed as a threat to Operation Watered down," said Jack. "It will be interesting to know what they will do with Big Joe: give him a course in remedial personnel elimination, or feed him to the fishes? These guys mean business. Lot's at stake apparently."

Sam followed the van discreetly to Big Joe's ranch. Rather than circumnavigate the hill upon which the mansion rested, the van took a service road around the hill toward the back. Sam decided to park her car behind some trees and follow on foot. She told Jack what her plan was. For the umpteenth time, he told her to "be careful."

Sam found some boulders behind which to hide when she saw the van stop a short distance away. The two muscle men jumped out of the van and "escorted" Big Joe to a large cement pad. Big Joe was still recovering from the taser shot and had to be dragged to the pad. While two of the men held him, the van driver opened a well-head.

"Oh no," said Sam into the phone. "They are going to feed him to the fishes." She could hear the driver tell Big Joe, have you ever seen "our special water feature, Big Joe?"

Big Joe, screamed "No! I can't swim."

Stealing a line from Butch Cassidy one of the men said, "Don't worry, the fall will probably kill you." They shoved Big Joe into the aquifer well and quickly sealed the well head. They turned around and checked to see if anyone had seen them.

Sam crouched lower behind the boulder and held her breath. She could not see what they were doing. She worried that they would find her car and begin a search for her. She heard nearby footsteps. Her heart was pounding. She texted Jack and pleaded that he would get to her before they did.

Jack, texted back, "We are minutes away, Sam. Hold tight!"

Then she heard it. "Well what have we here," said one of the muscle men as he look over the boulder at Sam.

CHAPTER FIFTY-SIX

Sam looked up and saw the big man hunched over the boulder behind which she was crouching. "What are you doing here, young lady?" He asked.

Thinking quickly, Sam said, "I am a hydrologist searching for pockets of water."

"Pockets of water?" he repeated.

"Yes, it is part of a study I am doing for my Masters degree in water science," she explained.

"When you find these so-called pockets, what are you going to do with them?" he asked.

"I record them and enter them in a our university computer system," she responded.

"Have you found any here?" he asked.

"As a matter of fact, yes I have, and I found evidence of some gold," she said. "Look for yourself," she said pointing to the ground at her feet.

The muscle man came around the boulder, bent over and looked down at the ground in search of evidence that Sam indicated was gold. "I don't see any gold," he said as he looked at the ground. She unleashed a round house blow with all her might to his temple with a grapefruit sized rock. Down he went.

Sam prayed that the other two assailants did not hear what had happened. She peeked over the top of the boulder and could see that they were talking and pointing to the well-head, not in her direction. Soon they would be looking for their missing companion. Sam took the grapefruit sized rock and hit the prone victim one more time to make sure he was silenced, if not dead. Then she turned and retreated behind the boulder, and began to retrace her steps to her car. She knew that the two assailants would be looking for her once they found their injured companion. All hell would break loose.

"Where the heck are you guys," she thought wondering where Jack and Coop were.

After back tracking twenty-five steps, Sam turned and began running for her car. A shot rang out and she dove for cover in some bushes. No doubt they had found their injured partner, and her time was up! Carefully, she looked though the bushes, saw the remaining two split up and begin to flank her. Soon each of the assailants would be on opposite sides of her with weapons aimed at her. She found another rock and threw it as far as she could to her right side. She hoped that the noise would distract them and give her one more chance to escape.

As she turned to run with the expectation of being shot in the back, she heard the gun shot, but did not go down or feel an injury. Then she heard another shot and again felt no injury. She turned and saw Coop and Jack standing over two prone bodies.

"Am I glad to see you two," Sam yelled.

"You gave us a hint as to where you were when you said that Big Joe was going to swim with the fishes in his aquifer," said Jack. "Then we knew we had to get to Big Joe's famous water feature asap. What did you hit the other guy with?"

"I found a rock to my liking and gave him my best 60 mph softball shot with a grapefruit sized rock to his temple. I used to pitch for the women's softball team," said Sam.

CHAPTER FIFTY-SEVEN

They headed back to Los Angeles in search of Simon Wong. "One down and one to go," said Jack.

"But which one?" asked Coop.

"Simon Wong," said Jack.

"Is he the prey, or are we the prey?" asked Coop.

"I see what you mean," answered Jack. "Either one of us will be the end of the problem for the other. So we had better find him first!

"What did Henry, the librarian, tell us?" asked Coop.

"Just head to Chinatown," said Jack.

"Let's do it," said Coop.

Just then, Jack's phone rang. "Hello," he said. "Sam, what's up?" Jack listened intently and pondered what Sam was sharing while she drove back to Tulare in her car.

"Sam, has been thinking about Operation Watered down," Jack told Coop. "She thinks the Operation will be most effective if there is a catalyst, a stress placed on the water system."

"What kind of stress?" asked Coop.

"She thinks that if a wildfire occurred, and water resources were strained, maximum damage could be done," Jack explained. "She described the Mafia in Italy weaponizing wildfires to achieve insurance payouts, zoning reconfigurations and other advantages for those seeking them."

"Weaponizing wildfires," repeated Coop. "I have never heard of that."

"In California with the annual multitude of wildfires, weaponization should not be too steep a hill to climb," thought Jack aloud.

"With the Santa Ana winds, if properly predicted, a horrendous wildfire could be started," predicted Coop. "Heck, Simon could hire a couple of guys to drive through the high end homes of the Palisades and throw road flares out the windows of a car driving near bone dry grass. The Santa Ana's will do the rest."

"So maybe the trigger point is the Santa Ana's," said Jack. "If we know when they are likely to occur, we can predict when Simon will unleash Operation Water down. We had better find him fast as it is that time of year when the winds begin to blow!"

They found the Chinatown Gateway and meandered toward the Central Plaza. From there, they got their bearings and headed to N. Spring Street. Checking the numbers as they walked. "There it is," announced Jack as they found 821 N. Spring Street.

"Do you think he will buy it?" asked Coop.

"He should," answered Jack.

It was a small office bearing the name Chinese American Almond Growers Association in both English and Chinese. Jack and Coop entered the office and approached a receptionist who said, "May I help you?"

Jack responded, "We hope so. We are looking for Simon Wong" and presented her with his card.

She looked at the card and said, "One moment please." Thereafter, she picked up the phone in front of her, dialed a number and said, "Two people here to see Mr. Wong." After listening for a moment, she said, "Ok, I will." Please be seated as she pointed to a sofa near the front door. "Someone will be with you shortly," she said.

Jack looked at Coop and shrugged his shoulders. Without speaking, the questionable gesture was returned as if to say, "We are after Wong, not 'someone' else." After 5 minutes, the door to the office behind the receptionist opened and two muscular men appeared.

"The first man out the door asked, "Are you the guys looking for Mr. Wong?"

Jack looked at Coop. The two of them then looked around the office as if to say, "It must be us stupid, because no one else is here!" Instead, Jack simply said, "yes."

"Well, he ain't here for yous."

"How can you tell he is not here for us. He doesn't know who 'us' is?" Jack responded.

"He ain't here for nobody. Get that? And get lost!" the muscle-man continued.

"Are you sure? We have a present for him," said Coop.

The lead muscle man looked mystified and turned to his partner with questioning eye as if to say, "What do we do now?" As he turned back to confront Coop, he was cold cocked by Coop who gave him a right cross that connected solidly against his left temple. He staggered backwards and fell over the reception desk. The receptionist screamed. The second muscle man sized up the situation quickly and pulled a .45 out from its hostler located under his left arm.

"That's enough. You shouldn't have done that to em. Keep

it up and yous guys will eat some bullets. As my partner said, "Mr. Wong ain't here, but now maybe we can arrange a meeting with him and yous two. Step right this way," the gunman said motioning with his gun toward the back door from which they entered the reception area. Coop and Jack followed his instructions thinking that they would now be introduced to Simon.

The interoffice they entered was large and nicely furnished with an antique desk, fashionable chairs, a meeting table for 10, and a side table with coffee and pastries. "Mind if we have one?" asked Jack.

"Keep movin, yous guys," ordered the one with the gun. They passed a flat screen TV mounted on the wall next to a large maps of China and California facing the desk. Other than the four of them, no one else was in the back office. The muscle men pushed Coop and Jack to the back of the office where there was a door. The door opened into an alley. They were told to keep walking as they exited the office back door.

Down the alley they proceeded until they we instructed to stop opposite a stairway leading down from the alley to an unmarked door. "Get down there and wait," the gun man said. They thought of escaping, but the stairs, a railing and the .45 kept them at the entrance to the cellar door. The gunman took out his cell phone and dialed a number. "It's Louie, he said into the phone. We have two. Open up." Soon the alley door opened, and Jack and Coop were ordered inside.

Quickly they were shoved against the cement wall and told to "spread them." One of the men patted down each of them and announced that they were "clean." Then they were pushed into two chairs that were in the middle of the underground cellar. Each chair had an overhead light aimed at it. The chairs were of sturdy metal frame and bolted to the floor at each leg. Jack and Coop glanced at each other and telepathically said, "This doesn't look good."

Their hands and feet were zip locked to the chairs with little room to move arms, hands, or legs. Then duct tape was applied to arms and legs around the chair's arms and legs. Another rope was placed around their chest and through the back of the chair. Securely bound, they were told that someone would be with them soon and hoods were placed over their heads.

An hour later, they heard the alley door open, and someone walked into the cellar. Then they heard a familiar voice say, "Mr. Armstrong and Mr. Cooper, why are you looking for me?"

Jack answered, "We'd like to discuss Operation Watered down with you."

Speak up Mr. Armstrong, "I am having trouble hearing you."

Jack shouted through the hood over his head, "We'd like to discuss Operation Watered down with you!"

"That's better Mr. Armstrong," Simon said. "What is it about what you call Operation Watered down that you would like to discuss?"

"Is it true that you intend to disrupt the flow of water to Southern California during a cataclysmic wildfire?" Jack shouted.

"That is none of your business, Mr. Armstrong," Simon responded.

"We are here to warn you," shouted Jack.

"Warn me?" answered Simon. "Warn me about what?"

"There will be consequences if you commence Operation Watered down," Jack shouted.

"Yes, yes, I may have trouble getting my car washed, or my dog bathed in Los Angeles, Mr. Armstrong," said Simon sarcastically.

"Joke as you wish, Mr. Wong," Jack shouted through the hood. "Why would the Chinese government be interested disrupting Southern California water?"

"What makes you think, Mr. Armstrong, that the Chinese government wished to disrupt Southern California water?" Simon asked.

"You do, Mr. Wong and your ties to Big Joe and his syndicate," Jack shouted.

"Pretend, Mr. Armstrong, that you are correct. What are you going to do about it?" asked Simon.

"Take this hood off of me and my partner, and I will tell you," Jack shouted hopefully for the last time. Simon motioned for his muscle men to remove the hoods from Coop and Jack. They blinked and adjusted their eyes.

"The hoods are off, Mr. Armstrong. What have you to say?" asked Simon.

"Three words, Mr. Wong. Three Gorges Dam!" said Jack.

"The Three Gorges Dam in China?" questioned Simon.

"Yes, there is an article in my back pocket that may be of interest to you," said Jack.

Simon motioned to his men to search Jack's back pocket for the article. They handed it to Simon who read it. It was a

Reuters report:

"Early today the world famous and giant Three Gorges Dam in China suffered a total power blackout. It is the world's largest power station (22,500 MW). Completed in 2006 the dam has 32 main turbines with two smaller generators which provide power to the plant itself.

"In addition to generating electricity, the dam was designed to increase the Yangtze Rivers shipping capacity and reduces the potential for flooding downstream, which historically plagued the Yangtze. Made of concrete and steel, the dam is 2,554 yards long 607 feet high. It restrains 410 miles of Yangtze water with a surface area of 403 square miles.

"The main generators each weigh approximately 6,000 tons and are designed to produce more than 700 MW of power each. The dam's generators account for 14% of China's total hydro generation. Although the dam's hydro generation has been stopped, the dam appears to not be breached. Even so there are cracks evident in the facing. Experts are working feverishly to return the dam to normal hydro power and checking structural safety. Officials have no idea what caused the outage or the cracks."

Simon finished reading and re-read the article. "Mr. Armstrong, what do you know about this incident?"

"Interesting development isn't it, Mr. Wong?" answered Jack. "I wonder if a fuse has blown at the Three Gorges. Fuses can be tricky."

"Don't try to be cute, Mr. Armstrong, if you know what's good for you and your colleague," said Simon.

"Do you think that the Premier would be interested in learning how this happened? And whether it might happen again, perhaps elsewhere in China? Maybe, he would like to know who is responsible?" asked Jack.

"What if he learned that the U.S.A. cyber security force had a hand in what transpired, can duplicate the outage again at Three Gorges, and elsewhere, and only did so because of the information given to them by Coop and me about the threat that you and Big Joe presented to Southern California water?" added Jack.

"You made your point, Mr. Armstrong," said Simon.

"Perhaps your muscle men can untie me and Coop, and we can take a walk so we can discuss the situation," offered Jack.

Simon motioned to his men to release Jack and Coop. Turning to Jack he asked, "Where would you like to go?"

"I thought that we could stroll down Spring Street. The sun is setting, and it is a nice evening for a walk," said Jack. "Don't you think so?"

Off they went. As they turned onto Spring Street, Jack said, "Isn't this the street featured in the final scene of the movie Chinatown?"

"I wouldn't know," answered Simon with a perplexed look on his face.

"Mr. Wong based on what we say, our countries can unleash massive cyber-attacks on each other's country causing significant harm to each, or we can stand down and return to normal," recognized Jack. "What say you?"

"You make a good point Mr. Armstrong," answered Simon.

"Shall we seek détente then, Mr. Wong?" asked Jack.

"Yes," answered Simon.

"There are a few things that I must insist upon," said Jack. There shall be no disruption of water or the infrastructure carrying water or generating electricity to Southern California, Northern California or anywhere in the U.S. If your Premier agrees, Mr. Wong, then we will achieved détente.

"I will deliver the message to my Premier, Mr. Armstrong, but I do not control our government," said Simon.

As they parted, Jack turned to Coop and said, "I hope it works. Lord knows we did the best we could. If we fail…".

Coop responded, "Forget it, Jack, it's Chinatown."

The author wishes to acknowledge my daughter, Heather, for her love and literary support as well as her husband, Tod, for his valuable knowledge in helping to publish *Watered down* and *The Niantic Caper*. Finally, I wish to extend a special acknowledgment to Nick Silverman who provided excellent editorial insight for *Watered down*.

SOURCES FOR WATERED DOWN

Books

Caste by Isabel Wilkerson
The Great Displacement by Jake Bittle
The King of California by Mark Arax, Rick Waltzman
The Library Book by Susan Orlean
The Niantic Caper by James Woods
The White Album by Joan Didion
The End of the World is Just the Beginning by Peter Zeihan
Rock Me on the Water by Ronald Brownstein
The Worth of Water by Gary White, Matt Damon
Cadillac Desert, Revised and Updated Edition by Marc Reisner
The Dreamt Land by Mark Arax
River Notes by Wade Davis
Out of the Fields by Ramon, Resa, MD
California by Kevin Starr

Los Angeles Times

Cracks, hack, attacks: California's vulnerable water system faces many threats, Hayley Smith, May 8, 2023

On a brutal summer day, one California town ran out of water. Then the fire came, Diana Marcum, Ian James, July 13, 2022

One of American's hottest cities is down to one water well. What happens if the taps go dry? Ralph Vartabedian, July 20, 2021

The reality of legal weed in California: Huge illegal grows, violence, worker exploitation and deaths, Paige St. John, September 8, 2022

Man who bombed Los Angeles Aqueduct reveals his story, Louis Sahagun, October 30, 2013

With the land sinking, they persist in pumping, Susanne Rust, Jessica Garrison, Ian James, January 6, 2024

Clashes over water increase globally, Ian James, January 11, 2024

Groundwater levels dropping around the world, Ian James, January 26, 2024

Newsom unveils trimmer plan for delta water tunnel, Susanne Rust
California drought pits farmers vs. cities. But neither is the biggest water
victim, Hayley Smith, October 2, 2022

Deadly results as dramatic climate whiplash causes California's aging
levees to fail, Hayley Smith, Louis Sahagun, Jessica Garrison, January 5,
2023

Los Angeles is running out of water, and time. Are leaders willing to act?
Hayley Smith, October 13, 2022

A dust battle could cost L.A., Louis Sahagun
L.A.'s quest for water leaves costly bill: Higher rates for customers, choking
air pollution, Louis Sahagun, November 8, 2022

Entire region under drought emergency, Hayley Smith, Ian James
L.A. lets rain flow into the Pacific Ocean, wasting a vital resource. Can we
do better? Hayley Smith, January 6, 2023

15-day watering ban in portions of L.A. County due to pipeline leak,
Hayley Smith, August 15, 2022

Paper records and steel vaults: Can California water rights enter the digital
age? Ari Plachta, December 27, 2021

Look out: Wall St. takes bets on water, Michael Hiltzik, January 3, 2021

Household water wells are drying up in record numbers as California
drought worsens, Doran's Pineda, Gabrielle Lamar Lemee, December 8,
2022

Full-on crisis: Groundwater in California's Central Valley disappearing at
alarming rate, Ian James, December 22, 2022

'Fast paths' for the water below: From the air, scientist may underground channels that could help replenish aquifers, Ian James
'It's a disaster,' Drought dramatically shrinking California farmland, costing $1.7 billion, Ian James, November 23, 2022

A frenzy of well drilling by California farmers leaves taps running dry, Maria L. La Ganga, Gabrielle LaMarr Le Mee, Ian James, December 16, 2021.

100 years of interstate friction over a river, Michael Hiltzik
The Colorado River is overused and shrinking, Ian James, Molly Hennessy-Fiske, January 26, 2023

At the heart of Colorado River crisis, the mighty 'Law of the River' holds sway, Hayley Smith, Ian James, February 3, 2023

Colorado Basin among the most water-stressed, Ian James, August 17, 2023

The shrinking Colorado River, Ian James
Growing fears of 'dead pool' on Colorado River as drought threatens Hoover Dam water, Ian James, December 16, 2022

Ever wonder where your drinking water comes from? A reader asked and we answer, Rachel Schnalzer, September 27, 2021

Who else was stealing? Conspiracy plea deepens mystery in San Joaquin Valley Water Heist. May 28, 2024

Inside L.A.'s desperate battle for water as the Palisades fire exploded, Matt Hamilton and Ian James, January 16, 2025

Inside L.A.'s desperate battle for water as the Palisades fire exploded, Matt Hamilton and Ian James, Jan. 16, 2025

New York Times

Drinking Water Disappears, Rebecca Noble, August 29, 2023

America Is Using Up Its Groundwater Like There's No Tomorrow, August 29, 2023

When One Almond Gulps 3.2 Gallons of Water, Nicholas Kristof, May 13, 2023

Trillion Gallon Question, Christopher Cox, June 22, 2023

A Drought So Dire That a Utah Town Pulled the Plug on Growth, Jack Healy, Sophie Kasakove, July 20, 2021

Small Towns Grow Desperate for Water in California, Thomas Fuller, August 14, 2021

The Central Valley Town That Keeps Sinking, Lois Henry, May 25, 2021
Wall Street Eyes Billions in the Colorado's Water, Ben Ryder Howe, January 3, 2021

How China Transformed Into a Prime Cyber Threat to the U.S., Nicole Peiroth, July 20, 2021

Arizona Is in a Race to the Bottom of Its Water Wells, With Saudi Arabia's Help, Natalie Koch, December 26, 2022

These are the Winds That Turn Wildfires Deadly in L.A., Raymond Zhong and Zach Levitt, Jan. 28, 2025

Washington Post

U.S. announces more water cuts as Colorado River hit dire low, Joshua Partelow, Karin Brulliard, August 16, 2022

Arizona city cuts off a neighborhood's water supply amid drought, Joshua Partlow, January 16, 2023

How a Saudi firm tapped a gusher of water in drought-stricken Arizona, Isaac Stanley-Becker, Joshua Partlow, Yvonne Wingett Sanchez, July 16, 2023

Leaked files from Chinese firm show international hacking effort, Christian Shepherd, Cate Cadell, Ellen Nakashima, Joseph Menn, AaronSchaffer, February 21, 2024

China's cyber army is invading critical U.S. services, Ellen Nakashim, Joseph Menn, December 11, 2023

Why a Taiwan election upset could be a U.S. blessing, Jason Willick, January 5, 2024

Here's where water is running out in the world—and why, Veronica Penney, John Muvskens, August 16, 2023

CNN

Wells are running dry in drought-weary Southwest as foreign-owned farms guzzle water to feed cattle overseas, Ella Nielsen, November 5, 2022.

How the Mafia is weaponizing wildfires, Laura Paddison, January 27, 2025.

FBI Director warns that Chinese hackers are preparing to "wreck havoc" on critical US infrastructure, Hanna Rabinowitz, Sean Lyngaas, Jan. 31, 2024

WIKIPEDIA

Pyramid Lake (Los Angeles County, California)
California water wars
California State Water Project
Chinatown (1974 film)
Los Angeles Department of Water and Power
Palm Springs Aerial Tramway
Coachella Valley Water District
Joshua Tree National Park

MISCELLANEOUS

The Biggest Potential Water Disaster in the United States, The New Yorker, David Owen, May 11, 2022

The Well Fixer's Warning, The Atlantic, Mark Arax, August 17, 2021

This Sign on the California I-5 has puzzled SF and LA drivers for years. Where did it come from?, SF Gate, Joshua Bate, September 30, 2021

Water utilities grapple with cybersecurity woes: Hacking an agency in a Pennsylvania town prompts U.S. officials to warn about protecting supplies, Associated Press, Marc Levy, reprinted in the LA Times, January 11, 2024

Nasdaq Velez's California Water Index

Joint Operations Center, U.S. Department of the Interior, California Great Basin Region.

Beef Research.org

Operations Control Center of the California State Water Project, Sacramento Bee, Ari Plachia, June 13, 2023

FBI chief says China has bigger hacking program than the competition combined, Reuters, Raphael Sater, September 18, 2023

China-Linked Hackers Breached a Power Grid—Again, Wired, Andy Greenberg, September 12, 2023

China-backed hackers spying on US critical infrastructure, says Five Eyes, US News, May 24, 2023

California Agricultural Water Use: Key Background Information prepared by the Pacific Institute, April 2015

Are tarantulas in the California desert, Desert Sun, James W. Cornett, January 29, 2024

A Self-Guided Tour of the Los Angeles Aqueduct, KCET, Eldon Trinidad, November 4, 2013

Groundwater Gold Rush, Bloomberg Green+Markets, Peter Waldman, Sinduia Rangaraian, Mark Chediak, April 12, 2023

California's Water Supply, A 700-Mile Journey, KVPR, Amy Quinton, Capital Public Radio, October 13, 2013

Layperson's Guide to Groundwater, Prepared by the Water Education Foundation, updated 2011

Satellites reveal the secrets of water guzzling farms in California, NPR, Dan Charles, October 18, 2021

California farms produce a lot of food—but what and how much might surprise you, Orange County Register, Kurt Snibbe, July 27, 2017

Thieves are stealing California's scarce water. Where's it going? Illegal marijuana farms, Cal Matters, Julie Cart, July 20, 2021

Where does Southern California's tap water come from? Bureau of Reclamation California—Great Basin, April 19, 2023

Restoring the Columbia River: Reliable Water for SW United States, Steven Dietz, 2025

Made in the USA
Middletown, DE
03 April 2025

73545015R00173